DIDN'T STAND A CHANCE

A Stella Kirk Mystery #2

L. P. Suzanne Atkinson

lpsabooks
http://lpsabooks.wix.com/lpsabooks#

Copyright © 2019 by L. P. Suzanne Atkinson
First Edition — March, 2020

All rights reserved

No part of this publication may be reproduced in any form, or by any means, electronic or mechanical, including photocopying, recording, or any information browsing, storage, or retrieval system without permission in writing from the publisher.

This is a work of fiction. Names, characters, and incidents either are the product of the author's imagination or are used fictitiously.

Cover Design by Majeau Designs
Editing by Tim Covell

ISBN
978-0-9958696-6-0 (Paperback)
978-0-9958696-7-7 (eBook)

1. Fiction, Mystery/Detective-Cozy/General
2. Fiction, Mystery/Detective-Amateur Sleuth
3. Fiction, Mystery/Detective-Female Sleuths

Distributed to the trade by the Ingram Book Company

Table of Contents

Recurring Characters: 1
Chapter 1: I Was Fine an Hour Ago 3
Chapter 2: Jacob is Moving Away 7
Chapter 3: People Are Bound to Talk 13
Chapter 4: There Are No Words 23
Chapter 5: I Do My Part 33
Chapter 6: I'm Worried for His Mental Health 41
Chapter 7: No One Was Aware 51
Chapter 8: Investigative Protocols 61
Chapter 9: Did You Kiss? 71
Chapter 10: She Had No Idea 81
Chapter 11: I Still Have Questions 91
Chapter 12: Were We Right? 99
Chapter 13: It's Difficult to Point a Finger 107
Chapter 14: You People Have Missed the Point 115
Chapter 15: I Burned a Few Bridges 125
Chapter 16: If I Go Under a Bus 133
Chapter 17: What Does She Want? 141
Chapter 18: I Forced Him to Compare 149
Chapter 19: Where Did You Get the Samples? 159
Chapter 20: Are You Done, Yet? 167
Chapter 21: Don't Search Me for Answers 175
Chapter 22: Accidents Happen, Right? 183
Chapter 23: Lots I Want to Understand 191
Chapter 24: Are You Here to Arrest My Sister? 199
Chapter 25: Debriefing the Parties Involved 209
About the Author 217

"No one has the patent on you"
Katie St. Claire

"I will not delete pieces of me to please you"
Bryanna Dawn

Other works by L. P. Suzanne Atkinson

~Creative Non-Fiction~
Emily's Will Be Done

~Fiction~
Ties That Bind
Station Secrets: Regarding Hayworth Book I
Hexagon Dilemma: Regarding Hayworth Book II
Segue House Connection: Regarding Hayworth Book III
Diner Revelations: Regarding Hayworth Book IV
No Visible Means: A Stella Kirk Mystery #1

For David, always

Thank you to Wyneth, Kat, Barb, Marguerite and Beverley
for your insights when I needed them most, as well as to my editor, Tim.

And my mother.

Recurring Characters:

Stella Kirk	Owner of Shale Cliffs RV Park; amateur sleuth
Aiden North	RCMP Detective
Rosemary North	Aiden's wife
Nick Cochran	Park Manager; Stella's love interest
Alice & Paul Morgan	Park Employees; brother & sister
Eve Trembly	Park Employee; Del Trembly's granddaughter
Duke (John) Powell	Park Security
Kiki	Duke's Pomeranian
Trixie Kirk	Stella's sister
Brigitte & Mia Kirk	Trixie's daughter & granddaughter
Norbert Kirk	Stella & Trixie's father
RV Park residents	Mildred Fox, Buddy McGarvey, Curtis Walsh & Elroy Brown, Louise & Bob Stone, Sally & Rob Black

Chapter 1

I Was Fine an Hour Ago

November 18, 1980
Shale Cliffs RV Park

His father called today—nine days early for American Thanksgiving—odd. He suggested Nick travel to Florida for a visit after Christmas. Apparently, Tobias Cochran has some financial scheme brewing and wants Nick to invest the money he inherited from his aunt. *If he goes, will he come back? Will he need me to return the money he used to buy into the park this year? What the hell is he thinking?*

Toenails dig into Stella's thigh, interrupting her spin into the familiar abyss of negativity. A wet nose, partially obscured by a red turtleneck, pokes out from under the Hudson's Bay blanket providing extra protection from the chill. Stella and Nick sip wine in front of the fire. Kiki attempts to snuggle in further than her present position permits.

"Why are we harbouring the mutt again?" She can't prevent an element of indulgence from creeping into her attempt at a stern tone. "I still haven't decided if I'm happy you volunteered to dog-sit."

Nick chuckles while he gives Kiki an ear rub. "She loves you, Stella."

"Of course—walks in the frigid weather, kibble scattered from one end of the kitchen to the other, she expects to sleep in our bed, and she doesn't always smell so great."

"You're a good girl," he croons. "Auntie Stella didn't mean it." He turns his attention to Stella. "Duke's mother should be discharged in a few days."

Stella's aware Duke wasn't permitted to take his dog to Mrs. Powell's unit at the care home in the northern part of the province. He was staying there while he visited her in hospital. He was in a real bind, so they relented. She's teasing, of course, but Nick's expression is as mournful as Kiki's.

Stella squints at their charge. Kiki's eyes are closed while Nick rubs her ear. "Alice is her favourite person, but beggars can't be choosers, eh Kiki?" She touches the fluffiness of the Pomeranian's small head and resists the urge to coo.

Nick peeks at his watch. "Supper will be ready in ten minutes."

"Cooking is another one of your assets." She can't stop the blush from flooding her cheeks. His list of positive qualities always serves to make her feel less than adequate. Involvement of his family undermines her sense of security.

****

Painter Farm

"Back in a few. Off for a walk over to the house. Need a breath of fresh air."

"What?" Opal emerges from the kitchen. She wipes her hands with a stained dish towel. Her expression of disbelief is easy for Lucy to interpret. "Cavelle will be home soon."

Lucy ignores her sister-in-law. She slams her tiny feet into a pair of rubber boots that must be three sizes too big. Then she relents. "I'll only be gone a few minutes. I want to see the progress on the basement walls."

Hester, dressed in a long wool skirt soiled with dirt and whatever she last ate, shuffles up to the back-porch entry and peeks out from behind her more imposing sister. "Come, too?"

Lucy turns around and faces the hauntingly beautiful woman who has made the timid request.

Opal intercedes. "No, Hester. The air has a chill—you can't go." Her arm becomes a railroad crossing gate in front of Hester.

"Next time, I promise." Lucy wraps Jacob's barn coat around her small frame. The oily textured fabric hangs to her ankles and smells like cow shit, an homage to the days when the Painters kept animals. She hauls her long blond curls out from under the corduroy collar.

"Take a flashlight, Lucy. The ground is rough."

A familiar prickly sensation tickles her hairline—Lucy's uncontrollable response to Opal's abrupt and authoritative tone. She opens the storm door and picks her way down the stairs.

Despite her resolve and recently developed stubborn streak, she knows Opal was right. She stumbles across the frozen stubble where the machinery has torn up the topsoil. Her feet slide around in the heavy boots. A pale amber glow, cast by a floor lamp near the dining room bow window, is her single light source.

She stops to adjust her boots and turns back toward the noble American Foursquare farmhouse, built by Jacob's father who passed away eight years ago. The imposing home was finished in 1933 when Leon and Velma Painter were married. Velma died a few days after she gave birth to her fourth child and only son, Jacob, in 1951. *The house is too big and boorish. Jacob says our home should be my style—cute and petite. He's right. I want to be out from under his sisters. The sooner the better.*

I need to sit. She turns toward her destination and wobbles her way to the basement of their three-bedroom bungalow. In the gloom, the cement walls blend with the frozen earth. Once she can clearly make out the shadows of new concrete, she relaxes. The plywood forms, used to hold the cement in place while it cured, have been removed. When the back-filling is complete, the front entry will be level with the ground. She wants her house to have a flat entrance with no more than a threshold. *The family house has too damned many stairs. You can't grow old in a home with lots of stairs.*

Clutching Jacob's heavy, smelly coat around her, she ponders her husband of not quite three months. For two nights in a row he's been out to meetings—farmers and cattle ranchers. They get together at the fire hall for a supper put on by the ladies' auxiliary, while they discuss feed prices, fertilizer, and animal auctions. She wants him home. The source of her anxiety mystifies her, but she needs his support.

Lucy sits on the frigid concrete basement wall. The icy hardness bleeds through Jacob's heavy coat. She steadies herself with one hand on the rough stone surface. Damp wind off the water whips her long hair around her flushed face. Her feet are ice cubes floating inside the cavernous rubber boots dangling over the wall and into the empty hole eight feet below. Nonetheless, she's thankful to be away from Opal's watchful eyes.

Discomfort clouds her focus. The cement has cured despite the cold, so the framers should be out to the property any day. Lucy knows she doesn't have an abundance of patience, and if it begins to snow, construction is sure to stop until spring.

She didn't go to work today because she was sick when she woke up. She was better by the afternoon, so she called her boss to pick up a shift, but it was too late. All the At-Home Care clients who required help from a practical nurse were scheduled with other staff. Now she's as sick as she felt this morning. *What is wrong with me? Do I have the flu? I'm so dizzy and nauseous. Supper was good. I was fine an hour ago.*

Despite her silent criticisms of Opal's rigidity and over-bearing attitude, Lucy acknowledges her oldest sister-in-law is a great cook. Since she married Jacob and moved out to the Painter farm, challenges have been frequent, but food has not been one of them.

Ouch! God in heaven! What is the matter with me? Lucy holds her side and winces. *Once the pain eases, I'll go back to the house and rest.* She balances on her cement perch. She shuts her eyes and hopes the dizziness subsides enough for her to return across the yard without toppling over.

Chapter 2

Jacob is Moving Away

August 30, 1980

"I still can't believe Opal and Cavelle Painter have allowed their little brother Jacob to marry Lucy Smithers." She doesn't try to disguise her sarcasm.

Stella stands while Nick buttons the twenty-four pearl fasteners on the back of her pale pink silk blouse. "Could be fun," he muses while he hovers over the bottom half of his task. "Jacob has a third sister who's odd somehow, correct?"

"Hester. Yeah. She's thirty-nine, I think. Never went to school. First her mother taught her and then Opal after Velma Painter died. Hester's not social. She's highly intelligent but in specific areas. Loves books." She fidgets and tries to stay still. "I remember her bedroom when we were kids. The whole space was set up with bookshelves on each of the walls and another row of shelves from front to back, as if we were in the stacks at the Port Ephron Library."

She exhales her anxiety. "Are you operating in slow motion on purpose? I want to meet with Alice for a minute to make sure she has reservations and lot assignment under control." Continuing to muse, she adds, "I enjoy Hester's company. She's unusual, but intriguing unusual, if you know what I mean. When I visited the Painter place as a teenager, I always tried to spend a few minutes with her. Most of the girls steered clear."

Nick fails to react to her last remark. He taps her on the shoulder to indicate he's finished and turns toward the entry door of her apartment. "Going to a shindig on the Saturday of the Labour Day weekend is not the smartest plan, you know." He graces her with a broad grin before he makes his way down the stairs. "I have to go check on Paul," he yells over his shoulder.

The wedding is at three o'clock. The drive takes a mere ten minutes to get around the bay. Stella can see the Painter property from the balcony off her upstairs residence. Nick Cochran, whom she has always introduced as her park manager, will be her official plus one for the first time. A blush warms her cheeks.

Nick accepted the job soon after she assumed ownership of Shale Cliffs from her father. Norbert Kirk's memory loss made running the business impossible for him. She knows she could not have taken up the reins without Nick's help. They make a good team. Now he's bought into the place to the tune of ten percent. He paid to have the water system upgraded. She and her sister, Trixie, managed to secure a loan to get the electrical updated as well, but the job won't happen until October. Busy times.

Stella checks her lipstick, worn only on very special occasions, in the mirror. Not bad for an old girl, despite her recent visit to the hair salon and the less than adequate trim she received from the new girl. Her short, straight, and dirty blond hair has started to turn grey at the temples. She chose cream coloured palazzo pants which hang to the floor in soft folds. She slips her feet into brilliant red leather sandals guaranteed to create a fashionable clash with the blouse. Trixie is the expert in such topics. Her unrequested guidance must be rubbing off. She rams tissues into a small sequined clutch her impractical sister gave her for Christmas one year, and hurries toward the main floor.

"Fabulous!" Alice mans her post in the office but stands in the doorway to admire Stella when she appears. "Nick will be back in a minute."

"We'll be full by the end of the day, right? Do we expect many more to check in?"

Alice, ever efficient as Stella's office manager extraordinaire, bobs her red locks. "The majority arrived yesterday. We have two spots up here on the top row, but that's all. Room for the odd straggler, but I'll refer anyone else to Port Ephron RV." She nods to her boss. "No problem. You go and have fun."

"Oh, and one little request, Stella." Alice's eyes twinkle. "Since Eve will be at the wedding with her grandmother, I need you to report how she looks when she's not cleaning bathrooms and weeding flower beds." She giggles. "Take your camera. I need to see a picture."

"I can't believe you want me to spy on Eve!" In a more conspiratorial tone, she adds, "I bet I won't even recognize her. Luckily, I've met Del Trembly many times because she lives in Harbour Manor, the same care home as Dad."

"Okay, Stella." Nick catches his breath, glances at his watch, and interrupts. "Paul has done a spin around the park to make sure the fire pits don't have any garbage in them. He'll mow. Duke said Kiki's under the weather. You know Duke." He peers at Alice. "I think he expects to leave her up here with you when he starts his rounds."

Alice nods. "Reception is quiet, you guys. I can manage five pounds of Pomeranian, no problem. We're in good shape, Stella."

"What would I do without you, Alice? And, by the way, you'll find lots of food in the fridge." She winks. "I actually shopped."

****

They let the screen door bang and cross the parking lot to Stella's dilapidated Jeep.

The road to the Painter farm opens to ocean vistas on three sides, but the square brown farmhouse hides behind a line of half-century old red maples planted with precision to grace the approach. A simple low-wire fence, framed in wood, marks the dooryard perimeter. The top rail is festooned with purple and white balloons. The entry leading to the front porch is draped in purple and white bunting. Someone has taken great pains to decorate. Vehicles are parked side by side in the field to the left. Nick guides the Jeep into the next available spot.

Stella appreciates the security of Nick's arm as they make their way across the uneven ground toward the rustic gate. Little white arrow signs are strategically placed at the sun porch corner and the side of the house, to guide visitors in the right direction. They hear the din of voices, while spectacular ocean views at the rear of the property frame the setting for Lucy and Jacob's wedding.

"You're here!" Eve Trembly accosts them on their approach.

Her eyes fix on Stella's arm looped around Nick's elbow. *Surely, she's aware of Nick and me. Our relationship can't be a surprise.*

"I'm glad you've arrived. The wedding isn't for another fifteen minutes and I want you to meet my grandmother."

Stella nods at Nick, disengages as unobtrusively as possible, and starts to follow her youngest employee and most recent hire.

"I'll find seats," he tells her as he surveys the rows of white folding chairs.

"Gram, meet Stella Kirk, my boss. Stella, let me introduce my grandmother,

Delores Trembly. She's Jacob and the sisters' aunt."

"Hi, Del. Lovely to see you again." Stella shakes the old lady's hand. "Del and my dad, Norbert, are friends at the manor, right Del?"

Del's black Breton hat trembles as she replies. "Norbert and I go back a hundred years at least." The tinkle of her laugh is caught on the summer breeze. Her bowler-style hat, with the delicate upturned brim, is paired with a beige trench coat, not required today.

Stella is about to remark on Del's youthful appearance, but the old lady is distracted by an equally elderly woman who takes the seat beside her.

Stella turns her attention to Eve. "My goodness, you clean up well, I must say." When she works at the park, Eve piles her mounds of thick and black, curly hair in a knot on the top of her head. She tries to squish the mass into submission with a ball cap, sure to rise like the cream on top of a frozen bottle of milk delivered to your porch on a winter's day. She always wears a neon Shale Cliffs T-shirt and blue jeans or denim shorts.

Eve blushes and touches her hair where it hangs below her shoulders. "I don't suppose you've ever seen me with my mop combed." She lowers her chin and peers at her yellow sun dress. "Mom bought this for me in the spring, but I've never had a chance to wear it until now." She smooths the front.

"You look very nice." Stella glimpses Jacob off to the side, behind the trellis which is covered in purple bunting and white flowers. "I think they're ready to get the ceremony underway. Nick is waving at me. I'm sure we'll run into each other again before the afternoon is over." She touches Mrs. Trembly's shoulder. "Enjoy the ceremony, Del."

The Breton bobs a response.

Nick has chosen their seats at the far end of a row of chairs, near the back. As Stella approaches, the man with whom Nick has been chatting gets up to search for his own place. Stella takes the seat beside her love and they turn their attention to the ocean.

"Man, their view is breath-taking, Stella. I thought ours was great, but theirs is unbelievable."

His use of the word "ours" is not lost on Stella, warmed by the thought.

"I was talking to Borden Fisher. He's secured the contract to build a house for Jacob and Lucy, on the lot next door. He said they want a modest single-story, but the rear will be all windows and garden doors out to an enormous patio. What a spot!"

"I'm surprised they aren't expected to live in the farmhouse." Stella leans in to whisper. "God, Cavelle still lives here, and she's forty-two. She could easily find a place of her own if she wanted to, being a real estate agent, for heaven's sake."

"I bet Jacob took control because he wants to get out from under the interference of three sisters. I imagine Lucy is no different than any other young bride, wanting to set up housekeeping her own way. Hard to say." He pats her knee.

"A few of the guests are unexpected."

"Like who?"

"Paulina McAdams, for one. You know her. She owns Yellow House, the place with a bookstore and a little library in the front parlours. Brigitte takes Mia there for story hour. She was very welcoming when I moved back to town."

"Yeah. Nice."

"Paulina was dating Jacob's father, Leon, when he died, over twenty years ago. Ardith Holland, the nursing supervisor for At-Home Care Services, is here with her husband. I've never seen him before."

"And I thought Trixie would be here by now."

"Me too, Nick. She's good friends with Cavelle, but when the fish plant is busy, she works most Saturdays to get the extra hours. I'm pleased we found enough time for her to sign my loan papers—and help to solve Lorraine Young's murder, for that matter." It was a troubling summer, but Lorraine's murderers are in jail now.

A hush falls over the crowd when Lucy's brother, Glenn walks his mother along the centre aisle to take her place in the front row, to the right. Bitsy Smithers reflects her nickname at four feet, eleven inches in height. Her son, although a short person as well, looms over her. He resembles his mother since both are more round than tall.

Jacob, who has been waiting patiently, enters the area accompanied by his best man. The first strains of Mendelssohn's "Wedding March" float on the wind. A stereo speaker has been connected to a wire pulled through the kitchen window. Everyone turns as Opal, Jacob's oldest sister, walks with hesitant grace toward the minister. She's followed by Maeve Cavannah, Lucy's closest friend, and then the other two sisters. They are all dressed in deep purple satin skirts and white blouses with tiny purple flowers. They carry bouquets Stella is sure came straight out of Hester's garden. Cavelle follows Maeve. She gazes with confidence at the assembled guests. Hester shuffles forward, bringing up the rear. Stella fears she might get spooked and run away any minute. She stops and turns around. Stella can see Lucy nod to her and motion for her to go forward. Hester complies. Lucy reaches for her father's arm. Reid Smithers escorts his little girl through the crowd to meet her husband-to-be.

The ceremony is shorter than Stella expected. The reception is informal, with sandwiches and sweets, tea and coffee, as well as the obligatory wedding cake. Stella has been told Opal made the cake.

"Hi, Hester. Special day, eh?" Stella sits on a folding chair beside the youngest of Jacob's three older sisters.

She is focused on the wilted wildflowers in her lap. "Dead, now." She holds them up to Stella.

"Did you provide the bouquets today?"

"Lucy bought hers from a store." Her eyes light up. "But I did the rest."

Stella pats her hand. "A fine job, my dear. They were gorgeous."

"I was sad when I cut them because I had to kill them." Her momentary expression of delight begins to crumble as she returns her attention to her lap.

Stella tries another approach. "The ceremony was wonderful. What did you think?"

"Jacob is moving away soon." She doesn't lift her eyes.

"Hester, he'll be next door." Her attempt to comfort proves futile.

"Jacob is moving away to be with Lucy."

CHAPTER 3

People Are Bound to Talk

October 1, 1980

"I'm on my way out to catch up with the contractor, Stella."

"Good, Nick. The Port Ephron Electrical truck drove past the office a minute ago." Stella is in reception. September has flown by in a blur of estimates and plans. Now, the electrical company is here early to begin installation of the new panel, but no matter. Few seasonal campers remain after October 1. The end-of-the-year potluck is this Saturday and the park will be closed as of Thanksgiving Monday. Rigs have departed in a steady stream this week. Certain residents move their units to indoor storage while others prefer to leave them on site. The decision is up to the owners. Nevertheless, she is aware of how a harsh winter, out in the open, is hard on a trailer.

"I did a run through the bathrooms. Can I help you with any other chores before I go?"

"No. I miss the staff, but I think we can manage to muddle on. Kids require an education." She steals a quick peek around the door frame. "Aiden asked if you would walk him through the winterization process on Lorraine's trailer over the long weekend." She pauses before she corrects herself. "On the Holiday Rambler. I told him he was on your list because you did the work for Lorraine." Her heart twinges when she references her seasonal resident who was murdered in May.

"You're right. Tell him we can set up for holiday Monday, October 13. I'll be finished with the last of my group by then."

"Okay. See you for lunch."

Stella's plan for her day is simple. She wants to call Aiden to ensure he and

Rosemary feel welcome to attend the party. She needs to contact Trixie and beg an extra hand. Also, a trip around the park is necessary to determine how many of the guests plan to remain through Saturday. The weather's cooling significantly in the evening, and folks with older trailers often struggle with the cold. There will be no budging Mildred Fox until the last day, though. She will wrap up in that filthy comforter and sit by her fire. *If I let her, she'd stay out by her smoky campfire until Christmas.*

"Port Ephron RCMP."

"Stella Kirk here. Calling for Detective North."

"Hold on, ma'am."

"Stella. What can I do for you today?"

"Good morning, Aiden. I wanted to tell you Nick says he's happy to provide you with the information any responsible owner needs to learn so they're able to close a unit. Will Thanksgiving Monday work for you?" She wonders if he appreciates the finer points involved in cleaning a trailer septic system and draining the water lines.

"Sure. We're invited to Rosemary's sister Toni's place for holiday dinner." He chuckles. "Gives me a good excuse to be late. I'll drop Rosie off at Toni's house before I come over."

"One word of advice."

"What?"

"Leave time to have a shower after you finish up here." She doesn't elaborate.

"Okay. Could get messy, you think?"

"Definitely. Nick will coach you through every task once the honey wagon leaves. Another question. Shall I expect you both for the potluck this Saturday? You're seasonal campers, now. Can you come?"

"Are you kidding? Rosie's excited. I haven't seen her this involved in years. She didn't want to move home last week. You were right. The trailer has been great for her—independence away from her hovering and well-meaning sisters. She says she's not an invalid. She also said she'll cook a ham."

"We enjoy Rosemary out here at the park, Aiden—and you, too, of course." She hesitates as the words float along the phone line. She and Aiden were close in high school—eons ago. Neither mentions those days, but their love affair existed, even if thirty years have passed.

"Saturday afternoon it is, Stella. Call us if you need any other help."

Did his voice sound softer than normal? She isn't sure. As a homicide detective, Aiden is excellent at his job, but interactions with the residents of the isolated community of Shale Harbour often put him at a disadvantage. Stella knows her ability to get the locals to cooperate proved invaluable when he investigated Lorraine's murder.

"Trixie, I thought you were off today but when I called the house, Brigitte said you were at work." As usual, Trixie has answered the phone at the fish plant. She is the receptionist and a typist for the business. Her daughter and granddaughter remain at home.

"I switched so I can come to the party."

Recognizing the undertone of sadness she detects in her sister's voice, Stella attempts an upbeat approach. "Great! I'm relieved, because I need your help. By the way, what's the matter?"

"Well." Her voice sounds muffled. Stella imagines she's turned her back and covered the mouthpiece to hide her conversation from the busybodies in the office. "I planned to bring my new man, but damn if he hasn't been called out of town." Stella notes the whine in Trixie's tone.

"Happy to hear you found yourself a fresh mark." Stella keeps her tease gentle. Trixie mocks her affair with Nick. Stella interprets the behaviour to be more regret than jealousy because Trixie finds herself so often alone after a failed relationship. She avoids putting the spotlight on her personal happiness right now, in an attempt at kindness toward her sister.

"Yes, and he isn't ten years younger than me, Stella. He's my age and very respectable. He's a Human Resources Management Consultant, and travels to consult."

The tone of her voice makes the word "consult" sound very posh. Her explanation seems rehearsed. Stella ignores the dig. "What's his name? How did you meet him?"

"Russ Harrison. He moved here from out West somewhere and bought a summer house through Meredith Tompkins. He winterized the place and now he can use Shale Harbour as his home base." Her voice becomes excited. "I met him by accident when I went to pick up Cavelle Painter for lunch. He was at Grey Cottage Realty to meet with Meredith." She mews. "He was so romantic."

"How so?" Stella struggles to sound interested. Trixie's stories are usually exaggerated.

"Cavelle told me he called the office the next day and asked them who I was and where I worked. He showed up at the plant and we went for supper over at the hotel the same night. He's away a lot, but we've hit it off over the last couple of months." She exhales in a theatrical gush.

Stella's sure she understands what "hit it off" means. "Well, I'm sorry we won't meet him on Saturday, but I'll arrange a dinner soon with both of you, the Norths, and us—after the chaos settles and I'm not up to my elbows in electrical contractors and water pumps."

"God, Stella, where do you get the patience? I'll be at the park early on Saturday to help. I might be able to scare up a few lobsters for a big salad."

"Thanks, Trixie." Stella is relieved her sister will use her fish plant connections to find a special treat for the dinner, despite the fact she's always hated the business. They are partners, but Trixie stays out of the picture if she gets her stipend the end of each month.

****

The golf cart, their contraption used to whiz around the park in what she considers a highly efficient manner, is snuggled in near the rear veranda and not in the hands of her security person, Duke Powell, today. Duke, whose real name is John, prefers the John Wayne character name of Duke. He will return to his motel efficiency unit in Port Ephron after official closure. He insists he must be the one to manage the gate and check on the residents until the last campfire goes out. He takes his position seriously. Stella puts up with his idiosyncrasies.

She hums her way toward Mildred Fox's little 1956 Cardinal trailer, and parks upwind from the old woman's smoky fire. Mildred, grubby and no doubt loaded even though it's eleven o'clock in the morning, waves. "Hey, Stella. To what do I owe a visit from on high today?"

"Now, Mildred. Don't be a smarty pants. We close, officially, on October 13, so I stopped by to find out when you plan to leave for the season, and if you're coming to the potluck this weekend."

"I'll come if I git a drive up to the house. Can I give you a few bucks to buy rolls? Cookin' ain't what I do." She lifts her glass in salute.

"No need to cook. Your job will be to show up. I have lots of grub. When do you expect your guy to close the Cardinal?"

"Oh, he'll be here next Sunday, the twelfth, he said. Then I guess I'm back to the seniors' for the winter. Hate the thought."

"Well, we'll camp again next year. I'll send Duke to fetch you Saturday afternoon. Are you keepin' warm?"

"Enough. I stay by the fire and have three big blankets inside. Snug as a bug, Stella. No need to waste your worries on this old girl." Her cackle bounces in the breeze as she pats her belly. "I got insulation."

Stella marvels at how a woman of her age manages to put up with the inconveniences of life in a minuscule trailer until late in the season. Most of her elderly residents want to be at home with the electric heat cranked sky high.

"Later, Mildred. Have a few more stops." She purrs across an empty lot and points the machine toward Sally and Rob Black's big rig. Sally, wrapped in a fisherman's knit sweater that could accommodate three other people huddled inside, is sweeping the deck as Stella pulls in.

"Stella! I suppose you want the date for when we'll be headin' home. Rob wants to stay for your party on Saturday. He'll disconnect us Sunday morning and then we're gone." She glances back toward her trailer. "I hate to think of her stored in the barn. Despite the difficult spring with...." She gestures in the direction of the 1978 Holiday Rambler at the end of the front roadway, purchased by Aiden and Rosemary from Lorraine's estate. Her blond curls shudder. "Anyway, the rest of the summer was great."

"Where's Rob this morning?" Stella can't help but notice when their diesel truck isn't parked in its usual spot.

"Oh, he ran into town to get me more potatoes. I thought I'd do a potato salad for the party." She smiles. "Less work for you if I do the potatoes, right?"

"Aren't you sweet? Potato salad is a crowd pleaser. I'll do the coleslaw—the benefits of a team." She waves. "I'm off, Sally."

On her way up to touch base with Curtis Walsh and Elroy Brown, she drives past Buddy McGarvey's tent trailer. He's moved out, but said he'd be back for the party and to pick up the unit. No tent trailers get left for the winter. Park rule.

"The boys," as they have been nicknamed by their neighbours, are busy as one folds lawn chairs and the other stows the barbecue. "Will you two pull out before Saturday?"

Curtis straightens up. "Good morning! Didn't hear you roll in. Yes. We expect to be on the road at dawn tomorrow morning. The old girl here," as he refers to their ancient Winnebago motor home, "doesn't fly the way she used to. We take our time."

"Sorry to hear. Drive safe, if I don't connect with you before you leave. And you'll be back, eh? Alice told me your fees are paid for 1981."

Elroy rounds the corner after he closes a lower compartment. "Oh, we'll be back. We love Shale Cliffs RV Park, Stella. You folks are family, aren't they hon?"

Curtis winks at Stella. "Yes, El—family."

On the way over to catch up with Louise and Bob Stone, Stella spies Ted Metcalfe standing in the lane watching the guys from Port Ephron Electrical.

He catches sight of her and sprints over to the golf cart—a healthy jog for an old fellow well past eighty. "Hey, Stella! Nick's left for the house. Said it was near lunch time and he wanted to fix you a bite to eat."

Stella can't tell if the information is a tease or a fact. "That's Nick for you—always trying to get on my good side. Are you comin' to the potluck on Saturday, Ted?"

"The party's a tradition. The chef at the hotel is gonna make me a pumpkin pie to contribute. Hope a pie meets with your approval." His devilish expression clouds. "Wish my wife was here to create one of her fancy desserts, but no more."

His eyes puddle. Stella pats his arm. "The pie sounds great, Ted. When are you pulling up stakes?"

"Sunday, I'm back to the seniors' apartments." His eyes have a wistful glow—recalling happier times.

"See you Saturday. Keep an eye on those workers for me." She hums off along the path.

Louise and Bob Stone are from Alberta. Over the last couple of years, they've dragged their trailer to and from Calgary, but asked Stella, earlier in the season, if they could leave their unit in place for the winter. They'll drive home in their truck and enjoy luxury hotels along the way.

"Bob's tired of the set-up and disconnect every day, if we tow," the stunning Louise confided when she came up to pay next season's deposit. Louise was a beauty pageant winner many times over. She is tall; a vivacious redhead who could be two decades younger than her seventy years. Bob's age is more obvious, with his skin wrinkled by the sun and his knob-like bones riddled with arthritis.

Stella knocks on the trailer door, closed against the ever-present wind off the water.

"Come in, come in." Louise, always gracious, motions Stella into the kitchen.

The scent of tuna assaults her. "Hi. Wanted to double-check. You'll be here on Saturday, right?"

Bob is stretched out in his lounger, busy demolishing a sandwich. "Yeah, we'll be over, Stella." Bob manages to get the words out between munches. He takes a swig of cola and reaches for a pickle.

Louise's expression is indulgent; motherly. "I thought I'd cook lasagna—a hot dish, okay?"

"Of course! When are you off home?"

"Monday morning." He pauses to chomp on a handful of chips he's scooped from a wooden salad bowl placed within arm's reach. "Wish we could stay here instead of makin' a drive into colder weather."

"Bob wants to go straight to Florida—a discussion for another time." Louise acknowledges her husband's wishes. "We have grandchildren we need to visit, or they'll forget who we are."

"Well. I'm glad you'll be here for the party. Gotta run. Rumour has it Nick is making me lunch."

****

"Most of your stuff is moved up from the old cottage, right?" Stella sits with her elbows on the kitchen table. She examines the dilapidated condition of the white plywood cupboard doors while Nick struggles to balance at least four tablespoons of strawberry jam on a piece of toast. The crisp fall day tumbles in through the over-sized windows. This must be what a contented cat experiences when it's stretched out in the sun.

He munches and reads her mind at the same time. "People are bound to talk. Are you ready?"

She sits up straighter, propelled by a sudden flash of insight. "The fact of the matter is, I don't give a rat's ass what anybody thinks. If you were to move into the house for good, and not just for the winter, nothing would please me more." Peeking over at him from behind her coffee cup, she's fully aware the twinkle in her eyes is giving her away.

"You want to make sure I stick around to help with the clean up from the end-of-the-season party last night. You can't fool me." His chuckle is more of a rumble.

"Yes. Of course. A maid is what I need." She sets her mug on the table's rough surface.

"Seriously, though, most of my stuff is here already. The staff and Trixie have us figured out. Your poor father thinks I own the place and I was your plus one at Jacob and Lucy's wedding. I figure we're public." The muscles of his jaw relax. "Can I hold your hand when we go to Cocoa and Café for lunch? Can I put my arm around your shoulders when we walk down the street in town?"

Warm flushes of pink creep up her cheeks. Not demonstrative by nature, she is keenly aware of her challenges with overt affection. "It might be okay, but I'll take a while to get used to the couple idea out in the real world."

Her chair scrapes the Lino when she pushes the ladder-back away from the table and takes the two steps necessary to reach his side. She places a gentle kiss on the top of his head. "Break is over. The house needs a good cleaning today. Most of the seasonal residents will be packed up and gone by tomorrow morning, a week early, and then we can plan a winter paint project for the kitchen! Pale yellow cupboards?"

"This is my reassignment—the live-in handyman?" He holds her fingers. "Sounds perfect."

She relaxes.

****

By Sunday noon, the main floor is back to normal. She still wants to organize her office, but the cozy winter months loom ahead with a promise of snowy days, sub-zero nights curled up by the fire, new books waiting to be read, and a long list of tasks put aside in anticipation of freedom from the required summertime public interaction. She counts on many hours to address the chores she always manages to shove aside over the busy summer.

As she putters upstairs, her thoughts turn to Florida. Nick will no doubt take a trip south to visit with his parents after Christmas. She tries not to permit anxiety about his return to overshadow the support she wants to provide.

"Are you in the kitchen, Nick? Can you get the door?" She's heard the chimes rattle, indicating someone has entered reception. Her curiosity is piqued.

"Stella? Mr. and Mrs. Painter stopped in to say hi." The emphasis on the introduction is no doubt Nick's welcome to the newlyweds.

She runs down the stairs from the apartment to greet Jacob and Lucy. "Well! To what do we owe this honour? You two must be run off your feet, what with harvest, honeymoon, and house. I am pleased you found a minute to drop by."

After quick hugs, she leads the way into her communal main floor living room.

"You're in time for after-lunch tea. Care to join us?"

Stella provides Nick with an appreciative nod. He is the consummate host.

"Sounds wonderful." Lucy removes her windbreaker before she sits on one of the two sofas arranged perpendicular to the stone hearth. "Jacob and I wanted to visit and thank you both for the quilt. Opal tells me the design is a traditional star pattern."

Touched that they came to the park instead of sending a note, Stella gushes, "Oh, I'm thrilled that you like your gift. The Harbour Crafting Guild made it, and when I stopped by the hall to check if they had a quilt in stock I could buy for your wedding, the stars were perfect."

"My plan is for it to become the bedspread in our guest room if our home ever gets built and I have a guest room." Lucy tosses her blond curls over her shoulder when she turns to give Jacob a look Stella interprets as impatience.

"What's the story with your house, you guys?" Nick delivers their tea as he asks the question. "Borden Fisher told me his contracting company is building your bungalow. I talked to him at the wedding."

Jacob squirms as he directs a shrug toward Lucy and frowns at Nick. "Borden said a commercial job came up and he needed to do it first. He's promised me they'll have the basement poured and the place weather tight before snow flies, but here we are at the week before Thanksgiving. In our neck of the woods, fall and winter storms are right around the corner."

"If I can help in any way, give me a shout. Are you able to handle any of the work yourself?"

Nick takes a seat on the sofa across from their young guests. Stella warms to the sensation of his thigh resting against her own.

Jacob leans forward. "I want to contribute once they get inside, but Lucy says I should leave the construction to professionals. I guess decisions depend on how delayed we get."

"Every detail has to be perfect." Lucy squints at Stella. "You understand, Stella."

Chapter 4

There Are No Words

"Lucy sat in our living room six weeks ago. We discussed the new house and drank tea." Shocked at their activity today, Nick's silent support provides strength. Clad in a suit jacket reserved for serious occasions, his arm is positioned parallel to hers. The Port Ephron Funeral Home is an old-fashioned combination of thin carpets, office stacking chairs, and boxes of tissue placed with strategic precision on various end tables throughout the space. The chapel smells of dust and tears.

Her casket is closed. The wood is dark, and the handles are polished brass. The service attendees have assembled in what once was the Victorian parlour, while the family is clustered in a converted sun porch—the mourners' room. Stella remembers when her mother died, and they sat out in that same drafty vestibule. She and Trixie stared at one another until the service finished. The ritual made her angry. The reason remains a mystery.

"I've been over with Cavelle and the rest of the family." Trixie slides into the empty chair beside Stella.

"How are they? Lucy's death has shocked the whole community."

"Jacob might as well be catatonic. He sits and stares at the floor while Hester pats his knee."

"Opal and Cavelle?" Stella keeps her voice to a whisper. Recorded organ music, designed to fill voids in conversation, drones through speakers wedged in upper corners near the ceiling.

"Cavelle manages, as she always does." Trixie's breath seeps into her ear. "Opal is uptight. Her posture is rigid—a statue with a blank expression focused straight ahead—no help to Jacob whatsoever. Surprisingly, their Aunt Del is the supportive one in the bunch. Eve brought her."

Stella nods.

"Anyway, Del hobbles around on her cane, patting and hugging, whispering words of sympathy. The old lady is their closest relative."

"And the Smithers? Bitsy must be devastated."

The crowd stands as the funeral director leads Lucy's family, as well as the Painters, to their seats at the front. The warmth of Nick's hand soothes when his fingers intertwine with hers.

Lucy's service is brief, like her wedding. They line up to shake hands and express their condolences. "I am sorry for your loss." Tearful nods accompany Bitsy's handshake which includes a shredded and soggy tissue pressed into her palm.

"Reid, Lucy's death was such a terrible shock." More nods to match his clammy touch.

"Jacob, there are no words." She hugs him and pats his back. He stares at the floor, in a posture more reminiscent of a lost boy than a bereaved husband.

"Glenn, my sympathy." Lucy's brother takes her hand in both of his and thanks her for attending—a typical salesman's approach she finds odd considering the circumstances.

"Opal, my deepest condolences."

"One must carry on, Stella. Jacob and Hester need our care." She brushes arthritic fingers across her forehead while she assesses the line of attendees. "The family appreciates your support."

"Cavelle, I am sorry."

"Thanks." She reaches out past Stella to touch Trixie, who grasps her hand. "My friend, here, was a godsend."

Stella is struck by how each woman's personal style is similar to the other. A designer might refer to their fashion sense as low-key flash, today. Their heels are not *too* high. Their skirts are not *too* short. Their tops don't reveal *too* much, but neither one held back in the big and chunky costume jewellery department.

"Are you okay?" Stella wraps her arms around Hester, who looks lost and startled. Stella is reminded of a trapped and scared rabbit she once found under the veranda.

"Lucy's gone. She fell in the hole and died."

"I know. I am sorry. May I visit you one day soon?"

Hester bobs her head. "Eve, too. Eve is nice to me."

"Eve might be in school, but I'll drive out to the farm in a week or two." Before she moves along the line, Stella catches herself patting the trembling woman much as she would a stray kitten.

The final greeting is to Leon Painter's aging sister. "Hi, Del. We are so sorry for your loss. Long day for you. Is Eve sticking close by?"

"Yes, and yes. She's disappeared in search of a chair for me." The familiar black Breton hat quivers when she talks.

"May I take your coat for you and hang it up? I imagine, as more people crowd in to see the family, the reception room will get warm."

"No, I'm always freezing. Poor circulation. The doctor says my ticker isn't in the best shape."

Stella glances behind as the remainder of the attendees file in. "Well, I've held up the line long enough."

Del clutches her sleeve. "Please come speak to me later, once this mess," she flutters a trembling hand at the funeral attendees shuffling behind Stella, "is over."

"Of course. Nick and I will stick around for a while. You send Eve to find me when you're ready."

"Too many people," Del mutters, as Eve wiggles through the throng clutching a chair for her grandmother.

After they mercifully reach the end of handshakes and sympathy, Stella senses Nick's touch on her shoulder. He leans in to whisper, "I saw Borden Fisher over by the sandwiches a minute ago. I thought I might speak with him. Construction on Jacob's house must be causing him concern. I'll be right back."

As he starts to manoeuvre his way toward the contractor, Trixie materializes at Stella's elbow. "Lots of people, eh?"

Stella wraps her arm around her sister's shoulder and gives her a little hug. As usual, she imagines she resembles an unmade bed when positioned near Trixie. Stella knows her fashion sense is more RV park than designer runway. She experiences a sudden and overwhelming urge to be close to family, so ignores their obvious differences.

Trixie flew into her yard last Tuesday night, well after midnight. Stella was scared when Nick turned on the veranda light and she saw her sister in the amber glow. Her niece, Brigitte, and grandniece, Mia, were the first to come to mind.

Breathless and anxious, Trixie managed through gulps and tears to convey her news. Opal found Lucy's body in the basement of the new house. Cavelle raced home from work and called Trixie, who jumped in her van and drove out to the farm to support her friend. Before she returned to her house, she stopped at the park to tell Stella. The gesture was thoughtful.

Nick and Stella did not go back to bed after Trixie's departure. They spent the rest of the night awake, comforted in the knowledge the other was nearby.

"Did I ever thank you for driving out to the park to tell us about Lucy's death, Trixie?" She gives her sister's shoulder another squeeze. "If I didn't, then thank you. You went out of your way and it meant a lot. A sudden death rattles the soul." The stark reality of her own words gives her pause. "Such sadness. Lucy was young and anxious for her new life to begin with Jacob."

As they stand together, off to the side, Eve approaches. She pops out of nowhere since she's short enough to move around unnoticed in a large group. She nods toward Trixie. "Stella, Gram wants to know if she may come out to your house for a visit later in the week. She says the parlours are too crowded to conduct a decent conversation."

"Of course, Eve. I'm always happy to talk with Del. If she prefers the park instead of the care home for some reason, fine. Give me a call to schedule a time."

Eve thanks her and disappears into the bedlam. Stella telegraphs her thoughts over heads to Nick with a simple nod. Since their obligations are fulfilled, they can retreat to Shale Cliffs.

****

Stella is mystified as to the reason Del Trembly asked to see her.

Eve supports her grandmother's arm as the old lady struggles on the veranda stairs. She's much taller than Eve. She doesn't stoop when she walks. As a result, an observer might assume her to be less fragile than is the case, because she is dangerously unsteady on her feet. She uses her cane while leaning on her granddaughter.

"Hi, you two. Come on in. At least the wind's blowing off the land today. We aren't getting that wet bite which seeps into your bones whenever it rolls off the water."

Del bobs her Breton and enters the big living room. Stella manages the door. "Sit here, Del." She points to one of the sofas. "Nice to see you under more pleasant circumstances compared to Monday. Can I get you a cup of tea?"

"Wonderful idea, my dear." Stella supports Del's elbow as she drops onto a couch flanking the fireplace. "Eve will make us tea."

Stella turns to Eve and furrows her brow in a silent attempt to ascertain Mrs. Trembly's point.

"I brought schoolwork, Stella. I'll make you guys tea and then read in the kitchen. Gram wants to talk with you alone."

She replies to another quizzical expression from Stella. "I have no idea what is on her mind."

"I can still hear." The old lady interjects. "You are not aware because our conversation is none of your business. Find us some tea and I will talk with my friend, Stella." Del snuggles her behind deeper into the leather cushions.

Without further discussion, Stella sits. Eve needs no direction in the kitchen after she spent the summer as an employee here at the park. "Okay, Del. What can I do for you today?"

"Stella. You worked with Detective North to determine what happened to the poor young woman found dead the end of May, correct?"

"Well, yes, I guess I did, Del. Her case has been settled." Stella tries to exercise patience.

"I am a very troubled aunt with serious misgivings regarding one of my nieces. I hope you might consider an investigation related to my concerns."

"An investigation into what, Del?"

Always efficient, Eve returns with two mugs of tea on a wooden tray. She has assembled sugar, milk, spoons, and napkins. She obviously discovered Nick's stash of Fig Newtons hidden in the pantry, because Stella counts six cookies on a glass plate.

Del peers at Stella from over the frame of her glasses but remains silent.

"Thank you, Eve. Don't tell Nick you found his cookies. I expect he'll be back anytime. He took the Jeep into town for gas. You can use my office. The desk is more comfortable than the kitchen table."

Eve smiles and her hair, knotted in a heap on the top of her head, trembles in much the same way as Del's Breton hat. "I'm comfortable. I've studied in worse spots."

Once they're alone, Del whispers, "You are friends with my nieces, correct?"

"Of course. Opal and I attended school together. We're the same age. Trixie is two years younger than Cavelle, but they are close, now. We are both fond of Hester, despite her challenges."

"I'm worried. I think she hurt Lucy." Del takes a sip of tea and reaches for a cookie.

Stella hesitates. "Why do you think Hester might have hurt Lucy?"

"It's in her nature. You said yourself she has challenges."

"What do you suspect?"

"Maybe Lucy didn't fall."

"Del! You suspect a crime was committed? You can't believe Hester pushed Lucy into the basement of her new house."

The elderly woman hesitates. "Opal and Cavelle have covered for her in the past. They might confide information to you. I am their father's sister and an old lady. You are a friend; a high school chum."

"Have you contacted the police and expressed your concerns?" Stella is confounded by her visitor's accusation.

She doesn't answer the direct question. "Speak to Hester. Check her books."

"Don't talk in riddles, Del. Hester has a library for a room and if what Cavelle tells Trixie is true, she has volumes throughout the house as well. Hester loves her books more than she loves her garden."

Del sips her tea. She stares over Stella's shoulder in the direction of the veranda entry door, closed against the wind. At the same moment as the knob turns and Nick bursts in with a gust of chilly air, she redirects her attention once more toward Stella. "Investigate for me, Stella. Do an assessment. Calm an old lady's fears, if nothing else."

Nick hustles inside and quickly closes the door against the ever-present wind. "Well, if it isn't Del Trembly sitting in the living room with one of my Fig Newtons in her fingers. To what do we owe the honour today?"

"Hello, Nick. Nice to see you." Stella does not miss Del's inquisitive glance in her direction.

"We're discussing Lucy. Eve's in the kitchen." She tries to project a "don't stay" look. "She made tea."

****

On the day of Lucy's funeral, Stella promised Hester she would visit. It's been two weeks and Stella's worked hard to find a moment to get away. The snow hasn't settled in yet, so she and Nick are busy. They stacked the picnic tables. Half will require a paint job before the new season begins. They stored a dozen in the shop for repairs. The old truck rims, used as fire pits, were picked up and sorted a few days ago. The rusted ones are useless. Others become damaged and misshapen when campers drive over them by mistake. She's asked the tire company in Port Ephron to keep their cast-offs and she'll pick them up in the spring. Real fire pits are a big investment. She has enough on her plate right now.

When she left to visit Hester, Nick was replacing weather stripping on each of the outside doors in his fight against the icy blast of winter's fast approach. She hopes to be home in time for tea.

The Painter property is no longer hidden by maples and floats against an ocean backdrop. The trees are sticks in the grey sky. In the summer, she purchases fruits and vegetables from the Painter gardens and preserves from Opal's kitchen, but she hasn't been to visit in a while, unless, of course, she counts the wedding.

She climbs the front steps and enters the icy and damp porch where she knocks on the door separating the unheated and unused space from the main house. Opal's heavy tread thuds along the hardwood hallway as she approaches.

"Stella. Glad you could visit. I waited for you before pouring our after-lunch tea. Come in." Stella enters the gloom of the foyer. The front rooms of homes in this style are continually dark because of the closed-in porch. The shadows appear worse when the day is overcast.

"I promised Hester, at the funeral, I'd stop by. Usually, we visit when I shop at the vegetable stand once your market garden is open. I haven't been to the house since the wedding."

Opal closes the door before she mutters her response. "We don't discuss the funeral, or the wedding for that matter. Any talk upsets Hester."

"Oh. Sorry. Where is Hester?"

"Reading or sorting her books upstairs." She turns to Stella and smiles. "Hester is our live-in librarian."

"Yes. I remember her room when we were kids."

There's a hint of resignation in Opal's voice. "Hester doesn't change, Stella. She is always the same."

"Well, I'm happy to be here."

"Hester's been fond of you ever since we were teenagers."

"I'm fond of her, too, Opal. Where's Jacob today?"

Opal flaps a limp wrist in the vague direction of a crop of outbuildings flanking the farmhouse. "In the barn where he likes to putter—no different than our father, when he was alive. Jacob always discovers a piece of machinery to be oiled or greased, or a part to be picked up in town."

"Is he able to cope?"

"He's fine. He's young. He'll survive. We are a family. We will stick together no matter what. Shall I run and fetch Hester, or do you want to go?" She busies herself with the tea. "I'm sure you can still find your way."

Stella, ever alert to nuances in the language of others, detects an abruptness in her tone. Does Opal think the purpose of her visit is to interfere? Has their Aunt Del voiced her concerns to the family before? "Oh, I recall."

She drops her jacket and Jeep keys on the nearest kitchen chair and backtracks through the hall to the staircase. "Hey, Hester. I'm here for tea. Will you come downstairs, or shall I come up?"

She's halfway up when she hears a weak response to her shout. "Here, first."

Stella stands and surveys the five doors which open off the upstairs hallway—four bedrooms and a bathroom. Hester always occupied the big room at the rear of the house. She assumes Cavelle and Opal enjoy separate rooms now, since their father died eight years ago.

The door is ajar and Stella peeks inside. She addresses Hester, who is sitting in the middle of the floor surrounded by books. "Hi. Will you come for tea and visit with me?"

Hester holds her hand up and motions for Stella to enter and close the door. Stella complies, curious why Hester has not chosen to sit on her bed or at her desk. "What are you up to?" She succumbs to an unrequested need to whisper and joins Hester on the floor.

Stringy brown hair hangs into the younger woman's eyes. Her sweater is green wool. The arms and body are too short. Stella thinks it shrank in the wash and suspects Opal tried to throw the garment out innumerable times. Hester meets Stella's gaze. "I need to fix my books. They are not in order. Is Eve downstairs?"

"No. I'm sorry. She's back at school. Do you want your books to be in a special order, Hester?"

"Yes." Her response is flat. She picks at a stain on her brown wool skirt. "The yellow is mustard."

"Shall we go to the kitchen now? Do you and Opal have any of your yummy strawberry jam the family makes every summer? I hope there are still a few bottles to sell."

"Lucy is gone. She fell in the big hole."

"I know."

"Jacob is very sad. He doesn't talk to me anymore. I want a dog."

"He'll be better in time. Be patient."

Hester looks across the piles of books and papers—not at Stella, but toward the window over Stella's shoulder. "Lucy was sick."

"What do you mean?"

"Lucy was sick," she repeats.

Stella's unable to garner more. After additional cajoling, she persuades Hester to accompany her downstairs for tea.

"I thought you two forgot I was here." Opal is sullen, but the kitchen table has been readied with tea, mugs, and scones, nonetheless. "Hester, why must you wear that ugly sweater and dirty skirt?"

She doesn't wait for an answer. Stella thinks Opal needs to point out, to visitors, those elements of Hester's behaviour she's unable to control.

Hester's response is to pat her tummy. "My favourites. Is there jam in the basement? I want jam now and Stella wants jam to take home."

"I told Hester I hoped I could pick up a few bottles of your strawberry jam, if you aren't sold out."

"Stella wants jam and I want a dog."

Opal turns to Hester and scowls. "You had a dog. Remember how it died? We said no more dogs." She turns her attention to Stella. "You are in luck. I put more away a few weeks ago from extra berries we froze in the summer. I'll run down to the storage room and find you what—two, three?"

"Three bottles will be perfect."

As Opal makes her way to the basement, Hester turns to Stella and places her index finger on top of Stella's hand. "Lucy fell in the big hole and hit her head. She was sick, you know."

Chapter 5

I Do My Part

The next day, Nick and Stella drive to Harbour Manor. Stella is preoccupied with Del Trembly's suspicions. Nick tags along to spend a few moments with Stella's father, Norbert.

"I don't imagine Dad will recognize me today. Every time I visit, his dementia is worse," she laments. "Trixie said she might as well not come at all." She observes Nick's lean profile. "On her last visit, he asked her to empty the garbage and told her she was overdressed to be a cleaner."

Nick's eyes are focused on the road. "Poor old fella. I let him natter on and don't correct him when he insists I bought his park. No harm done." He moves his right hand across the worn bench seat to pat her knee. "You have your talk with Mrs. Trembly and then come find me. We'll stay in his room—too breezy for a walk outside."

The air at the manor always smells the same—an unpleasant mix of antiseptic and dirty diapers. Stella understands their attempts to create a substitute home for their residents, but the wide corridors, bright lights, and wheelchairs parked in various corners, are a constant institutional reminder.

Stella gave up her job, albeit not a fulfilling one, to return to Shale Cliffs and run the business. Norbert required long-term placement. Options were scarce. The touch of Nick's sleeve against her shoulder provides unexpected solace for her quiet resolve.

He turns into Norbert's room. She pauses for a moment to listen to her father's reaction. "Well, if it ain't Nick Cochran come to visit an old guy. How's the park doin'? Are you makin' any money?"

"Not this month, Norbert. Not in December. No campers now. How ya been? Are they treatin' ya good?"

She struggles to cope with the strangeness of their circumstances. Norbert Kirk recognizes Nick but not his own daughter. He always wanted a son and Nick fills the void. She shakes off her sadness when she turns at the end of the corridor and approaches Del's tiny space.

"Knock. Knock." The wide hospital-style door is ajar.

"Come in. I'm happy to see you today."

Del Trembly is positioned in her recliner by the window of her room. Her bed is made, and although your typical hospital issue, the frame has been lowered close to the floor and covered with a multicoloured handmade quilt.

"Sit here beside me. One of the girls fetched me another chair." Del points to a red, leatherette stacking version situated nearby. "I told her I expected company."

"Thanks, Del." Stella sits and refrains from removing her jacket. She doesn't expect to be long.

Del smooths the front of her purple velour lounging suit—a contradiction paired with her quaffed and sprayed hair. Stella can't remember ever encountering Del without her hat pulled level with her ears.

"Tell me what you discovered in your investigation." Del leans toward Stella, as if she's intent on discussing a government conspiracy theory. Her heavy breasts press against her thighs.

"Del, I visited with Hester and Opal yesterday and didn't detect any behaviour I could label as out of the ordinary. Hester is struggling with Lucy's death. She repeats how Lucy fell in the hole and died. Opal is the normal protective oldest sibling. Hester and Opal both appear fine, given the circumstances."

In a tone sharper than Stella has heard before, Del reveals, "I spoke to Cavelle; expressed my concerns. I want you to talk to her, Stella."

"I am more than happy to have a visit with Cavelle, but to what end? Does she agree Hester hurt Lucy?"

"She's studied Hester's condition. She understands the sorts of topics that hold the girl's interest—her books and plants." She picks at an invisible piece of lint on her pant leg.

"Del. Be honest with me. Is there a remote possibility the girls would cover up details related to Lucy's death?"

The old lady becomes evasive as she did when Eve accompanied her to the park. "Jacob wasn't home. He was out at a meeting—for the second night in a row. I'm sure the story is more complicated than Lucy fell in the hole, hit her head, and died."

"I will talk to Cavelle." Stella stands to leave. "Nick is visiting Dad. Want to take a walk with me along to his room?"

Del pushes on the arms of her lounger to stand. Stella steadies the elderly woman with a hand to her elbow while she leans out to reach for a cane. They toddle toward Norbert's together. As they approach, Stella can hear the guffaws of both men through the open door.

"Norbert is such a happy man. He must have been a wonderful father to you and Trixie."

"Hi, Dad. See who I brought to visit?"

"Come on in, Del." Norbert gives a quivery wave. "Have you met my friend Nick, here? He owns the RV park I used to run." Stella anticipates what's next as he looks up at her while she remains poised in the doorway. "What are you waitin' for? Don't you have work to do?"

Stella silently pleads to Nick before she returns to the bright lights of the corridor. She takes a deep breath and tries not to absorb the sting of his loss.

****

"Aunt Del must have engaged your investigative services, did she, Stella?" The three women—Trixie, Stella, and Cavelle Painter—are tucked in around a corner table at Cocoa and Café waiting for their curried cream of squash soup and cheese biscuits to be served. Each woman nurses a cup of cranberry tea. The dreary December day called for a drink with more comfort than coffee. "Is she still stuck on the notion my mentally disabled sister hurt Lucy?"

Stella shifts in her chair. Cavelle has diminished Del Trembly's concerns with a simple sentence. "She's worried, Cavelle."

"Aunt Del is a nuisance. She voiced the same cockamamie idea when Dad died. She said she was suspicious Hester killed Dad. Come on! I was the one who found him—in the barn; on the floor. He suffered a heart attack, or a stroke. The doctor never spelled out the cause of death in detail. I remember Dad complained of indigestion a few days before his death. Then, for all intents and purposes, he dropped dead." The expression on Cavelle's oval face, which is made up with professional care, changes like the light when a cloud crosses in front of the sun. "Poor Dad."

Challenge slides into sadness. Neither Kirk sister interrupts. They wait in polite silence. Stella watches Cavelle gather her emotions back to where they can be discussed and not displayed. Stella understands.

"Dad dated Paulina."

"Paulina McAdams, from Yellow House?"

"Yes. She visited the farm on a regular basis, but what was even nicer, she often invited Hester over to her library where the girl stayed for hours on end. The time she spent with Hester was a great help to Opal, in particular. Paulina and Hester became very close."

"Brigitte takes Mia to the library every week. She's never mentioned Hester."

"I'm not surprised. Hester never crossed Paulina's threshold after Dad died. In her mind, she blamed Paulina, I guess. Geez, Dad's been dead over twenty years." Her bright red lips smile, but her eyes reflect deeper thoughts. "Jacob was eight." She acknowledges the waitress, a young woman familiar to Cavelle, as she places their soups with quiet care in front of them. A basket filled with biscuits follows.

"You girls have been through hell, ever since your mother passed away." Stella picks up her spoon as she talks.

"Mom died two or three days after Jacob's birth. I was thirteen. I didn't understand what happened. I stuck close to Dad. Opal was sixteen, and she took over the house. She looked after Hester, who was ten, and Jacob, of course."

"Did Opal teach Hester? She never attended any school, right?" Trixie reaches for a biscuit.

Cavelle emits a huge breath. "Opal has dedicated her whole life to Hester, Jacob, and the farm. She ran the market garden and vegetable stand alone until Hester started to show an interest. She even did the barn chores with Jacob after Dad died. Poor little Jacob toddled along behind her. He wanted to learn and to help."

She focuses on Trixie and then Stella. "I admire my older sister more than words can convey. Her dedication enabled me to have a career. She's never had a chance for one, herself." In an obvious attempt to lighten the mood, she adds, "I often remind my dear friend, Trixie, here, how you saved the day with the RV park and she needs to be forever grateful for your sacrifice."

Stella sputters and sneaks a peek at her sister. "Oh, we manage to share the load, Cavelle. Each of us does what we do best when it comes to Dad, right Trixie?" Her effort to be magnanimous goes unnoticed.

Trixie reaches for her second biscuit and nods. In a tone of voice Stella has heard before, she simpers, "I do my part."

"Back to Del." Stella attempts to engage Cavelle once again. "She imagines Hester might have pushed Lucy and Opal wants to protect her. Your aunt's idea isn't plausible, Cavelle?" Persistence is necessary, at least for the moment.

"Opal says Lucy insisted on going off to look at the basement by herself. Hester asked to go, but Opal wouldn't let her. Why would Opal lie, Stella?" The frustration is audible in Cavelle's voice. "Hester is incapacitated in many ways. Even if she did push Lucy, she didn't know what she was doing."

"I understand, Cavelle. The question of competency is paramount in any court."

"The idea his sister killed his wife of three months would put Jacob over the edge." Trixie peers across the top of her mug.

"Correct." Cavelle drops her soup spoon into her empty bowl. "And what motive did Hester have? She has issues, but only specific events or occurrences set her off, Stella. She doesn't hurt people. The girl is as non-violent as you or I."

Stella pauses. She reminds herself their topic of conversation is Cavelle's siblings, and not a random case she's troubleshooting with Aiden. She tries to be cautious and parses her words. "Hester told me, on the day of the wedding, that Jacob was going away to live with Lucy. Maybe, in her mind, her brother intended to leave and toss their relationship aside."

"She might have feared Jacob would abandon her, Stella, but he would *never* abandon Hester. He has always made time for her, regardless of his other responsibilities. I am confident he will never change."

"Hester told me on Monday, when I visited, how Jacob won't talk to her now. Does she make up observations? Could she be mad at Jacob, and you or Opal aren't aware?"

Trixie's voice is soft. "Don't push, Stella. Lucy's death, the funeral, her family—the circumstances have been very challenging for Cavelle."

"I'm sorry, Cavelle. Have I upset you?" Stella rushes to ensure she hasn't pressed too hard.

"No, Stella, but Aunt Del gets an idea in her brain and she can't be budged."

"My sister's the same way." Trixie reaches out to touch Cavelle's shoulder.

"Stella can be a terrier with a bone. She never knows when to let go."

They change the subject and focus on the real estate market as well as the annual fundraiser fashion show Grey Cottage Realty sponsors on behalf of the community centre. Stella's contribution will involve a cheque—the limit of her expertise.

Tea is refreshed. The light drizzle has thickened into a cold rain poised to turn to sleet as the temperature hovers near freezing. Trixie has the day off. She has Wednesdays free in the fall and winter but goes to the fish plant part-time on the other weekdays. Cavelle's job slows this time of year, too. Most people shop for a new home, a cottage, or a plot of land in the summer months. The women linger.

"Were you aware Lucy was sick?"

"Stella, are you starting again?" Trixie's annoyance is palpable.

Cavelle speaks with what Stella interprets as renewed interest. "What do you mean? Who said she was sick?"

"Hester told me."

"Oh, Stella." Cavelle slumps back into her chair. "Hester spouts weird remarks on a regular basis. The odd one might be sensible, but most aren't." She reaches for her purse and prepares to approach the counter to settle her bill. "I'll talk to Jacob and see if she mentioned to him Lucy wasn't well. She could have felt dizzy and fallen, which makes significantly more sense than the theory that Hester pushed her."

"Call me after you have your discussion with Jacob, okay, Cavelle?"

Cavelle waves her goodbyes and Stella returns her attention to Trixie. "Do you have a few more minutes? My little dinner party is in ten days. Is your new man able to come with you or will Brigitte be your plus one, yet again?" She tries to tease.

Trixie, in her enthusiasm, misses Stella's point. "Yes. I can't wait. Russ says he has no scheduled business between the end of the week and the New Year. Saturday, the twentieth, is perfect." Her sister has managed a swoon as she talks. She must be more enamoured than usual with her most recent beau.

"There's no requirement to contribute. Supper won't be a potluck."

"What? Is Nick the cook?" Trixie giggles.

Stella whacks her on the arm. "No. The chef at the hotel will make tourtières for me as well as a cranberry and apple torte. I'll add roasted veggies and we'll be good. Is my menu okay with you?"

"Of course. You'll invite Aiden and Rosemary, right? I love her."

"I'll call Rosemary as soon as I get home but confirm with Aiden to be on the safe side. Poor Rosemary. If a message gets screwed up, she's had a hand in the confusion."

"I wonder what she'll wear. Honest to God, Stella, her get-up at the end-of-the-season park barbecue was smashing."

Stella recalls the lime green capri pants and polka dotted sunglasses, which she kept on her face for the evening. She played the role of a celebrity, incognito at a party held by her fans. Rosemary conducts her life as if she's still in high school. Aiden explained to Stella earlier in the year how his wife's depression is debilitating, but when she assumes the persona of her teenage self from the 1950s, she manages to become a social butterfly. Trixie, the fashion guru of the family, is inspired by Rosemary's style.

"Aiden needs to feel comfortable and confident she's accepted by us. No one makes 'crazy lady' comments behind her back. You might want to give Russ fair warning."

"Sure, no problem."

As is Trixie's habit, when it's time to leave, she wiggles her fingers at Stella on the way out the door. She managed to leave money for her tab on the table.

Later in the afternoon, Stella takes time from calculating her 1981 projected expenses to contact Rosemary. "North residence. Rosemary speaking."

"How are you today?" Stella can hear Annette Funicello belting out "My Little Grass Shack" in the background.

"Oh, hi Stella. Let me turn down the volume on my record player. Aiden says I always play my songs too loud."

After a moment, she returns to the phone, breathless. The music isn't much lower.

"I called to invite you to Nick's and my pre-Christmas supper a week from Saturday."

"Goodie." Her response is instantaneous. "We will come, of course."

Stella is cautious. "Do you need to double-check with Aiden?"

"No. I want to attend. Will your sister be at the party?"

"Trixie is invited, along with her new boyfriend, Russ Harrison."

"Oh, fabulous. She's a sweet girl. I love her. You are lucky to have Trixie for a sister. Mine can be very demanding." She pauses for a moment.

"Sweet girl" is not a particularly apt description of Trixie, and according to Aiden, Rosemary's sisters are a huge help to her. Rosemary's view of the world is entirely her own.

"What time? I'll write a message for Aiden."

"Dinner will be Saturday, the twentieth. Come to the park any time after five. We'll plan supper for six-thirty."

"What can I cook?"

"Not a crumb. I'm organized."

"Thanks for the invitation, Stella. See you next week. Bye."

Before she can react, Rosemary's gone, and the dial tone hums in her ear. Stella smiles. The abrupt end of the phone call mirrors Trixie's annoying habit of hanging up without saying goodbye. Aiden must have his hands full even if her two sisters help him when his hours are unpredictable.

"Detective North, please."

"Hi, Stella. It's Moyer. I recognized your voice. Hold on a minute and I'll get him."

"North."

"Aiden, Stella here."

"What's up?" He pauses. "I hope your call isn't work related."

"No, not right now, but I want to discuss Lucy Painter with you soon. The reason I've called today is to tell you I spoke with your charming wife and the two of you are invited out to the park for a pre-Christmas dinner party on Saturday, December 20, any time after five. Are you writing the information down?"

"Didn't you give Rosie the details?" His laugh is apologetic. "Okay. Okay. I have made an official back-up note. Thanks for the invite. Now, what about Lucy Painter? She fell into the basement of her bungalow under construction, hit her head, and died. Her sudden death was a tragic accident, Stella."

"I'm troubled. I know the family well, but Del has gotten me thinking. If we find a moment when you're out at the house, we'll talk."

"Why not have a visit on another day, after your party?"

"Good idea. Will you show me the autopsy report?"

He hesitates again. "The information is straightforward. The results were discussed with Jacob. I guess no harm will come from sharing them with you now."

"What's 'discussed with Jacob' supposed to mean?"

"It was a tragic fall, Stella. Sad but true."

Chapter 6

I'm Worried for His Mental Health

"I talked to Jacob—well, the whole family. I've eaten warmed-over supper almost every night for the past month, but I made a point to join the three of them on Saturday."

Stella hears remorse gurgle in Cavelle's throat. She's desperate to learn how Jacob has managed after Lucy's death, but the voice on the other end of the phone sounds defeated and lost. "What keeps you from eating dinner with your family, Cavelle?"

"Often, I stay at the office until I'm certain they're finished. The Painter farm is not the greatest place to be right now. Opal always sticks a plate in the warming oven for me."

"How does Jacob cope?"

"I was honest with them, Stella. I reported how Aunt Del has meddled in our affairs in the same way she did after Dad died. Hester doesn't understand—but Opal was pissed off. She wanted to go to the nursing home and give Aunt Del a piece of her mind."

"Del was concerned, Cavelle. She's an old lady."

"That's understandable but let her worry about Eve or another of her relatives for a change."

Stella repeats her initial question, which Cavelle has yet to answer. "How does Jacob cope? What was his reaction?"

Cavelle's exasperation wafts into the telephone connection. "Jacob was quiet through the whole discussion. Hester even asked him if he was mad at her. He studied her for a second, then whispered 'no' and stared at his plate. To be honest, I'm worried for his mental health."

"Does he need to see a counselor?"

Cavelle guffaws in Stella's ear. "Listen, Jacob's support system is a barn full of equipment and a bunch of farmers who meet for coffee twice a week. He's not the type to talk to a professional. God! He won't even talk to us."

"Could he suffer from guilt for any reason?" Stella doesn't want to antagonize Cavelle, but Jacob's behaviour, when in the company of his sisters who love him, doesn't appear normal.

"What's the reason for his guilt, Stella? He wasn't home when Lucy died. He was in town at a dinner meeting. Your investigation is focused on a nonexistent problem. You requested I speak with Jacob, and I did my best."

Stella lowers her voice and concentrates on projecting calmness. "Thank you, Cavelle. I appreciate your patience. Did Opal or Jacob mention an illness related to Lucy at any time before her death?"

"No. I asked the question. Opal rejected the idea out of hand. She emphasized Lucy's healthy appetite."

"Are you able to describe Jacob's reaction?"

Cavelle takes a deep breath. "Jacob looked surprised for a second, but his eyes were very sad. I'm convinced I made the situation worse because Hester began to bleat about how sick Lucy was." She groans. "By the end of the meal, I felt I should have stayed at the office."

"I'm sorry I stirred matters up for you."

"My dinner table tension isn't your fault. Aunt Del asked you to 'investigate;' to ask questions. You respected her wishes. Lucy's death has been tragic. I hope Jacob will figure out a way to move on. I don't imagine he'll be free from his grief anytime soon, though."

"Thanks for your time, Cavelle. I appreciate how difficult the conversation was, but it was important to follow up on Hester's remarks."

"Well, you know Hester. Between Hester and Aunt Del, reality can be difficult to decipher." Stella detects a hint of a chuckle in her voice.

The tension has been diffused. "We'll talk soon, Cavelle. Please encourage Opal not to give poor old Del a hard time."

"I'll do my best, but I would gather you've figured out I do not have a great deal of influence with the Painter crew, despite my efforts. See you, Stella."

"Take care, Cavelle."

She appreciates Cavelle's interpretation of the conversation with her family, although she isn't prepared to accept the information at face value. Jacob's behaviour is uncommon for a young man not yet thirty. To exhibit an element of anger, in addition to his sadness, is expected but he didn't ask questions related to the state of his wife's health before her sudden death; abnormal, to say the least. Del's suspicions may be well-founded but misdirected.

"Nick." She yells out the door of her office. He's busy in Alice's little reception area. She hears the sander as he readies the counter for a fresh coat of paint.

The sander shudders to a stop. "I'm right here. Ready for tea?"

"Yes. May I run a thought or two past you? I need a male perspective."

He takes the few steps necessary to traverse the distance between them and produces one of his grins guaranteed to cause her heart to twitch. "What? You're not waiting for Aiden on Saturday night?"

"Stop." She acknowledges his tease. Nick felt intimidated when Aiden first arrived to investigate Lorraine's disappearance. He insists he now realizes her old high school flame is not a threat. She hopes Aiden doesn't turn into Nick's excuse to leave for Florida and never return. "Listen to this." Her eyes widen as she reveals her news. "Aiden has promised to share Lucy Painter's autopsy report with me early next week. I wanted to talk with him at the party, but he doesn't want to discuss death at a dinner party, or in front of Rosemary, I guess."

She stands up from her desk. "Let's go in the kitchen and I'll ask my questions while you make me tea." She wraps an arm around his waist when she reaches the doorway. "Imagine Lucy was murdered."

Nick's eyes narrow. "Is there evidence? Is this why you're so anxious to see the autopsy report?"

"Here's my theory. Hester pushed Lucy into the basement where she died. Opal found them both in the yard, observed Lucy was dead, settled Hester inside, and called the ambulance and police. She contacted Jacob and Cavelle, who both tore home."

"A plausible series of events, Stella, except the story is Lucy walked over to the construction site by herself."

"Correct." Stella watches his ass while he makes the tea. The two behaviours have become synonymous habits somehow. "Let's say Opal tells Jacob the truth once they're alone. Consequences for Hester would be minimal because she's incompetent. Cavelle is none the wiser. Opal and Jacob are left to keep the secret."

"Okay. What will you do besides read the autopsy report?"

"I'm puzzled and need more information. I wonder why Cavelle describes Jacob's behaviour as if he has a reason to be guilty. She says she doesn't think he's guilty, but her description of him tells a different story. Has Jacob buried his anger to protect his sister? Does he regret attending his meeting instead of staying home with Lucy? It was his second night out in a row. Events don't add up."

From across the table, Nick meets her eyes. "You didn't answer my question, Stella."

"I think it would be useful if Aiden and I conducted interviews with both families. First, I'll hear the obligatory lecture—I have no concrete evidence. We'll see. Good tea, by the way."

****

Precipitation sticks to the windows before it slides toward the sill. The pellets, for they are neither snow nor rain, stack against the glass. If the storm worsens, she might not be able to see the yard by supper time. Her party could be canceled for lack of attendees.

The jangle of the phone jolts her away from her musings. "Shale Cliffs RV Park. Stella Kirk here."

"Do you have snow or rain out your way?"

"A kind of cross between the two, Trixie. Are you calling to cancel?"

"Good grief! No! Russ has a four-wheel-drive truck." Her voice drops an octave. "He said there's no point in attempting to find our way back to town later tonight, and I'd better pack my toothbrush. I guess I'm invited to his place. The cottage is five minutes from the park."

"Oh, I am fully aware of his cottage's location. You haven't been there before, Trixie? I must say, I'm surprised."

"Now, Stella. Stop and think." She giggles. "Russ and I prefer to go to Port Ephron for services. Understand?"

"Trixie, you're a grandmother! You don't need to pretend you're twenty and involved in a lurid affair."

"Why not? We like to play. Nick is ten years younger than you. Have your fun your way and I'll have mine. Anyway, we'll be at your house, regardless of the weather. I can't wait to see Rosemary." She pauses for a breath. "I hope Aiden booked a room at the hotel. I doubt if he'll want to navigate across the isthmus tonight."

"I'll tell him, if he calls. See you soon...and behave!"

She can hear Trixie chortle as she replaces the receiver in the cradle.

Before crossing the kitchen to finish vegetable preparations, the phone rings again. "Shale Cliffs RV Park..."

"How bad is the weather over your way?"

"What am I, the CBC meteorologist, Aiden?" She doesn't wait for his reply. "Worsening by the minute. Since we're near the water, I can see sleet mixed into the snow. I talked to Trixie and she said, from the looks of conditions in Shale Harbour, you two should arrange for a room at the Harbour Hotel."

"We already decided to stay at the hotel. We've booked a spot, but we might be late for dinner. Rosemary is flummoxed regarding attire. Any suggestions?"

"As usual, I choose comfy. She likes her pretty dresses. Tell her to wear whatever she wants but include a big cozy sweater in case we lose the power and our heat source becomes the fireplace. Helpful?"

"You have no idea. She's excited and anxious now, soon to be followed by distracted and unreasonable. Be warned, my friend."

"Don't worry. Trixie and Russ are coming. She and Trixie are kindred spirits. We'll have a fine time." Stella softens the mood. "I love the park when the weather's gruesome, which means I'm pleased the two of you are not considering the trip back to Port Ephron later tonight. Tell her I'm thrilled she'll be here."

Aiden's voice loses its edge. "Thanks. I'll relay your advice. See you soon."

The phone goes dead. She turns around to find Nick with both hands in the dishpan as he peels vegetables for the roaster. "Do we have enough for the six of us?" The expression on his face warms her to her very core. "I don't care if we have leftovers. My favourite part."

"Potatoes, turnips, and carrots will suffice. They take a good hour. We can warm up the oven and get them started around five. Aiden called. Rosemary's experiencing a fashion meltdown." She attempts to smooth her wrinkled heavy cotton pants. "I need to change."

"You look fine to me. Be comfortable. Rosemary will be the 1950s movie star and Trixie will be the...guess I won't say." He saunters over, knife in one hand and potato in the other. He places his elbows on her shoulders. "You, my dear, are beautiful in whatever you choose to wear."

She blushes. She always blushes, and he can elicit a similar reaction with a moment's notice. "Good. Happy you appreciate my ensemble, lover boy, but I need to clean up and at least change my sweater." She balances on the toes of her suede moccasins while she brushes his lips with her own. "I won't be long. Thanks for the help with the veggies." She pauses and turns. "By the way, let's pull out the dining room table from the wall and eat in front of the fire instead of in here."

"Great idea. We can set the furniture up when you finish whatever you intend to do. Away you go, now."

He hustles her from the kitchen and returns to the sink. She takes the stairs two at a time. *Instead of being so anxious, I must remind myself more often what a wonderful man he is.*

****

Their knock sounds weak because the wind is at a crescendo pitch. When she opens the old oak inside door and balances the screen with her other hand, she finds the Norths huddled against the shingled siding. "Get inside, you two. Our storm is getting worse."

The couple lurches into the great room. Rosemary starts to chatter the second she's out of the weather. "Thanks for the invitation, Stella. The park is real nifty with the snow and ice. You live inside a postcard. I adore the place, even in the winter." She removes her swing coat with the pleated high waistband and hands the garment back to her husband without looking. He catches the heavy wool fabric before it hits the floor. "Your tree! Gorgeous!" She turns for a moment. "Merry Christmas, Stella. Give her what we brought, Aiden."

Aiden's expression is sheepish. Laden with coats, he silently appeals to Stella for help.

Stella reaches under her guest's maroon coat draped across Aiden's arm and retrieves a festive bag. "Thanks, you two. We can never have enough wine, especially on a night as blustery as tonight. Let me take these coats. I'll put them in reception." She watches his face relax.

Nick pushes through the kitchen door as Rosemary approaches.

"I wondered where you were." Her tone has a sing-song quality.

"Stella likes to keep me busy. Now, aren't you the foxy lady tonight?" Nick has thoughtfully recalled their previous conversation about Rosemary's indecision.

Rosemary has chosen a red party dress. The fabric pattern depicts the Nutcracker which includes toy soldiers, presents, ornaments, queens, snowflakes, and stars sprinkled throughout. It's cinched at the waist with a belt covered in the same fabric. The neckline is a sweetheart design, and the bodice has minimal cap sleeves. Trixie will adore this outfit. Rosemary took Stella's advice to heart and has a heavier white sweater which she wraps over her shoulders.

She twirls around the room in response to the attention from Nick.

"Was that a knock?" Nick waves a hand in Stella's direction.

"Let me check." She opens the big oak door once again to find Trixie and Russ rummaging in Trixie's purse. "No need for keys. We're here. Come on in."

As they rustle themselves out of their coats, Stella assesses Russ Harrison with her standard efficiency. He could be forty-five. He's clean-shaven and his hair is grey. Although he obviously takes care of himself, describing him as attractive would be an over-reach. He is normal; average; the kind of guy who blends in.

"Sorry to be late. Russ wanted to pick up a few groceries to take out to the cottage tonight. Stuff for breakfast." Trixie's stage whisper would still be audible if the two women were outside in the wind.

Stella extends her hand. "You must be Russ. I'm Trixie's sister, Stella. Allow me to introduce Nick Cochran, our other partner here at the park, as well as my partner in crime." She winks at Nick as she turns her attention to the Norths. "And we are joined tonight by Aiden and Rosemary North, who live over in the Port."

Russ meanders around the big living room and shakes hands with each of Stella's guests in turn. She hears him mutter, "Russ Harrison. Nice to meet you," three separate times.

Nick to the rescue. "Okay. Shall I pour drinks? Supper will be in thirty minutes. Right, Stella?"

She glances at her wristwatch. The vegetables need another twenty minutes. "Yes, let's get drinks. Supper in a half hour."

When they return with beverages, conversation has already started to flow.

"What has brought you to our part of the world, Aiden?" Russ leans forward as if Aiden is the most important person in the room. "Retiring by the sea?"

Russ is what Stella would describe as a smooth operator. He's slick. He searches deep into your eyes. He reminds her of a politician hustling for votes. Stella notices how Trixie watches him with a mesmerized and loopy expression on her face. *She's smitten.*

"Not retired, yet, I'm afraid."

"I wish he was," Rosemary interjects.

"I've taken on the lead detective role at the RCMP station in Port Ephron. It will be my last post."

"We want to retire right here with Stella, don't we, Aiden?" Rosemary wiggles her behind closer to her husband and hooks her arm in his. "We have a trailer here at the park. We bought our unit from the estate of a girl who was murdered in May."

Stella cannot control her compulsion to clarify. "She didn't die in her unit, or even here at Shale Cliffs."

"No, they found her in a drainage ditch beside a field."

Aiden must not shelter her from as many details related to his work as I assumed.

Russ stares at Rosemary with rapt attention. She basks.

"And what do you do, Russ? Stella tells me you bought a cottage nearby." Rosemary's index finger is on her cheek while her thumb is under her chin. Her lips smile, but her eyes contain an eerie blankness.

"Yes. Renovated and winterized before cold weather, thank God." He glances at the snow-covered window for effect.

"You managed to find work around here?" Aiden refocuses back to his wife's earlier question.

Stella can sense a change in Aiden's tone. She's seen him interview enough suspects to interpret when his conversations are no longer casual.

"I consult. Human Resource Management."

Trixie inserts a remark into the conversation. "Russ travels for work. He's away lots."

"Sounds interesting." Aiden's voice is flat.

Stella senses Aiden has more questions deliberately not asked.

Dinner is a decided success. The chef at the Harbour Hotel outdid expectations with both the tourtières and the cranberry-apple dessert. Even the veggies get rave reviews. The storm rages on. The wind howls around the old house. The shingles shudder and the veranda creaks under the pressure of snow mixed with freezing rain building up along the eaves.

"Time to take off, right, Russ?" Trixie winks at Stella.

"Sure, babe. We're only five minutes away, but I imagine the roads are gruesome."

Stella trots out to reception and retrieves their coats. "Give me a call, Trixie. Merry Christmas, you two. Thanks for making the trip out on such a stormy night."

Within minutes, they're gone. The pickup truck roars to life. Stella peers out the side window and sees the box fishtail as the lights disappear on the way up the road.

"I suppose we should face the elements, too, my girl. The highway to Shale Harbour will be plowed, but the freezing rain has challenges." His perpetually tilted head acknowledges Nick and Stella in turn.

"What a wonderful evening, Stella." She hugs Nick. "Peachy, Nick."

Stella hands her the maroon swing coat.

"Don't forget to put on your gloves, honey. The car is cold for the first couple of minutes."

"Isn't he swell? Aiden always takes care of me, ever since we started going steady." Her eyes appear moist with the memory.

"Thanks again, you two. I'll call you Monday, Stella. We're fast approaching Christmas, but maybe we can have our talk. I'd prefer to come out here—too many ears at the Cocoa and Café."

"No problem. Nick and I will be around."

Nick shakes Aiden's hand. "My assignment is to repaint Alice's office *before* the holidays. The boss lady also has plans for the kitchen." He wraps a warm arm around Stella's shoulder.

Chapter 7

No One Was Aware

Aiden should be at the park any moment. The coffee is ready. The plow came an hour ago, and Nick is outside shoveling walks. Snow fell with a steady determination throughout the weekend, and they've devoted Monday morning to cleaning. She hears Nick shout out a greeting as Aiden's blue sedan lumbers into the parking lot.

"Navigating your big old car along my lane was a challenge?" She greets him as he stamps his feet and steps into the her living room.

He nods and bends to pull off his boots. "Needed to shovel my way out of the yard in Port Ephron," he grunts. "There were several vehicles in the ditch, and I wondered if the road across the isthmus might be closed, but I persevered." Cold air lingers around his coat. He hands her a tan manila folder. "I expect today to be quiet. Not many laws get broken when the weather's miserable and the roads are slippery."

She clutches the thin file while she acknowledges his observations. "I guess criminals don't want to shovel any more than the rest of us."

Nick opens the screen door as Aiden moves further into the room and removes his coat. "This coming from someone who hasn't shoveled today." The bluster of the wind matches his remark.

She gives him an affectionate punch. "Have a seat, Aiden." She squints when she peers over at him. "I assume you drove this far out of your way for a cup of coffee. I'll be right back."

"We can start there. I may need to spike my drink with rum, if you observe more in the autopsy report than I do."

When the three are comfortable on sofas, with warm pottery mugs of hazelnut-flavoured brew distributed, Stella reviews the documents. Her stomach is tense. She's nauseous. The room is dead quiet while she reads. She's aware of Nick's attention as he holds his mug and watches her. Aiden stares at the fire.

When she closes the file, Nick asks, "What does the report say?"

"The pathologist states she fell in the basement and died." The additional information is shocking. "She was pregnant. I had no idea."

"We've concluded no one was aware, not even Lucy."

"What makes you certain?"

"We talked to Jacob. He was flabbergasted when we told him. A bereaved husband couldn't fake the kind of response he exhibited. We spoke with Lucy's family doctor and he had not seen her in months. She didn't have a pending appointment. I discussed the issue with Ardith Holland, her supervisor from At-Home Care Services. She said Lucy missed a few shifts at work, including the day of her death. We were informed regarding November 18, but not the other days."

"The information explains why Hester repeated how Lucy was sick."

"Yes. The general opinion of the pathologist states she was dizzy from pregnancy symptoms, lost her balance, and toppled into the basement. The bruises on her body matched her position when she was found. We're sure she wasn't moved."

"Have you considered she was hit first and thrown into the basement afterward?" Nick says out loud what she's thinking.

"No. Forensics determined she died where she fell. We've sent blood, urine, and tissue samples away for analysis. Results could take at least a month, maybe more."

"What are they testing for?" Stella wants all the answers right now.

"The report indicates her liver and kidneys appeared damaged. The plausible explanation is the impact caused the anomalies. The lab wants to make sure she didn't have additional complications which precipitated her loss of balance and subsequent fall."

Nick interjects. "Are we to understand the fall killed her, but we don't know why she fell...yet?"

Aiden sips his coffee. "You're right. We're certain of the cause of death. Her pregnancy, or a specific symptom, might have caused an episode of dizziness."

Stella's voice is soft. "She could have taken drugs or been shoved."

"Possibilities, Stella. The position of the body tells us a great deal. The pictures are under the report. I brought them in case you wanted to look. They indicate she slid down the wall. She must have sat on the cement before she keeled over. If she was pushed hard, she would have been further from the side. Then again, if she were nudged...."

"I'm still puzzled, Aiden. Even if she wasn't aware of her pregnancy, Opal or Cavelle must have learned she was sick. They all live together. If Hester noticed, then why were the other two sisters not suspicious? I want to understand what they observed. How often did she miss work? How was her appetite? Was she throwing up?" Her questions start to tumble over top of one another.

"Don't get ahead of yourself, Stella."

Nick's cautionary words serve to slow her. She purses her lips as she meets his gaze. "You're correct, of course, but the investigation remains open, at least until the analysis is completed. We can still interview people involved, right Aiden?"

The police detective refills his cup from the carafe on the coffee table before he replies. "Yes. In the strictest of terms, the investigation is still open, although there appears to be no motive, or hard evidence, for that matter, of anything untoward." He leans back into the sofa. "I agree regarding revisiting Jacob, his sisters, and Lucy's boss, though. If you accompany me, we can talk to the family together. I'll need further history. I'm interested in your impressions, but we must remain extremely low key. To be honest, I don't know if Jacob told the Smithers family Lucy was pregnant."

"You mean Reid and Bitsy have no idea their daughter was expecting when she died?" Stella is horrified. "No one spoke to them?"

"Not as far as I'm aware, Stella. Perhaps Jacob has talked to them by now."

She sits up straighter on the couch and reaches for the carafe. "If Lucy suspected she was going to have a baby, she discussed the possibility with Bitsy first. A clear way to ascertain whether Lucy knew she was pregnant is to talk to her mother. This could change everything."

Aiden nods. "We can do interviews after the holidays, but we'll describe them as follow-up because it was a sudden death."

****

Since Stella moved back to Shale Harbour, Trixie and her daughter have hosted Christmas Eve dinner. Stella likes Christmas morning at the park. She makes chowder for lunch. She and Nick want to create traditions together. Trixie and Brigitte enjoy a raucous celebration with Mia in the morning, so the sisters settled on a compromise. The festive time works for everyone. They include Norbert in the family dinner and then he enjoys the celebrations at Harbour Manor on the twenty-fifth.

As they bounce up the plowed drive to retrieve Norbert from the manor and take him to Trixie's dinner, Stella harnesses her emotions. Norbert won't recognize her although he loves and remembers Nick. When he needs encouragement to get into the Jeep, his relationship with Nick will help. She bought him a sweater jacket—a brown, washable wool blend with pockets. She wrapped the box with red foil and added a big bow. He'll no doubt thank Nick and tell her to empty his trash.

Nick has heard her sigh and pats her leg as he turns off the vehicle. "I'm fine," she replies to his touch. "Let's get going." She climbs out, waits for her love to circle the Jeep, and hooks her free arm in his. She hands him the package. "You might as well give him his present."

"Not a chance. Remember, Stella, there are days when I come over for a visit when he asks after you." Nick averts his attention from the salted path and holds her tighter. "I told him I married you." The ring of his laugh is crystal clear in cool night air. "I married his daughter and own the park, too."

"What? He believed you?"

"Hopefully."

"Geez, Nick. We'll need to find a way to make sure Trixie and Brigitte are in on your scheme."

"No problem. I briefed them when Trixie called to confirm the time."

"Secrets, mister. You are full of secrets." She isn't cross. She learned years ago, where circumstances relate to her father and his dementia, options are few. She takes a deep breath when they reach his door.

"Hello, Norbert. Ready to go to Christmas Eve dinner at Trixie's?"

"Nick. Glad you're here. Well! You brought your bride." He extends a gnarled and liver-spotted hand. His fingers always appear longer than might be expected for a man of his stature. "Norbert Kirk. Awful nice to git to meet you."

Stella decides, at that moment, to play along. He has remembered Nick has a wife, but he doesn't see her as his daughter. "Great to meet you, too.

I'm Stella Cochran. This present is from Nick and me." She sets the shiny red foiled box on the bed. "You can open your gift now or wait until tomorrow."

"Well, aren't you sweet?" He rips into the foil, pulls up the lid, and exposes the rich brown knit. "Here. Help me put it on. It's great. Just what an old guy needs in a drafty building like this one." Rheumy eyes focus on each of them in turn. "Thanks. I'll wear my new sweater tonight." He shoves his hands in the pockets. "Where are we goin', again?"

Trixie's rundown two-bedroom rental house sits near the centre of Shale Harbour. Entrance is through an unfinished and uninsulated front porch, which serves to break the wind. The snow has been scraped off the gravel of her short driveway. Even so, the result is barely enough room to pull the Jeep in behind Trixie's 1970 VW Microbus. As Stella alights from the passenger side of the front and opens the back door of the vehicle for her father, she regrets her unspoken criticism of Trixie's accommodations. Since the VW van won't last much longer, Trixie's prime location might prove convenient.

Norbert starts to clamor out but ignores Stella's proffered arm. "I'll wait for Nick to help me. Need a strong guy when I walk over the snow."

Nick skids around the back bumper as Stella moves out of his way. A year ago, she would have argued and felt slighted, but no more. She waits while Nick helps her father and then she closes the vehicle door while still clutching Mia's parcel in her free hand.

Her sister's shabby kitchen is decorated with multicoloured twinkling lights. The rickety table is paired with a folding contraption which might have once served her parents for card games. None of the chairs match. They are surrounded by the holiday smells of turkey and summer savory.

Stella relaxes. Their simple rules have been followed. Dinner is not potluck as are many family meals. Trixie cooks and Brigitte makes the dessert. No presents are exchanged, except for Mia. Stella brought a book: *The Velveteen Rabbit*. Stella's Christmas wish is for the heartfelt story to be read to Mia over and over again in the years to come. If the child wears the book out, she will buy her another.

"Dinner was wonderful, Trixie." Stella smiles her gratitude across the table.

Mia sits wide-eyed on her mother's knee. She caresses her new book while she waits for the people to leave. Brigitte and Mia have a plan to read together later.

Trixie, sparkling in a red sequined tank top and a long black skirt, preens. "Dinner is my contribution for a holiday family night, Stella. Most of our occasions happen at the park. Tonight's celebration is from us." She pats her daughter's hand.

"Where's Russ? I heard him say he intended to be around over the holidays." Nick has started to help Norbert on with his coat as he talks.

Trixie pouts. "He's home. I invited him, but he figured my dinner was too much family too soon." She shrugs her shoulders. "Oh well, his loss. He plans to come by on Boxing Day to meet Brigitte and Mia." She frowns. "I don't understand his problem. He's already met you people. God give me patience."

On the return drive, Stella decides to explore whether her father remembers the Painter family. Her parents were friends with Leon and Velma at one time. "Dad. Sorry. Norbert, do you recall the Painter family?"

"Sure do. Leon and Velma built the farm over on the point. Both gone now."

"Right. Do you remember their kids?"

"Yup. Dorothy and me—we had two girls, and they had three. Theirs stayed near home while ours moved away. Kids."

She twists around and sees, in the shadowed light from the dash, strands of his thin grey hair sliding from side to side. He shakes his head in what must be aggravation related to a perceived slight from years ago.

"There was one weird kid; everybody said she was stupid."

"Hester? Do you mean Hester, Norbert?"

"Yeah. Her name was Hester. Velma kept her home. My Dorothy thought she should be in school with other kids."

"Why did she disagree with Mrs. Painter?"

"You can't tell a book by its cover. Dorothy used to say you can't tell a book by its cover."

****

Christmas Day, Boxing Day, and the weekend were perfect. Stella holds her warm thoughts close while she makes coffee and prepares leftover cinnamon buns along with scrambled eggs for breakfast. For a second year, they exchanged books. Nick gave her Jeffrey Archer's *Kane and Abel*. She bought him John LeCarré's *Smiley's People*. They read. They watched sappy Christmas movies while the television flickered and blurred with the wind.

They kept the fire well banked as the snow blew and swirled around the windows. They intended to depend on the answering machine, but the phone never rang. On their first official Christmas as a couple, they managed to take full advantage of both their time and their privacy. She senses the heat on her cheeks again when she hears his heavy tread on the stairs.

"Good morning, madame. I trust you slept well?"

She blushes again. "It's Monday. Back to work." Deflection is her go-to option.

"Oh. You mean time to start painting? Will you help?" He wraps plaid flannel arms around her shoulders.

"Nope. I expect to hear from Aiden any minute. We might visit Reid and Bitsy Smithers today. I wonder if they suspected Lucy was pregnant?"

Nick sneaks a piece of cinnamon bun. "Not a chance. Bitsy is a chatterbox. Keeping quiet isn't one of her qualities. I don't imagine you'll have an easy time. Bitsy's the emotional type."

As he reaches for another chunk of the mangled bun, the racket of the ringing phone interrupts their conversation. Aiden is on his way.

They have a quick coffee together. Aiden makes a call to Lucy's parents' home and confirms they are welcome to drop by near ten o'clock. "Is our goal to determine if they understood Lucy was pregnant?" Stella is aware of how precarious the emotions of Mr. and Mrs. Smithers are likely to be.

"I don't want them to assume we've opened an investigation—at least not yet. We can't jump to conclusions. The evidence points to a simple fall. She was dizzy because of her pregnancy and she fell."

"Might I ask the parents if she expressed any concerns regarding her move out to the Painter farm, or the family in general?"

"As long as we don't suggest foul play. I told them the protocol is to talk to people who were important in her life while we wait for toxicology. I said the reason our visit is six weeks after her death is because of the holiday and basic routines are no rush. I added that I asked you to accompany me because of your history with the Painter family and because I'm newly back to the area. I won't get away with adding that last bit for too much longer." His lips form a thin line although his eyes twinkle.

The Smithers live in a 1950s bungalow, on a residential street near downtown Port Ephron. They bought the house five years ago when they moved from Marathon, Ontario. They could have bought a larger and newer house in a subdivision, but this one is close to the Pontiac / Buick dealership. Reid is the manager, and their son, Glen, is a salesman.

Stella and Aiden trudge up the brick path to the front door, framed by glass block on both sides. The entry has three little windows across the top and the doorbell plays a tune Stella recognizes but can't, for the life of her, remember the title.

Reid counters the sound. "Hold your horses. On my way."

Stella and Aiden exchange glances.

The moment he swings the door open, Reid extends a manicured and mitt-like hand to Aiden. Ever the traditional car salesman, and although the calendar will soon indicate 1981, he's dressed in a brown suit with ivory stripes. A pair of spats and he could pass for a carnival barker from the 1930s.

"Welcome, Detective North. And Stella Kirk. Pleasure to have a visit with you."

Aiden clears his throat. "I still don't have a partner and, since I left town when I was a kid, Stella here helps me meet people."

"No problem. Bitsy said the two of you were poppin' by. Besides, I'm tryin' to encourage Stella to trade that old Jeep of her father's." His voice booms. "Bitsy, honey, the company's here."

Stella raises one brow toward Aiden and then, as she tends to do, completes a quick assessment of the entry way and living room as they move nearer the sofa. Christmas decorations are subdued to say the least. They have trimmed a small tree by the front window, but there are no lights. They must have struggled to do the little they did. Three sympathy cards remain on the mantle. Stella attempts to brush aside a pang of guilt washing over her as she recalls her own cozy and loving holiday.

Bitsy appears in the arched entry separating the living room and dining area from the kitchen. She's wiping her hands on an apron which would fall to mid-thigh on Stella but hangs well below Bitsy's knees. She is very short. Her bum is her only large feature. She waddles in. "Stella, how nice of you to come along with the detective. Detective North, I'm Bitsy Smithers. My name's Elizabeth, but everyone calls me Bitsy. Pleased to meet you. Have a seat. Can I get you tea, coffee?"

She reminds Stella of an anxious hen.

"No thanks, Bitsy." Aiden is gracious as he sits. Stella chooses a chair to the side. The Smithers both perch on an antique settee to the right of the tree.

Aiden continues. "We thought it important to share a piece of information learned from the autopsy report, and to ask a few questions related to Lucy prior to her death." Bitsy's eyes instantly puddle. "I hope we haven't intruded."

She drags a tissue out of her apron pocket and dabs at her eyes. "I'm fine. Go ahead. I cope the best I can." She attempts a smile through the glaze of her tears. "I've decided life will be difficult from now on. I am in despair."

"What did you want to tell us, Detective North?" Reid attempts to keep the conversation moving despite his wife's overt emotions.

Aiden clears his throat for a second time, and glances toward Stella.

With Aiden's unspoken permission, Stella cuts to the chase. "Did Lucy confide in you that she was pregnant?"

"Pregnant! What? Our Lucy was expecting? Oh Reid. How unbearable." She leans into her husband who wraps a big arm around her shoulder.

"There, there, honey. No, we didn't notice any signs. Did she realize?"

Bitsy's head moves from side to side, perhaps in denial; perhaps in agreement with Reid.

"Maybe she suspected?" Stella interrupts before Aiden replies. "A girl might suspect but doesn't make an appointment with the doctor until she's sure."

"She never visited her doctor and Jacob was not aware either." Aiden's contribution to the conversation is reluctant at best.

Stella knows he's not prepared to reveal additional details connecting the pregnancy to the fall. She focuses her attention on Bitsy. "I understand how difficult the circumstances must be for you, but you and Lucy were close. Did she happen to mention any illness, or problems she might have experienced at home or at work?"

"No. No, of course not. She was a newlywed. She was blissful. She was soon to have her own house—a bungalow like ours. She couldn't wait." Bitsy pauses to sniff and dab at her eyes with her rumpled tissue. "She told me Opal liked to control the family, Hester was hard to talk to, and Cavelle was never home. But Lucy loved her work. She and Jacob were very happy." Bitsy lifts her head to catch her husband's attention. "There's nothing else. Right, Reid?"

Aiden and Stella get the hint. "Thank you both for your hospitality today. I hope you understand the need to follow protocols and ask certain questions."

"And we wanted you to hear the details from us," Stella quietly adds at the end of Aiden's thank you.

They are silent until Aiden has manoeuvred the car away from the house and in the direction of Shale Harbour.

"They're telling the truth, Aiden. The Smithers were unaware of their daughter's pregnancy. I suspect she didn't share any other possible concerns with them either."

"I agree. Depending on toxicology, there may be a need to talk with her brother, but for now, we'll interview the Painter sisters and determine where any additional information might lead us. To be honest Stella, I'm even more sure the poor girl fell in the basement and died."

As Aiden's sedan creeps into her parking lot, flurries are approaching from the west.

Chapter 8

Investigative Protocols

Winter has arrived with an unforgiving vengeance this first week of January 1981. Stella prefers the occasional temperate season when the storms come and go, but temperatures cycle to above normal levels on a regular basis. Her boots squeak on the packed snow in the driveway. She tucks her gloved hands deep into the pockets of her blue calf-length parka, and shuffles as fast as is safe toward Aiden's car.

She jumps into the front seat. Aiden rubs his hands together. A thin film of ice has formed along the frame of the windshield. "Good morning," he mutters through chattering teeth. "This wreck should go to the shop. The heater is crap."

"No kidding." She grins. "Good morning to you, too. Is Opal aware we're on our way?"

"I called and talked with her yesterday. Cavelle has to work, but the other three will be home." The big car crunches on the snow as Aiden negotiates the lot and moves the vehicle onto the road. "I've tried but I don't remember Opal in high school."

"She's the kind of person who blends into the background, Aiden. She quit in grade eleven after Jacob was born and their mother died. We were sixteen."

"After Velma Painter passed away, she left school and cared for the baby as well as Hester? How old was Hester?"

"Ten, if my math is right. Cavelle told me Opal has sacrificed her entire life for the family. Cavelle says the one reason she has a career is because Opal helped take care of the farm."

"When did their father die?"

"Jacob was eight. It was 1959." She glances across the front seat at his hunched profile leaned toward the windshield. "Will you let me ask a few questions? What's the plan for today?"

"I explained to Opal that there are investigative protocols after a sudden death. I mentioned you, and she expressed curiosity. Her attitude bordered on annoyance, so I told her that you are involved because of your familiarity with residents of the area." He frowns. "Funny. I guess I was nondescript in high school, too, because she didn't say a word."

Stella remains silent, long enough for Aiden to take his eyes off the road and check on her.

"Yes, you can ask questions. I'm interested in your observations, too. What's the matter?"

"I wonder why she was annoyed."

They park the car at the front of the farmhouse and scamper up the steps into the unheated sun porch. The walls, bereft of insulation, break the wind but not the cold. Before Aiden raises a fist to knock, the door creaks open and Opal's form emerges in the shadowed foyer.

Aiden extends his hand. "Good morning, Miss Painter. I'm Detective Aiden North."

Opal's expression remains blank, although Stella notices a quick eye movement in her direction. "Yes. I remember you. We were in high school together. You ran with a faster crowd." Her eyes dart back to Stella.

"Glad you could receive us today, Opal. Is the temperature colder than yesterday, or is my imagination frozen, too?" She tries to lessen the tension.

"Your imagination has always worked overtime, Stella." She turns toward the living room, which runs into the dining room. The spaces consume half of the downstairs, from front to back. "Come in here," she directs. "Coffee?"

"Sure," Stella pipes up. She chooses to ignore the veiled slur regarding her imagination. "Hester. How are you?"

Hester is tucked into the built-in seat of the dining room bow window. She is surrounded by books and catalogs of various vintages. She waves but does not lift her eyes from the book in her hands.

"Come and meet my friend, Aiden North, Hester."

"No. Hello. I will stay where I am. Opal gave me permission to read here, but not to move."

Stella notices Hester's grooming today. Her hair is combed, and her complexion lacks the red and mottled characteristics often present. "You look very nice, Hester."

"Thank you," she replies, although she remains focused on her book. "I had a bath and dressed in clean clothes." In an unpredictable move, she lifts her eyes from the page and points out the window. "Lucy fell and died out in the yard. She fell in the hole and died."

"Stop, Hester. I told you that if you are to stay in here, you must be quiet." Opal graces Stella and Aiden with an expression tethered between frustration and indulgence. She places a tray on the coffee table. "Please, sit."

"Thanks for your time, Miss Painter. As I mentioned on the phone, there are basic protocols after a sudden death. I hope you don't mind." Aiden's smile is tempered.

"Lucy fell in the hole and died," Hester trumpets from the dining room.

"Yes, Hester. I'll go sit with her, Aiden. You and Opal chat." Stella hopes her outward attempt at a calm facade will encourage the woman's cooperation. Opal's expression illustrates her confusion while Aiden nods his ascent.

Stella moves a dining room chair nearer to Hester. "What are you reading?"

"I'm not reading, I'm studying the banes. There are many and it's important to know the differences."

"What are banes, Hester? Can you tell me?" Stella keeps her voice quiet, in the hopes she'll be able to overhear the conversation in the other room.

"One is dogbane. Another is wolfsbane. Cowbane grows here, but I don't believe henbane does. My dog died, but he ate wolfsbane, not dogbane." She leans off the window seat toward Stella. "My dog was a wolf in disguise." Her eyes enlarge, and she puts a finger over her lips. "Don't tell Opal. I want another dog. Jacob gave permission—almost."

"Are they each species of plants, Hester?"

"Bane means death. I must study all the details before Jacob will allow another dog."

She tries to keep her voice calm. "Tell me what you've learned."

"I could never tell you everything I've learned, Stella. I am very smart."

Stella acknowledges her remark with a soft chuckle. Hester's mind has a mysterious method of order. "I've never heard of banes. Do they grow around here?"

"Of course. Monkshood is quite common." She whispers again. "Monkshood killed my dog. There's water hemlock. It is easy to find. Farmers are afraid for their animals sometimes."

A glance toward Opal and Aiden assures her their exchanges appear civil although she can hear little. The conversation must be progressing well. He is calling Opal by her first name. "Hester, the two plants you mentioned—are they banes?"

"Yes, of course." She sweeps her hand across a series of small pamphlet-style books.

Stella notices the author names of Maud Going and Faith Fyles. Another thin volume is by an L. H. Pammel. The focus of each is poisonous plants. She can only see a few names. Hester has a dozen or more similar publications. "Wherever did you get your collection?"

"Paulina bought them for me at a government used book sale. They're old and no one wanted them anymore, but I am smart." She leans over toward Stella again. "Two of my books are from 1899 and from 1910. Books may be old, but plants don't change." Her unexpected laugh resembles the squawk of a duck. "If monkshood can kill a dog in 1899, it will still kill a dog now."

Suddenly, she pushes her body deeper into the window seat and further from Stella. "Opal says no more dogs."

"Will you tell me more poisonous plant facts, Hester?"

"Later, Stella. I need to plan my garden for the spring." She has refocused her attention on the Vessy's Seed Catalog and Stella's dismissal is abrupt.

Upon her return to the living room, cup in hand, Stella hears Aiden question Lucy's health. "Is it your opinion she was in good health?"

Opal sits very straight in a wingback chair opposite Aiden, who is seated on the couch. "She was healthy as a horse—and a big eater." She brushes a stray grey hair, which has managed to slip out of her bun, away from her face. "I must say, she often remarked on how much she admired my cooking. I try very hard to make hearty meals. Jacob and Cavelle work long hours and are tired when they get home." She sniffs. "I'm not sure if Lucy found her job difficult—to visit people in their homes and help them sort their pills. Nevertheless, she was a visiting nurse and travelled a lot. I guess she put in full days, too." She grunts. "No need to speak ill of the dead."

"Was Lucy taking advantage at work?"

"Well, she called in sick the day she died, but afterward she seemed fine. She ate a big dinner. She was a faker."

"Did you know she was pregnant?"

Opal's face turns the shade of putty. She twists a paper napkin between her fingers until only confetti remains. "Pregnant? No! Are you sure? Why did no one tell me? Did Jacob know?"

Aiden's voice is calm compared to Opal's shrill questions. "Jacob was informed right after the autopsy and Lucy's parents were recently informed. Our investigation suggests no one, including Lucy, was aware. She didn't contact her doctor."

Stella observes Aiden tilt his head even further toward his shoulder as he watches Opal struggle to control her emotions.

The back door clatters. "I'm back. I'll be inside in a minute after I wash up," Jacob yells from the kitchen.

"Jacob kept it from me." Opal's voice is now a whisper. Her words are hushed and reverent.

"Where is Lucy's baby?"

"No, Hester." Stella acknowledges Aiden's barely perceptible nod. "Lucy was expecting a baby."

"Was her baby still inside her?"

Opal's eyes fill with tears. One begins its journey down her cheek only to become tangled in a wrinkle near her lip line.

"Yes, Hester." Stella struggles to maintain her own composure, now. Opal's expression is haunted and full of pain. "Lucy was pregnant when she died."

Jacob catches their attention. He stands at the door to the dining room. He is dressed in blue jeans and a grey turtleneck. He nods to Aiden. "I gather they know. Once she told me you were coming, I figured I'd stay in the barn until you asked if she knew. Good timing, I guess."

"Why in hell did you not tell me Lucy was pregnant?" Opal spits the question at her brother.

"I didn't know, Opal; no idea. When Detective North told me after the autopsy, I was shocked. Didn't want to talk about a dead baby any more than a dead wife. I figured you'd find out soon enough." He approaches the centre of the living room. "Did you make more coffee? I'll go get us a refill." He reaches for the pot, turns on his heel, and leaves.

Hester abandons her books to sit on the needlepoint footstool beside Opal's chair. She pats her older sister's hand. "Don't cuss, Opal. We coulda had another baby if Lucy didn't fall in the hole and die."

The silence, while they wait for Jacob to return, consumes Stella. She's afraid the quiet will stifle further conversation. She holds Aiden's gaze with her own.

Aiden returns his attention to his notebook while Jacob adds milk to his mug and makes himself comfortable in a nearby armchair. "Anything more you can tell us, Jacob?"

"Not much to add, Detective. None of us knew her condition. She wouldn't have tried to walk across the frozen ruts out to the job site if she understood she was pregnant. She also thought she didn't need to take a flashlight. No way she suspected." He sips his coffee.

Lucy's death was tragic. His behaviour is remarkably stoic, under the circumstances. Although Cavelle described him as more grief-stricken, Stella imagines she is witnessing Jacob's attempt to cope. "Hester told me Lucy was sick," Stella then points out to the group.

Jacob directs his attention toward his sister. "Hester, old girl, what makes you so sure Lucy was sick?"

"She threw up on the wood floor in my bedroom." Hester's tone is matter of fact.

"You never said, Hester."

"Lucy made me promise not to. I'm a good girl. I can keep a secret. I never told anyone until after she died. Then I told Stella." She graces Stella with a toothy grin.

Obviously touched by his sister and her challenges, he clears his throat before speaking. "Did she say why she was sick, Hester?"

"No. She said it kind of came and went. She cleaned up her mess, so I didn't mind."

"You should have told me, Hester. I could have talked to Lucy." Opal's voice cracks with emotion.

Hester runs her index finger across her lips, locking them with an imaginary key. She wiggles her finger at the end.

"Okay, Hester, we understand." Jacob returns his attention to Aiden. "Hester can keep a secret. Often, we don't give her enough credit. Eh, old girl?" He leans over and touches her shoulder.

She beams when she looks up at him. "Can I come out to the barn with you later?"

"Sure, old girl. We've got some tractor parts to be organized, okay?"

****

After they struggle on with coats and boots, they make their goodbyes and scuttle to the car. Neither says a word until they are shut inside, and Aiden starts the engine.

He begins. "She was sick from her pregnancy but didn't understand the reason yet."

"Opal was shocked and devastated to hear the news. I felt sorry for her. I'm sure she was imagining the changes in their lives. What a sin. Jacob is speaking to Hester again. I expect his aloofness was all in Hester's head."

"Let me get you home. Who else do we need to talk to?"

"I want to speak with Paulina McAdams. She dated Leon Painter until he died. I can make one trip do because I'd like to discuss Hester and research local poisonous plants, as well."

"Research what?"

"Hester is studying local poisonous plants. She calls them the banes, which means death, by the way. She pointed out the different species—found right around here. Were you aware we have all kinds of poisons in our own backyard—plants able to kill people and animals?"

Aiden's expression is familiar. He assumes she has an idea and won't give up regardless of the facts, but she pushes forward anyway. "Hester told me her dog ate a plant and died. I want to understand what's around here. I pay no attention to the flora except when the gardens at the house need to be weeded."

"What are you getting at, Stella?"

"Del might be right and Lucy was sick because Hester poisoned her. Once I talk with Paulina and research the banes, you can get the lab to test for poisons. I'll let on my interests are personal for right now."

"This is no doubt a wild goose chase, but on the other hand, we shouldn't assume Lucy's sickness was due to her pregnancy." The hesitancy disappears from his voice. "And the old boyfriend? Cavelle mentioned this guy who is the son of one of her client's. It's in the file I gave you when we reviewed the autopsy. Do you remember his name?"

"William Sylvester. Shouldn't we speak with her brother, Glenn, as well? Brothers can be sounding boards. And her boss, Ardith Holland? You talked to her on the phone, right?"

"Yes. Only regarding sick days, but we can arrange an interview with her as well."

"Good. Maybe Ardith can shed light on how Lucy found her life at home. There was no doubt tension festering at the farm, and she might have confided in her boss. Let's visit Ardith now. This late in the morning could be quiet for her."

****

The offices of At-Home Care Services are housed in a tiny renovated house near the entrance to town. The plate-glass door clashes with the residential style of the building. Ardith Holland, stationed behind a large mahogany table with turned legs the size of tree trunks, startles when the buzzer sounds as they push the door open.

"Good morning. What can I do for you today?" She stands.

Stella realizes she might not be familiar with either one of them. She turns to Aiden, who takes the lead.

"Good morning. Miss Holland, correct? I'm Detective Aiden North and this is Stella Kirk. She often accompanies me on interviews."

Ardith's shoulders slide into a more relaxed position. "Oh, yes. Stella. You own the RV park, right? And Detective North? We talked on the phone. You must be here to discuss Lucy. We are still overwhelmed by her death."

"Of course. We are in the process of completing follow-up visits with people involved in her life—protocol. Our questions will only take a few moments of your time."

Stella does not miss Ardith's surreptitious glance. To clarify, she adds, "I accompany Detective North on occasion because I'm familiar with most of the residents in the community."

Ardith points to chairs across from the desk and plunks into her own with a thud. "You don't know me."

Stella, surprised by her abruptness, sits.

Aiden resumes. "Miss Holland, both Lucy's health, as well as her state of mind, are of concern to us. Was she sick much before her death?"

"She took a few odd days off, Detective. I gave you detailed information."

Aiden is undeterred by her attitude. "Did you suspect a cause?"

"I'm a nurse. I wondered if she might be pregnant, but I never asked. I assumed an appointment with her doctor was on the horizon."

"The autopsy determined she *was* pregnant. If she suspected, who might be her closest confidante?"

"No idea...but I'm positive she wasn't at the point where she was able to put two and two together."

"Okay, Miss Holland. On another topic, did Lucy ever discuss issues she encountered with her sisters-in-law? We are curious about her time at the Painter farm. She was anxious for construction to be completed on her new house."

"Constructing their bungalow made her giddy with excitement." Ardith eyes reflect her sadness. "She complained about the big old farmhouse and too many stairs. She wanted a house like the one her parents own in Port Ephron." The nurse supervisor's voice takes on a lecture tone. "We see countless people who can no longer stay at home because they aren't able to traverse their stairs. Clients are often forced to move as a result. Lucy was adamant regarding no steps although her wishes did not eliminate the stairs to the basement. She said Jacob insisted on a basement but agreed to place her laundry and her freezer on the main floor."

She gazes off over their shoulders and out the front door. "Ironic she should fall into the basement. Was she dizzy because of her condition?"

"We aren't certain, Miss Holland. We're awaiting the final toxicology report before we come to any conclusions. Thank you for your time today. If you remember any additional information, please don't hesitate to call me." He offers her his card.

Aiden drops Stella off at the RV park. They plan their next day. He will accompany her to meet Paulina McAdams at Yellow House. He refuses her offer to stay for lunch. She silently admits she's happy he took a pass, since she has no idea the state of her kitchen. Nick planned to paint. The old screen slams behind her. She closes the inside door and appreciates the warmth of the log fire. The difficulties encountered, as they try to keep her rambling century home comfortable in the winter, are endless.

"I'm in the kitchen," he sings out.

She rounds the corner to confront cabinets with no doors, their contents covered in tea towels on counters, and clouds of dust surrounding her remarkable Nick, sandpaper in hand.

He flashes white teeth in a face still tanned from the summer sun. "I made egg salad sandwiches. They're in the fridge."

Chapter 9

Did You Kiss?

"I don't suppose you've ever been here before." Stella, wrapped in her parka against the sharp bite of wind off the water, picks her way up the bricked walk to Yellow House. With her chin embedded in the collar of her coat, her voice is muffled. "There's sea glass snuggled under the snow at the foot of the first step. Paulina deposits her finds from the beach. She encourages children to search for treasures when they play at the shore."

"No, I've never been in, Stella." He doesn't sound impressed.

Before she makes her way up to the veranda, Stella turns toward Aiden. "Paulina is Rosemary's kind of girl. You'll understand." She hopes he glimpses the humour in her eyes before she rings the bell.

"Good morning, Paulina. I appreciate your time today. We need your help."

"Always a pleasure to see Mia's great-aunt." She peers past Stella and extends her arm to Aiden. "And this handsome gentleman must be Detective North."

She holds his hand for a few seconds longer than Stella judges necessary. *Did Aiden blush?*

"Come in out of the weather. Let me take your coats." She bustles around them, reminding Stella of the squirrels at the park.

Paulina McAdams resembles the popular singer from the 1960s and 70s—Juliette. Her dyed blond hair is coiffed to perfection. Stella expects she could stand in a gale and not one strand would be nudged out of place. She has not dressed for the conditions in what is a drafty house at best. She sports slacks known years ago as cigarette pants while her blouse is short-sleeved and fitted over an ample bosom. She has a cardigan around her shoulders. Stella sneaks a glimpse at Aiden. *Is he avoiding eye contact?*

"You're not off to Florida, Paulina? Your first January in Shale Harbour for what? Twenty years?"

The older woman giggles. "Well, I spent a few winters here when Leon was alive." Her eyes darken. "And one in New York a few months after he died. Not very many though. You certainly own more warm and serviceable clothes than I." She focuses on Stella's baggy knit pants and her heavy wool sweater.

"Hard to portray sexy when the thermometer says minus twenty Celsius." She knows her tone projects sarcasm instead of humour.

"Maybe for you," she responds, hips swiveling as she leads them into the business portion of the downstairs.

When built, the four primary rooms on the main floor of Paulina's Gothic farmhouse consisted of two separate parlours, one on either side of the front entry. The parlour on the right was designed to merge into a dining room separated from the kitchen, located across the back, by a pocket door. She converted the smaller parlour on the left of the staircase into a library with bookcases, comfy armchairs, and stained-glass antique standing lamps. The front room is full of children's books, antique toys, and a half-dozen tiny wooden chairs, along with a wingback to accommodate an adult. The formal dining room is now her little bookshop. Hester must have been in heaven when she spent time here with Paulina. What a shame those visits stopped.

"Let's go straight back into the kitchen. I've made coffee."

She turns to check and Stella nods. "Coffee sounds perfect."

"Thanks." Aiden looks at the floor and mumbles—dumbstruck by Paulina, apparently.

They wiggle through the organized clutter which is the bookshop and her minuscule office, on their way to a huge country kitchen complete with modern cabinets, a central island, a family room, and patio doors which lead out to what is now a snow-covered deck. The walls are covered in collectibles—baskets, kitchen implements from long ago, and calendars from the 1930s.

"What a stunning space. Were you the owner who contracted the work for the addition?"

"Oh, yes. Leon helped, of course. I wanted a living space downstairs but privacy despite allowing the house to be open to the public in the summer. I was reluctant to turn an upstairs bedroom into my sitting room, and Leon said he would worry at the thought of me running down the stairs because of customers, so we expanded the kitchen into my private space." She putters around the cupboards and the coffee pot. "I can't imagine how you need my help. You said you and your detective friend," she simpers at Aiden, "are doing research and you hope I can be of assistance?"

"Correct. I want to learn the characteristics of local poisonous plants. Hester told me you gave her a collection of old pamphlets and books a few years ago. I was curious if you have more."

"What's your specific interest, Stella? I still own references related to various aspects of agriculture. They're in the closet under the stairs. I bought the whole stack at a government auction, including many duplicates. From those, I chose a few for Hester." Her smile is wistful. "She was both excited and grateful. When her dog died, they suspected the poor little mite ate monkshood and that precipitated her interest."

"Is monkshood one of those plants she calls the banes?"

"Why, yes." Curious eyes study her guests. "Monkshood is commonly known as wolfsbane." She sets mugs of coffee on the island and places cream and sugar nearby, along with a pottery vase full of teaspoons. "You two help yourselves while I dig out the box and see what's there."

The woman disappears for five minutes. Stella can hear her shuffle and grunt out in the hallway. She uses the time to examine Paulina's décor and is particularly impressed with the tin letters, a P and an M, hanging on the wall above the stove. Aiden calls out to ask if she needs his assistance and she sings out a distinct "no" before he has a chance to vacate his stool.

Paulina breezes back with a stack of books and a few pamphlet-style documents. "I can't imagine what you could want with these, but you are welcome to sign them out or do your research here—whatever you prefer." She graces Aiden with a full-face smile.

"Thanks. This is marvelous." Stella thumbs through the top two journals. "May I borrow them?"

"Of course. I'll get my register and record what you take." Stella is unable to disguise her expression of surprise. "I don't give people time limits, but it's important to me that I keep track of who has my books."

"We appreciate your help. You are obviously a very valuable resource in the community." Aiden sips his coffee, remaining on the periphery of the conversation.

"My value was considerably greater when Leon was alive. I acquired most of the agricultural information because of him and his cronies—as well as Hester, of course. The woman is obsessed with plants and books; always has been." She turns her attentions to Aiden. "And how can I help you today? You're very quiet."

"Do you mind if we ask you what happened regarding Leon's death?" Stella is hesitant, but wants to hear Paulina's interpretation, nonetheless.

"No. His death was over twenty years ago now. Seems like yesterday." She emits a withered shudder. "Cavelle found him in the barn. The doctor said it was a 'cardiac event.' Leon told me he felt unwell a week earlier, but I didn't worry. Anyone can experience a bad day."

"Hester no longer comes to Yellow House?" Aiden's tone is curious.

Paulina's face clouds for a mere second before she gives her coif a tiny shake. "No, she doesn't. Opal likes to be in control." Paulina's voice is devoid of both judgment and emotion.

****

Stella follows Aiden past a dented blue Chevette toward the Sylvester residence. She has no personal knowledge of William Sylvester and could have skipped this interview, but Aiden requested she tag along to observe. To prepare, Stella asked Trixie to pick Cavelle's brain and find out what she knows regarding this previous boyfriend.

Trixie's research was limited. William is the primary caregiver to his mother, who has multiple sclerosis. He considered himself to be Lucy's boyfriend although Lucy insisted their interaction was professional and there was no personal connection. Her role as the At-Home Care nurse was to visit weekly, assist with medication management, and report Mrs. Sylvester's condition to her doctor.

Aiden rings the bell. The door is opened by a frail young man who reminds Stella of a raven. His face is pointed, led by an out-of-proportion nose. His jet-black hair hangs in strings across his high forehead. His eyes are hooded, and his nails are dirty. Aiden wants her to assess. She begins immediately.

"Good morning, William. We talked on the phone. I'm Detective North." He gestures a gloved hand in Stella's direction. "This is Stella Kirk. She assists me in interviews."

William opens the door wider. He doesn't speak, but nods to them.

They enter a minuscule foyer where both struggle out of their boots. Despite no gesture on William's part, they remove cumbersome parkas and lay them across the banister at the foot of the stairs.

He leads them into a combination living room and dining room where the latter has become the bedroom for his mother. Mrs. Sylvester sits slumped in her wheelchair. She peeks up at them from under heavy bangs which drag in her eyes.

When Stella sees the woman struggle to interact, she crosses the room and touches her hand. "Good morning, Mrs. Sylvester. I'm Stella Kirk, from out at the RV park. Detective North and I are here to discuss Lucy. You remember Lucy?"

The bangs tremble as she tries to lift her gaze.

Stella squats.

Mrs. Sylvester rocks back and forth. "Nice girl. Good nurse." Her words are slurred but Stella understands.

William interrupts. The sound is shockingly deep for a person his size. "My mother was fond of Lucy. She was a big help. The new nurse doesn't take the time to visit. She shows up, checks the pills, and leaves." He turns toward his charge. "Want to lie down now?"

Miriam Sylvester attempts a nod.

Without any acknowledgment of their obvious presence, William approaches his mother from the front. He leans over to raise her arms and place them around his neck where she clasps her hands. He holds her around the waist, lifts her up, and they do a very dangerous shuffle-like dance to manoeuvre her the couple of necessary steps needed to reach the hospital bed. He lowers her to the bed, lifts her feet up on the mattress, adjusts her pillows, and pulls a light coverlet across her legs. "Are you okay for now, Mom?"

Her appreciation is authentic although her expression is more of a grimace.

He reaches up to grab the curtain used to separate the two rooms and draws the fabric closed, isolating his mother on the other side. Without another word, he sits on a needlepoint bench in front of the empty fireplace, and stares at them both.

"How long were you acquainted with Lucy Painter, William?" Aiden jumps in.

"My friends call me Cat. You know, Sylvester the Cat?" His expression is vacant. "She was Lucy Smithers when we met her, almost a year ago. Mom's pills were too complicated for me, and the doctor wanted a practical nurse to come in and make sure she took them right. Lucy came."

"You and Lucy were close, William?"

"I figured we were. She always stayed longer. She was good to Mom, but even nicer to me."

"How was she nicer?"

"Lucy brought me cookies she baked herself. She gave me a T-shirt she bought from a place she visited out West when she went on vacation." His hands hang between his legs. The cruel vigor with which he wrings and knots his bony fingers makes Stella wince.

After a quick glance at Aiden, she asks, "Were you a couple?"

William smiles. His teeth are the colour of corn. "I guess we were, if you don't count how I never took her anywhere. I'm stuck here with Mom. On Thursdays, the government sends a worker to sit with her, so I can get to the store, but there's no more help."

Were they ever intimate, or has the idea been conjured up by a lonely young man with limited contacts? Stella persists. "My question is personal, William, but we want to understand. Did you have any type of contact with Lucy? Did you kiss?"

His pale face blanches a lighter shade of putty. Aiden turns in his chair to caution her with a silent stare, but the topic requires addressing.

"I wanted to, but it never happened." William whispers, "I told my friends we did."

"Oh." Aiden takes a deep breath. "What happened when she became engaged and was married?"

"It was awful. I pretended the news was a surprise, but it wasn't. I knew there'd be no invitation for me, and I couldn't go, anyway." He glances over toward the dusty grey curtain limply separating them from Mrs. Sylvester.

"How did you learn she died?" Stella tries to steer the conversation past his obvious humiliation.

He wipes sweaty hands across his grubby shirt. "A friend of her brother told me. I was already upset. She was supposed to be here, but a substitute came. I guessed she was mad because I called her at home."

"Exactly how many times?" Stella can hear the strain in Aiden's voice.

William's expression is defiant. "I had permission when she was single. She gave me her number in case Mom took a spell. After she married Painter,

I called her. She asked me not to contact her at home again. I did as I was told. What difference does it make? She's dead."

Aiden stands. "We follow up on any sudden death event. We talk with the person's friends and acquaintances. We were told you dated her before she married Jacob Painter, but I gather the story was not accurate." An impatient thread is buried in Aiden's tone, indicating little or no sympathy.

William moves across the living room toward the door. "She was a nice girl, but there'd be no big farm or new house comin' from me. She was gonna get the stuff she wanted." His voice drops to a whisper. "All I own is a sick mother."

"Thanks, William. We appreciate your time." Stella wiggles her chilled feet back into her boots. The Sylvester home is cool. She suspects money is scarce.

Once in the car and on their return trip to the RV park, she asks the question she knows they must consider. "Was he upset enough to kill her? Do you think William knocked her into the basement?"

****

"Do you want to come with me to town this morning? I'll buy you lunch."

Stella is curled up on one of the sofas in front of the fire. It has been two days since she collected the reference books from Paulina at Yellow House. They're spread out around her on both the other couch cushion and on the floor. She's anxious to study the banes. "Pass, Nick." She beams up at him. "But I'll heat the leftover chicken soup in the fridge and set the table by the time you get back."

"You'd make lunch for me?" He attempts a swoon but resembles a drunk who can't navigate the room.

She grins as she stands to give him a kiss before he ventures out into the blustery morning. She says a silent prayer that this cold snap ends soon. "Be careful on the drive. Remember your list?"

Nick pats his pocket. "See you in an hour." He pulls the inside door tight but lets the screen slam.

Wandering out to her kitchen, she surveys the half-finished paint job. The improvement will be huge once the work is completed...whenever. She pours her third cup of coffee, unplugs the empty pot, and returns to her nest of pillows and books.

She is immersed in the information she's uncovered, and therefore shocked when Nick and a blast of frigid air burst back into the house. "Are you home so soon? What time is it?"

"Hi. Yes, I am. Near noon." Nick retrieves the bags he placed on the floor while he removed his boots. He then makes a beeline toward her, leans over to kiss her cheek and whispers in her ear, "I don't smell any chicken soup."

"Oh my God!" She knocks him off balance when she jumps up and races toward the kitchen.

Total indulgence is written on his handsome face. "Nick, I'm sorry. I was caught up in the poisonous plant books and lost track of the time."

He rests a still-chilled hand on her shoulder. "You put groceries away. I'll get lunch. Considering your reading material, maybe I need to watch what I eat more carefully from now on." He chuckles. "I'm curious, though. What did you discover? Most killer plants are found in the deep south, or Africa, or some such place, right?"

"No. I was surprised. Hester was right when she told me many native varieties, for example the banes, can be found nearby."

Nick stirs the soup while Stella places cheeses, crackers, and silverware on the table.

Once they settle for their meal, she resumes. "While you were gone, I read excerpts from two books Paulina loaned me. Hester has copies of the same ones. The first is called *A Manual of Poisonous Plants*, copyrighted in 1910 by L. H. Pammel, and the other is *Principal Poisonous Plants of Canada* written in 1919 by Faith Fyles."

"Man, those are old, Stella."

"Right, although Hester emphasized how the books may be ancient, but plants don't change."

"Point taken, but could Lucy get into a poison at the farm by accident—in November?"

"No idea. Symptoms of poisoning by banes found nearby are similar but different. Cowbane is often referred to as water hemlock. The plant resembles carrots or parsnips and is the most poisonous plant in North America. Death is fast, but if you were to drink water hemlock tea, repressed respiration might take forty-eight hours."

"I suppose they named the weed cowbane because cows die if they eat it?"

"Precisely. And there's lots of wolfsbane, or monkshood, too. Hester said monkshood killed her dog. The flowers are a pale blue shade. Ingesting any part of the plant can cause severe vomiting and you eventually die of asphyxiation."

"Sounds grisly. Did the autopsy indicate Lucy was poisoned?"

"The toxicology report hasn't come back, but Aiden suggested they need to test for specific chemicals. People and animals can die from eating monkshood and water hemlock." She begins to stack their dishes by the sink. "The one observation which troubles me is the initial autopsy questioned the condition of her liver and kidneys but did not link it to a fall of eight feet. None of the information, in what I've read so far, indicates any of the banes could cause the organ damage."

"I suppose you'll want to find a plant that hurts your liver." He giggles. "Maybe there's a whiskey plant. Everyone understands what whiskey can do to a liver."

"Be serious." She chortles regardless. "Aiden wonders if William Sylvester might be involved in Lucy's death, but I'm more inclined to follow Del Trembly's lead. More studying is in my future. Lucy could well have been poisoned."

"Stella." Nick walks up behind her and wraps his arms around her shoulders while she stands at the counter. "Poor little Lucy felt dizzy and nauseous because of her pregnancy, fell in the hole, and died. Sad and simple."

CHAPTER 10

She Had No Idea

Familiar bits of colourful sea glass poke through the melting snow. Stella navigates the steps to Paulina McAdams' front door on Monday morning. Paulina has agreed to see her again. She wants to discuss Paulina's relationships with the Painter children in more detail. Paulina's observations about their interactions, despite the fact Leon has been dead for twenty years, will be helpful. In addition, she needs to educate herself regarding local poisonous plants other than the banes. The initial autopsy suggested possible liver and kidney damage. Her goal is to present Aiden with potential toxins for the pathologist to test.

Paulina answers the moment she knocks. She no doubt waited by the sidelight for the Jeep's approach. "Come in. Come in. Warmer today. We may be gifted with a January thaw."

"Let's hope. We might run out of wood for the fireplace before spring at the rate we're burning." She removes her boots, places them on the tray near the door, and lays her coat across the banister at the foot of the stairs.

"Come into the library. I've made coffee." Paulina leads the way into the cozy room. "It took time, but I assembled all my poisonous plant references in addition to the banes, as you say Hester calls them. The most predominant options besides the banes are mushrooms. Did you read the various mentions of mushrooms in the Pammel book I gave you?"

Within the silence left by Stella's lack of an immediate response, Paulina pours coffee. She sits and adjusts her blue sweater set so both sides of the cardigan are even at her belted waist. Her trousers are a duplicate of the ones she wore last week, except the colour of rich cream.

"No. I searched for descriptions of banes. If I'm not mistaken, he discusses monkshood and water hemlock."

"And the Amanitas, Stella. You aren't paying attention," she chastises. "Amanitas are poisonous mushrooms. They are full of amatoxin and there are species common here in the East, although, for the life of me, I can't figure out why you're interested."

"For right now, Paulina, my task is to educate myself." She tries to make her voice sound light and airy. "Once spring comes, we'll be back to the grindstone, and any research has to wait. I'm anxious to learn about...what are they, again?"

"Amanitas," Paulina taps her spoon on the table. "Two come to mind. Bisporigera is the most common. Another variety is Virosa. People call the group destroying angel mushrooms. If you want poison, your most accessible option around here is the destroying angel. They are pure white and, I hear, taste musky and wonderful although many who experience the flavour will die eventually." She sips her coffee, then dabs her lips with a flowered paper napkin. "You can slice and dry them to save for later. Of course, wolfsbane and cowbane roots dry well and remain effective if ground to a powder."

She leans in toward Stella and widens her eyes. "Share with me, my dear, whom do you wish to poison?"

Stella wants to squirm. The sensation annoys her. "There are lots of folks from away who come into the office and want to be told what species of snakes to avoid and what plants are poisonous. I always tell them garter snakes are harmless and our climate doesn't support plants able to kill you. A camper last summer was anxious to inform me that I needed to bone up on local flora." She hopes her lie sticks. "I guess I need to improve my education."

"Well, those campers were mean-spirited. Maybe next season, you can make them creamy mushroom soup." She throws her head back and emits a squeaky mouse-with-its-foot-in-a-trap laugh.

Time to change the subject. "Paulina, I realize twenty years has passed since you hung out at the Painter place, but could you give me your impressions of the four kids and how they got along?"

"Sure." She sounds cooperative, but hesitant nonetheless. "They were all young at the time. Opal was twenty-four when Leon died. She was protective of Hester and Jacob. She ran most aspects of the farm. Leon visited me in the evenings, and if I mentioned chores, he'd say Opal had the work in hand."

Paulina's expression is wistful when she mentions Leon—obviously her one great love, despite their age gap. Of course, Stella is ten years older than Nick, and they manage, but twenty-five years seems insurmountable, even in the 1980s.

"I never developed a relationship with Cavelle, regretfully. She studied every day. She attended night school in Port Ephron to get her real estate papers. I remember a big to-do about Jacob's attendance at elementary. Opal wanted to teach him at home, the same as Hester, but Leon refused."

"Did Jacob come here with Hester? Were you close to him, too?"

"Leon often dropped off Hester for an afternoon with me, but Opal rarely let Jacob out of her sight." Paulina's voice becomes hushed and sad. "Opal was sixteen when Jacob was born, and Velma died. People said she took over as Jacob's mother from the day Velma passed away. She even quit school."

"Yes. We were in the same grade."

"Right!" Paulina leans back into her armchair. "Of course, you remember."

"Was Hester's problem ever revealed to you, Paulina? She's always been different. Was she diagnosed with a specific condition?"

"Not to my knowledge." Paulina leans forward again. Stella can detect annoyance reflected in her eyes. "The girl's not stupid—far from stupid. She's one of the smartest people I've met. Her issue is she can't relate to the social cues in her immediate environment...but Hester's remarkable, nevertheless. My God, she could teach university courses about plants and gardens. I often asked for her advice."

"You must miss her, Paulina."

"I did for a long time. I see the Painter family only on occasion now although I was thrilled to be invited to Lucy and Jacob's wedding." She pats her blond hair.

"Before I forget, Paulina, I'm fascinated by your initials hanging on the kitchen wall. I spied them when we were here the other day."

"Oh, those. They're antique cake tins. Leon found them at an auction and hung them for me. I've tried to collect more over the years, but apparently, they're highly valuable and hard to find. I located two numbers—now stuffed in a box in the back-porch pantry. I don't go to auctions these days, but my love life has improved, so that's a bonus." She giggles. "I currently enjoy a new beau and he's filled the emptiness I struggled with for years after Leon's death. We keep a low profile," she whispers. "Our romance presents a few complications, but it's worth staying in town for the winter." She squeaks again.

****

"Call this interview 'protocol after a sudden death' if you want, but I'm convinced Jacob Painter offed Lucy because his sisters made him."

Aiden and Stella sit on straight-backed wooden chairs across from Maeve Cavannah, who insists she was Lucy Painter's closest friend. When she contacted the station, Aiden arranged for them to meet her at noon to accommodate her split shift schedule today. She's a practical nurse with At-Home Care Services. Maeve crosses her long and heavy legs at the ankle while she perches on the edge of her dilapidated red velvet sofa.

As she takes note of the shredded arms, Stella knows she doesn't require the skills of a detective to determine the two obese orange felines balanced on the back are the culprits.

"Why was Jacob Painter instrumental in his wife's death, Maeve?" Aiden's voice is noncommittal.

"His sisters rule the roost—Opal, in particular. Lucy told me Jacob does whatever Opal says. I'm sure, if Opal instructed him to get rid of her, he would—no questions asked."

Maeve is a big woman, with horse-like features. When she slams her back into the sofa cushions, with unstated satisfaction, both pets vibrate but hold on for dear life. Cat hair fluffs through the air between them.

Stella looks at Aiden for silent permission and asks, "Did she tell you she was pregnant?"

"What? Pregnant? No, she did not." Her face has blanched.

"To your knowledge, was she aware?"

Maeve answers the question with one of her own. "Did Jacob know?"

"He says no."

"Then she had no idea." Her words come out of her wide mouth in a saliva-filled scoff. "We were best friends. If she had any inkling, I would be told, likely before Jacob."

Aiden positions his pen over his notebook. "Can you think of any other information, Maeve? We understand you two were close. We are sorry for your loss."

Grief shudders through Maeve's broad shoulders. "She and Jacob got along okay. Any tension appeared to be with the sisters—Opal, for sure." Balancing her elbows on her knees, she proceeds. "Now Hester is another story. She is one odd duck. She's a ten-year-old with a professor's expertise in plants. Lucy told me her whole bedroom is arranged in library fashion, with shelves down the middle. I've met her twice. She's weird, but Lucy liked her. They spent lots of time with one another. We ate lunch one day—Lucy, Hester, and me. Lucy promised Hester a get-together again soon." She leans back into the sofa once more. Her voice trembles. "I guess that's not gonna happen."

****

The two find Glenn Smithers at work. The Pontiac / Buick dealership isn't busy on a Tuesday in the middle of January. Glenn is happy to come inside, away from brushing an overnight dusting of snow off car windshields and roofs. He's anxious to pour himself a hot cup of coffee and willing to visit with them.

"Mom and Dad told me she was pregnant. Sad, eh? Don't think my mom will ever be the same again." He sits on the edge of his office chair, behind a desk which disguises how his feet struggle to touch the floor. Glenn has inherited the Smithers' family stature. He is an exceedingly short man, resembling his mother.

"As I mentioned on the phone, I ask Stella to tag along to interviews because I don't have many contacts in the area yet. Moved away after high school."

"Your questions have caused us problems at home. My mother's been upset since your visit. Let's cut to the chase. I'm afraid you two are the nickel holdin' up the dollar today, and I need to get back on the floor. Busy. Busy." He raises his eyebrows and chuckles.

The showroom remains quiet. Stella fails to appreciate his overt sales optimism. "We wanted to hear if Lucy ever discussed her life with Jacob and his sisters after she moved to the farm."

"Lucy was a bright girl. She was my sister, and I loved her, but we didn't run in the same circles. She never talked about the Painters."

Aiden interjects. "Are you friends with William Sylvester, Glenn?"

"You mean lovesick Cat? Not really, but a buddy of mine was in high school with him. From what I understand, he was fuelin' a rumour where he and Lucy were a couple." His guffaw rocks his chair and puts his coffee at significant risk. "What a loser! Lucy was cross. She was going to talk with him and put an end to his lies for good. She said that's what you get for tryin' to be kind to some poor soul. She was pissed!"

"Did she mention William's phone calls?"

"Oh, yeah. She was clear. Whatever he says when it comes to any association with her is a lie. I was to report that to my friends."

"And did you?" Aiden jots notes as fast as Glenn talks.

"For sure. Cat's pathetic. No need for Lucy to deal with his crap."

****

Later in the evening, Stella decides to touch base with Cavelle and calls Grey Cottage Realty, thinking she's likely working late.

"Grey Cottage Realty. How may I help you?"

"Cavelle. Happy I caught you."

"Well, what can I do for you, Stella? It's after-hours. I'm not required to answer." Her laugh is soft, almost sad.

"Oh, I took the chance you might be hiding out at work tonight, Cavelle. I can't imagine life at home is too great right now."

A withered groan rattles through the phone line and fills Stella's ear.

"Did she tell you she was pregnant, Cavelle?"

"God, no! I wish. Opal would not have permitted her to stumble around the job site in the dark if she had known. Jacob wouldn't have attended meetings two nights in a row, either."

"Does the family have plans for the house, Cavelle?"

"Strange you should ask. Jacob and I discussed the bungalow yesterday. I suggested getting the place completed for me. He showed interest in the idea. He has no desire to move in now."

"What's Opal's opinion?"

"Opal wants the basement filled in and to forget the construction ever existed. I guess we'll wait until spring before we decide. What's up with you? Can I talk you and Trixie into meeting me for lunch before the end of the week?"

"Sure. Any time. Give Trixie a shout and then one of you call me with the details. You need to pack up, my girl. Snow has started again."

Stella hangs up. She watches the snow swirling in the glow of the yard light. The question is who will benefit from the new house?

****

"Aiden. It's me. Want to meet today and talk poisons?"

"Still on that kick? Toxicology isn't back yet."

"Are you able to request tests for specific poisons?"

"I can, if we're able to indicate the exact substances. Tell me your concerns."

Stella understands her suspicions are based on a hunch, but she takes a deep breath and forges ahead. "Come over for coffee and I'll fill you in on my research and my second visit with Paulina on Monday. I called Cavelle last evening, too. She was still at work."

"I hope you didn't go overboard. I wanted our questions to remain discreet." Aiden's voice contains a thread of impatience that's difficult for her to ignore. "There's no hard evidence Lucy was murdered."

Having known one another for a long time, she ignores his tone. "Come out to the park for coffee, Aiden. We can talk here."

He arrives an hour later. Stella is sitting at her kitchen table admiring the refreshed cabinets when she hears his knock. "I'm on my way."

She takes big strides across the living room and reaches the door as it slides open to reveal Aiden North, his neck wrapped in a plaid scarf and his head covered in a wool cap pulled around his ears.

"Good morning. Too damned miserable to stand on the porch. I wish the weather would make up its mind to stay cold or warm. One or the other. What a roller coaster!" He stamps his boots for effect.

Stella patiently waits for him to get his rant behind him. "Well, a good morning to you, too. You're an old crank today. I expected the station to be quiet. After all, people don't break the law when the temperature drops, right?"

"So much for theories. The fish plant in Port Ephron was broken into last night."

He reacts to what she is sure is her shocked expression. "Nothing to take. The investigators from Robbery Division say they trashed the joint pretty good though."

"Great. The robbery will no doubt impact the local plant, and Trixie, as well. They might move work over to Shale Harbour. Are you involved in the case?"

"Unless a person was hurt or killed, they don't need me." He peels off his coat, scarf, and hat.

They make their way to the kitchen as Nick rumbles down the stairs. "Do I hear Aiden North and smell coffee, too?" He reaches out to shake Aiden's hand when they approach the staircase. "Great to see you."

"Join us, Nick."

"Perfect timing. I've put the last coat of paint on the bathroom vanity."

Stella turns to Aiden. "Nick is deep into winter works projects. Come admire my kitchen."

Aiden appears preoccupied and uninterested. Nick pours coffee. Kitchen chairs scrape the old Lino floor when they sit.

Stella jumps right in, afraid Aiden assumes she's given indications of her suspicions to other people. "I think there are two areas for toxicology to investigate. One is into what Hester refers to as banes. The most common plants near us are water hemlock or cowbane, and monkshood or wolfsbane. They are poisonous, available, and can be dried without the poison weakening too much. There are a few local deadly mushrooms as well—various varieties of Amanitas, according to Paulina. They can be successfully dried. Amanitas cause liver and kidney damage." She understands her research is their first significant link to the initial autopsy report where tissue damage was detected.

"A murderer collected local poisons, dried them up, and what?" His voice becomes shrill. "Dropped them in Lucy's soup? Are you kidding?"

The heat of her reddened cheeks distracts Stella from their conversation, but she swallows and perseveres. She struggles to force any volume out of her voice when she replies, "As a matter of fact, I do. The Painter place is filled with dried plants and flowers. They sell dried herbs and lots of dried wild mushrooms. Hester has a huge garden with dozens of species. If a person possessed the skills and knowledge, they could dry poisonous versions and set them aside." She knows her theory verges on lunacy.

Nick interrupts. "Can the toxicology lab use particular tests if they suspect a certain poison?"

"Yes. They can, although I doubt if every poison has a test." Aiden turns his attention back to Stella. "Do you honestly believe one of the Painter clan poisoned Lucy?"

"I can find a motive for each one of them. Cavelle told me yesterday how she might finish the house for herself since Jacob doesn't want to live there.

Hester's condition makes a hardcore reason unnecessary. She might have done a cockamamie experiment. I could suspect her of poisoning her dog to see how monkshood works. Maeve Cavannah says Jacob is capable of being pressured into hurting Lucy. As for Opal, her family was disrupted, which is reason enough for her." She reaches for the coffee carafe Nick brought to the table earlier.

"You make me crazy, Stella." Aiden has jotted in his notebook throughout their discussion. "I'll talk with the lab. I guess, if they can do any tests which indicate the presence of a poison, the evidence will provide sufficient reason to open a formal inquiry." He flips his notebook shut. "Dried mushrooms and organ damage? My job isn't getting any easier."

Stella knows he's not as annoyed as he sounds. She understands the investigation of a sudden death without potential complications makes circumstances simpler. "By the way, I never let on why I needed the information when I talked to Paulina. I told her there are often campers interested in native plants and I want to do research this winter and become more knowledgeable." She sees relief in his expression.

She purses her lips. Trust will be necessary if they are to work together. As much as her future relating to assisting with investigations remains unclear, there seems to be no formal partner for Aiden on the horizon.

CHAPTER 11

I Still Have Questions

Stella sips tepid coffee and listens to the sound of rhythmic drips as icicles above the kitchen window melt. The crunch of newspaper and the rattle of kindling in the bucket tell her Nick is building a morning fire. The outdoor temperature may have warmed up a degree or two above freezing, but the house is damp, requiring comfort and warmth.

His lean frame emerges in the doorway. He touches her cheek on his way toward the cupboard and a fresh mug.

"I want to pay a visit to Del Trembly this morning if you don't have chores for me. I still have questions."

"I always have chores for you." He attempts a leer but accomplishes an impish grin instead.

She tries to suppress her laugh. He needs no encouragement.

Pulling out a kitchen chair, he settles directly across from her. "Did Aiden get the toxicology report back from the lab?"

"Nope, but I want to see if I can garner a few more details from dear Aunt Del. Why is she suspicious of Hester, and not Opal or Cavelle? Lucy liked Hester. Maeve said Lucy was good to Hester. She took her places and included her as often as possible."

"Are you second-guessing your theory? Maybe Lucy fell in the hole and died, simple and sad, Stella." This has become a familiar refrain, from both Nick and Aiden.

"I hope you're right, but I'll call Harbour Manor and ask them to tell Del to expect me midmorning. I'm off to lunch with Trixie and Cavelle, too," she adds as he starts to get up.

"Man! Alone again. What's a poor guy to do?" He feigns a swoon.

"Seriously, I want to check the trim work around the park today. A few sections of lattice need fixing. The weather's warm right now, so I'll repair them." He pushes his chair out from the table. "I'll store any parts in the workshop until spring. A piece of eavestrough requires attention, too." He stretches across the counter to peer out the kitchen window. "And not a moment too soon, by the length of those icicles."

"There's a stash of cinnamon buns from Cocoa and Café in the freezer. Handing them over to you for your lunch will have to serve as my penance, because I intend to run off without you."

"You're my best girl." He kisses her temple. "See you for supper. I might make you a chicken pot pie and then, my dear, you will be forever in my debt."

He winks at her on his way out the door. She giggles. Nick never misses an opportunity to communicate that he finds her attractive. Although never totally convinced, she enjoys the familiar tingle his teasing creates.

"Good morning. Stella Kirk calling. Could you please advise Del Trembly I will be in to visit her at ten-thirty?"

"No problem. Friday mornings are quiet. I'll give her the message."

The old Jeep mumbles with the effort of starting in the damp. The drive out to the main road is slushy so Stella takes her time. Traffic on the bare, wet highway into town is light. She expects most people want to stay close to home until the sun has a chance to dry the blacktop. As she pulls into the parking lot at Harbour Manor, her thoughts drift to her father. There will be no visit with Norbert today, even as Mrs. Nick Cochran—maybe next week with Nick in tow.

Once in the familiar foyer and wide hospital-style corridor of the manor, she makes her way toward Del's room. As she passes her father's door, she steals a glimpse inside. He's dozing in a chair by the window. With a sudden realization of how much she misses him, grief washes over her—as if he were dead already. Tears prick her eyes.

She finds Del stretched out in her over-sized recliner, legs askew, and hands gripped to the sides as if she's trying to prevent lift-off. "Del! Did the staff tell you I was coming?"

"Absolutely. Can you help me? Damned old contraption! I push and push but can't get the front to fold in."

"Here. Let me." Stella bends to place her hands on the footrest. "Now push." As the elderly woman makes a grunt-filled effort, Stella leans against the footrest and Del's feet swing toward the floor.

"Whew! Now I know how a pinned butterfly feels. I need a new chair. This one is too temperamental." She pats Stella's hand. "Sit closer and we can talk. To what do I owe the pleasure of your company today? Did you visit with your father on the way in?"

Typical of Del, she wants answers immediately. "I didn't stop to see Dad. Did he tell you Nick reported to him that we got married?"

Del's face floods with shocked surprise.

"Oh no! Don't misunderstand. Nick told Dad he and I are married, to discourage Dad from assuming I'm a cleaner here at the Manor. I get a better response as Nick's wife."

"Norbert never said, Stella. Besides," she leans over and lowers her voice to a whisper, "you two should get hitched."

"The year is 1981, Del. Circumstances are fine the way they are. Nick has bought into the park though. Now we're an official team. No need for a marriage licence."

"Okay, my dear." Satisfied, Del changes the subject back to matters at hand. "What's brought you here today?"

"I want to have a private conversation with you—to hear exactly why you suspect Hester might have murdered Lucy. A toxicology report is in the works. I convinced the police to test for specific plant poisons." She adds for emphasis, "Remember, though, this discussion is between us. Don't tell anyone, okay?"

Del's mouth, highlighted by bright pink lipstick today, turns into a perfect bow when she sucks her rouge-tinted cheeks in surprise. "What can I tell you, Stella? Am I a witness?"

"No. I need your expert assessment, Del."

Bobbing her head, she replies, "Hester is a plant fanatic. She knows more about plants than any person I've ever met. She's also a social cripple." She waves her chubby hand, adorned with a ring on every finger, at Stella. "I mean no offense. She never went to school. Her obsessions were encouraged, and she has no understanding of consequences. The family protects her because of her condition."

"Leon supported homeschooling for Hester?"

Del scoffs. "Poor old henpecked Leon. He couldn't hold his own—not with Velma or Opal after Velma died. I tried a dozen times to convince him to send her to public school or a special institution, but he refused to stand up to Opal, who stood by her mother's wishes."

"Did you encourage him to send Jacob to regular school?"

"Not necessary. Leon refused permission for him to stay at home even though I thought Opal would go crazy at the time."

"It is impossible to talk with Hester alone. Opal won't let me," Stella complains. "She hovers, and her behaviour intimidates Hester. I'm interested in the extent of her knowledge regarding particular plants, and whether she possesses the skills to kill a person."

"Listen. I have an idea." Before Del finishes, she's distracted by an older attendant who slides through the space where the door is ajar.

"Hey, Del. Figured you and your visitor might appreciate coffee."

Del glances at Stella for a second. "Stella, meet Jack...Jack Lawson. She helps out here at the manor." She addresses Jack and adds, "You're a volunteer, right?"

Jack nods. Her straw-textured black and grey-streaked hair flutters around her face. "Important to keep busy. Lots of folks don't have any family, or nobody who cares. I help where I can."

"Nice to meet you. Jack must be short for Jacqueline?"

"People call me Jack. Did you want those coffees?"

"Not for me. Del?"

"No thanks. Appreciate the offer though."

The older woman nods and scuttles out to the hall.

Del ignores the interruption. "Here's my idea. Eve comes home in a week and she'll be around for a few days. I'll suggest Eve pick up Hester and bring the girl here to the Manor for a visit, but we'll come to see you, instead." She presses her broad shoulders into her chair and glances at the door. "Too many big ears in this place," she whispers. "You can ask her whatever you want, and Opal won't be around to get in the way, either. Good idea?"

Stella pats Del on the arm. "Your plan is worth a try, my friend. Aiden said he expects the report before the end of next week. Thanks for your help. I'll be in touch." She bends to give Del a hug before she leaves.

****

Cavelle Painter sits alone at a small bistro table in the corner of the café. She glances up from the bulky file folder in front of her in response to Stella's entrance and nods her recognition. Stella detects a problem. Cavelle's expertly made-up face is without her customary real estate agent "I am attentive to your every need" expression.

"You appear to be a woman with the weight of the world on her shoulders." Stella pulls a chair across the pine floorboards. "Troubles with a sale?"

"No. Work is rarely busy this time of the year, although I've been asked to put together a list of options for a couple from out West. They want a summer home with six bedrooms." She chuckles. "Not an easy task."

"I can imagine."

"Trixie should be here any minute. She told me she needed to do an errand." The door swings wide again. "Here she is." Cavelle lifts her hand in a fluttery wave as Trixie crosses the café in long strides.

"Good afternoon, ladies. Sorry I'm late. Couldn't pay for lunch unless I stopped at the bank. Did I miss much?"

Stella is determined to do whatever is required to maintain a stable coexistence with her sister. Trixie is a reluctant partner in the operation of Shale Cliffs RV Park. If she receives her cheque each month, she doesn't interfere. She agreed to co-sign the necessary papers for their loan and accepted Nick as their ten percent owner. The sisters have what Stella considers an uneasy truce, and their alliance has improved in recent months. Much of this, Stella believes, relates to Trixie's romantic involvement with Russ Harrison. The affair has mellowed much of her anxiety. She's never been happier. "No problem. I arrived a minute ago. Cavelle was explaining the challenges with a request from a couple out West."

"Six-bedroom houses are not easy to find in cottage country, especially not on our side of the isthmus."

"How's the atmosphere at the office, Cavelle?" Trixie bends in closer and lowers her voice. "Are they still at one another's throats?"

Stella has no idea what her sister means.

Cavelle glances at both women and winces. "I guess there's no harm done if Stella knows."

"Oh, for heaven's sake, Cavelle. Stella is good at keeping secrets. You can't pry information out of her with a crowbar. Take it from me."

The lines on Cavelle's forehead disappear as she relaxes. "They are oil and water. One word out of him and she's mad."

Trixie turns to Stella and translates. "You know the Tompkins. Meredith is on the outs with good old Farley."

Cavelle adds, in a hushed whisper, "Good old Farley got himself a makeover and Meredith is exceedingly suspicious. She accuses him of stepping out—making new friends—whatever. He says he's writing his memoirs and doesn't want to work as much. Our Mrs. Tompkins is not a happy boss, so I was pleased to come out for lunch today." She sits back in her chair, seemingly relieved to have gotten the drama of her workplace off her chest.

"I'm only acquainted with them from a distance." Stella shrugs. "Meredith is very outgoing at community functions. Farley strikes me as a shrinking violet."

"Times have changed. Right, Cavelle?" Trixie chortles.

Cavelle lifts book-matched eyebrows in response.

Trixie forges on. "Any word on the toxicology report from the RCMP? Hasn't it been a long time?"

Stella bites her lip. If Cavelle is involved in Lucy's death in any way, there might be a telltale reaction. She remains noncommittal. "Aiden agreed to ask the toxicology people to test for the presence of particular substances. The report should be available soon."

"What substances?" Cavelle's expression reflects horror mixed with curiosity.

Could she fake her response? Stella's uncertain. She launches into her basic explanation. "They are running tests for a few common plant toxins." She consciously avoids revealing other details.

"Is it your opinion that Hester made Lucy a bowl of soup with toxic flowers?" Cavelle sounds both exasperated and agitated.

"We have no idea. Lucy was unwell."

"She was pregnant, for God's sake." Cavelle turns toward Trixie. "You've been pregnant. Didn't you get sick?"

Trixie studies her plate of half-eaten salad. "Not as much as many girls, but I felt crappy on occasion."

"Okay, not the best example but you understand. Women have morning sickness early on when they're expecting—and not always in the morning."

Stella nods agreement. She hesitates but decides not to elaborate. "Cavelle, please understand. Our conversation is pure speculation. The autopsy report mentioned organ damage not related to the fall." *And Hester was busy researching 'the banes', as she called them.* "Toxicology probably won't find anything."

"There's no poison." Cavelle's voice has a tenor of obvious annoyance although she remains, on the surface, in control. "My sister has lots of problems, but Hester has never hurt a fly."

Hester's little terrier crosses Stella's mind, but she remains silent.

****

Saturday has been a quiet and cozy day for Stella and her love. They slept in, cooked breakfast, and spent the better part of this cold and blustery afternoon curled up by the fire. They ventured out earlier for a stroll around the park, but the wind off the water was stiff and icy, forcing them to cut their walk short. They are invited to the North's for supper. Stella was looking forward to their evening with Aiden and Rosemary, but isn't anxious, now that they're getting ready to set out for the isthmus and Port Ephron. She suspects their visit will be short to accommodate for deteriorating road conditions.

"Prepared for a good old-fashioned supper at the diner?" Aiden answers the front door of their bungalow in Port Ephron with an indulgent smirk on his normally serious face. His blue jeans are rolled up at the ankles. He's wearing a white T-shirt with a small box inserted in the sleeve. His white hair is stiff with gel.

"Are we off to a diner?" Stella wiggles into the vestibule and analyzes his attire while she hands him her parka.

"Not a chance, my friend. Rosemary, with the help of her devoted sisters, both Toni and Mary Jo," his eyes focus heavenward as he talks, "have recreated a 1950s-style diner here in the middle of our house. Milkshake?"

"Because this is a perfect night for a milkshake, right? Is she in the kitchen? I'll trundle out to find her while you two get organized." She leaves the men to hang up coats. "Rosemary! Where are you?" She hears the click of stilettos as Rosemary hurries up the hallway from the bedrooms.

"I'm here. Wonderful to see you. Glad you could come. Is Nick here? Did you peek into the dining room on your way past? The décor is extraordinary." She claps her hands together, reminding Stella of a typical six-year-old on Christmas morning.

Suddenly, Rosemary's enthusiasm disappears. She frowns and stares at Stella's stockinged feet. "You are in socks, Stella. Do you not have shoes?" Her tone has a whiny unfamiliar quality. "For my party to be perfect, you must have correct shoes and a kerchief around your neck."

"Rosemary, relax. Dinner will be wonderful, regardless of what I'm wearing."

Stella's arm receives an authoritative tug as her hostess leads her along the hallway to the master bedroom.

"Try my saddle shoes. They aren't dressy, but they'll do. They're too big for me but they should fit you fine."

The gloom of the closet has a dusty smell. "You want me to wear these?"

"Yes. Yes." Rosemary sounds distracted and flustered as she rummages through a drawer full of scarves. She pulls out a pink one resembling old crinoline netting. "Quick, Stella. Put on the shoes and let me tie this scarf around your neck."

Stella acquiesces. The fabric is scratchy and the shoes pinch, but she's decided compliance is easier than any potential alternative yet to cross her mind. When they emerge into the living room, she gives Nick full marks. He inspects her cozy slacks and sweater topped with a netted pink scarf and paired with Rosemary's vintage saddle shoes. He meets her eyes with an expression telegraphing indulgence coupled with empathy. He has rolled up his jeans to match Aiden. She loves him more in this moment.

Rosemary's evening is a sock-hop-style success. They eat hamburgers, hot dogs, French fries, coleslaw out of paper holders, and apple pie with ice cream for dessert. The stereo belts out rock-and-roll for three hours. They survive.

As they don their coats, Aiden whispers in her ear that he had a short talk with the toxicology lab. The report will be available next Friday.

CHAPTER 12

Were We Right?

The days until Friday dragged. Stella searched for chores. She assisted Nick with an electrical issue in the pump house—in January—in the frigid air. She baked cookies. She went to town and babysat Mia, consuming an afternoon with a visit to Paulina's. Aiden is expected to call this morning. The lab results will be submitted today.

While she waits for the call from Aiden, she sits at the kitchen table and watches her lanky Nick make hot milk buns from a recipe he claims was his great-grandmother's. Stella suspects the directions were found in one of the stacks of cookbooks collected long ago by her mother. The preheating oven warms her, and the smell of yeast overwhelms the space as it dissolves in the sugar and tepid water. CBC radio hums in the background.

She studies his broad shoulders as he scalds the milk. *What did I do to deserve this guy? He could find a better job in an instant. He could make more money and enjoy more free time.* She nibbles on a fingernail while she second-guesses their liaison yet again. Their status is one source of her anxiety. While the hot liquid cools, he opens the fridge to retrieve the eggs, and winks at her on his return to the counter.

"You're preoccupied."

Stella's convinced his simple statement has no ulterior motives.

"Are you happy, Nick? I can't help but ask myself why you stay here in a rundown RV park, in an out-of-the-way village, with a woman ten years your senior."

He places two eggs in the English yellowware mixing bowl, rediscovered in an upper cupboard when they emptied the cabinets to paint—no doubt a favourite of Dorothy Kirk's, long ago. He approaches her with his hands palms up and cups her cheeks. "You, kid, overthink issues." He leans his tall frame in to kiss her, with pressured intent, on the lips. "I happen to be madly in love with you, if you haven't noticed by now."

As he holds her face, she's captive inside his touch which she expects is his plan. Her eyes widen as she makes a vain attempt to squirm.

"I've never said those words to you." He releases her. "I expect you assumed I'm after your money."

They both laugh at once. The park earns little more than break-even, for all the work they do. Humour masks the terror that bubbles inside her. Her response is delayed, but she's off the hook.

"No need to react right away." He sits on the edge of the chair beside her. "Here's my plan. Let me finish the buns. Try one and I am convinced you will love me forever." He stands, kisses her once more, on the forehead this time, and resumes his task at the counter.

Her mouth hangs open while she stares at his frame.

"Don't just sit at the table and watch my ass. Go to the pantry and find the white flour. Buns won't knead themselves, and the scalded milk has cooled enough for me to finish."

She does as she's told. Inside the larder off the entry to the large family kitchen, she takes a moment to acknowledge the weakness in her knees and the flush in her cheeks. She reaches for the square glass jar with the green metal lid. Dorothy brought it to the park from her mother's house after Gran was admitted to the hospital and never came home. *He says he loves me.*

Returning with the flour, she sets the big container on the counter with care before she wraps both arms around Nick's neck. The phone jangles at the precise moment she opens her mouth to reveal her thoughts. Instead, she kisses him and turns toward the source of the interruption mounted on the wall near the door.

"Shale Cliffs RV Park. Stella Kirk."

"Good morning, Stella." Aiden chuckles. "I suppose you think this call is overdue."

"Did the report arrive? Were we right?" She faces Nick while she talks.

"Toxicology suspects amatoxins figured in Lucy's death. They say several criteria must be met. Her tissue and blood samples, along with results of liver and kidney examinations, meet the criteria." Without a pause to listen to her potential response, he continues. "I'll read you a paragraph from the

summary: *The condition of the subject's liver, kidneys, and intestinal tissue were analyzed with a reference to possible amatoxin poisoning. Blood and urine analyses were completed. Results were compared to the six criteria where the presence of three indicate poisoning. The subject's samples exceed the required three. There is no indication of water hemlock (cowbane) or monkshood (wolfsbane), except for where symptoms may overlap. Conclusion of the analysis: amatoxin poisoning of the subject was likely, if not probable."*
Aiden pauses.

The gravity of the information is unmistakable. Stella takes a deep breath. "Lucy could have been murdered, Aiden."

"Yes, but they use the word 'likely', and indicate conclusive proof can only be considered once her food intake history is clarified. If possible, they need to analyze mushrooms she may have been in contact with during the last week to ten days of her life. Definitive findings will not be easy."

Her excitement begins to ebb.

Aiden adds, "It's imperative to talk with the family and try to determine the menus for as many as fourteen days before her death. If there's no information to hide—if Lucy's death was an accident—the interview won't be a problem."

"Do you remember what you had for supper two months ago?"

"Stella, you were right when you voiced suspicion, but brace yourself for the idea we may never discover the perpetrator."

Stella tries not to sound anxious. "Do you need my help? Are we to interview the family again?"

"I've requested Jacob come in to the office this afternoon. I'll miss your observations of his reaction when he discovers toxicology suggests his wife was poisoned."

She struggles to hide her frustration in being kept away from the investigation. She expects his superiors advised him not to work with a civilian. "I guess I'm not invited." Annoyance filters into her tone.

His inflection sounds tolerant. Stella detects an undertone of amusement. "No...because I need you to pop over to the farm and interview Opal and Hester. In so doing, we will have an element of surprise when each family member discovers Lucy's probable cause of death. I'm not sure what to do regarding Cavelle, although I'm doubtful she was involved."

Her words tumble over themselves. "No problem. I'll call Cavelle and ask her to meet me at the Painter's this afternoon. She said she isn't busy this time of year. With any luck, she might be free to spend the rest of the day at home and I'll be able to speak with the three sisters at once."

"Okay. Good. We have a plan."

Stella focuses on his instructions. His tone has a lecture quality, but she doesn't care.

"How each sister reacts is important. Menus are crucial. Refrain from any identification of the poison for now. Each person is to be considered a witness, not a suspect. Remember, we are not into a formal investigation yet. No one is charged with a crime. We need to gather more information based on new evidence, as we did when we visited them before."

Stella's heart pounds. "May I take notes?"

"Of course. I expect you to list the food Lucy ate and meals they took together. Remember, your notations are considered evidence if we take a case to court."

"Okay. I'll talk with you later tonight, Aiden."

****

Cavelle had no appointments booked. She agreed to meet Stella out at the farm to review the toxicology report. Opal was more reluctant but consented when she understood Cavelle's inclusion.

As Stella pulls her Jeep into the yard, she sees Cavelle slam the door of her electric blue sedan and turn toward the front porch. Stella jumps out as fast as possible. Her parka, purse and notebook are cumbersome. "Cavelle! Wait." She pants her way across the frozen ground. "I'm thrilled you were free this afternoon. Aiden asked me to meet you, Hester, and Opal together."

"Are you on the payroll now?" She frowns. "This is Detective North's job. Why is he sending you on his behalf?"

Inner conflict is difficult to conceal. Stella's unaware if Jacob told any of his sisters Aiden summoned him to the detachment. She must be careful. "I think he has another task." She tries to appeal to Cavelle's practical side. "I hope you don't mind my involvement. I'll call him instead, if you prefer."

"Oh, for heaven's sake, Stella, stop being crazy. If he asked you to talk to us…then, fine. I think it's weird though. Let's go inside out of this blasted wind."

Stella allows Cavelle to assume control. She follows her up the steps and into the barely warmer-than-outside porch. Cavelle opens the heavy oak door. "Opal, we're here! I found Stella out in the yard. I hope tea is made."

Opal cruises around the corner. Her face is a mask of annoyance brushed with impatience. "Of course, there's tea. You must be frozen." Her focus is Cavelle.

She ignores Stella's half-hearted wave.

"I'm pleased you're home for the afternoon, Cavelle. When Stella told me you were taking the afternoon off, I made plans for a special supper tonight. Hester is thrilled."

"Hi, Opal." Stella tries to insert herself into the exchange.

Finally, Opal turns toward Stella. "I expect to see you when the garden is harvested, and the vegetable stand is open. Your visits have become a habit this winter."

Stella is sure the oldest Painter sister's remark isn't a joke or a tease. "I'm here at Detective North's request, Opal. I told Cavelle, earlier, if you want to hear the information from him, I'm happy to make those arrangements." Unintended abruptness seeps into her tone. "He might visit later today or tomorrow."

"Leave your coat on the banister and come in where it's warm." Opal turns with a swish of her wool skirt and proceeds along the dingy corridor to the kitchen in the rear of the American Foursquare.

The table is set with three cups and saucers. A brown pottery teapot, with only the spout and handle visible, is snuggled into a knitted cozy the colour of pumpkins. "Where's Hester, Opal?" Stella wants Hester to be a part of their conversation. She needs to understand what happened to Lucy as well.

"She's upstairs with her nose in a book. Don't worry. I'll invite her to join us after I listen to what you report. I always assess information before it's provided to Hester, so I can attempt to predict her reaction."

"Fair enough, Opal, but Detective North's instructions were explicit—the three of you are to be present." Stella chooses a chair and makes herself comfortable. "After I tell you both about the conclusions, we will inform Hester together."

Opal nods in agreement while Cavelle reaches for the teapot.

"Not to mince words, the report indicates poison likely caused Lucy to lose her balance and fall. Specific criteria need to be met when the lab completes their tests. When they examined her body fluids and organs, the threshold for toxins was reached."

Cavelle covers her mouth with her hand. Her face crumples. "Your suspicions were right, Stella. Someone poisoned Lucy. How? An accident? Why, for heaven's sake? And, who?"

Stella watches Opal stare at the cupboard on the opposite wall while Cavelle sputters. Her expression is blank. Her eyes are black and empty. She doesn't turn when she remarks, "You people think Hester killed Lucy, don't you?"

When Stella reaches out to touch Opal's hand with her own, Opal withdraws her arm. She will not be comforted. "I don't understand what happened, Opal, but I told Detective North I'm happy to help the best way I'm able."

"Is Jacob aware?" Cavelle's voice trembles when she asks the question.

"I assume." Stella keeps her tone as quiet as possible. "He's at the detachment right now."

Opal frowns at Cavelle. "He said he needed to attend to an errand in town. I didn't ask for details."

Stella sits up straighter in her chair and glances from one woman to the other. "Am I clear? Neither of you have any idea how Lucy could come into contact with poison?"

"No," Cavelle snaps. "What, Stella? You think we murdered our sister-in-law? Are you serious? Are you insane?"

Cooperation is important for the remainder of her visit, so she ignores Cavelle's outburst and refocuses her attention on Hester's inclusion. "I am here solely for information gathering. No one has accused anyone of a crime." She recalls Aiden's instructions. *The meeting is to collect information; not to accuse.* "Can Hester join us now?"

Without further discussion, Opal rises from her place and leaves the kitchen. Stella hears the leaden trudge of her footsteps as she makes her way up the stairs.

"I'm sorry I've upset you, Cavelle. Aiden requested I reveal the results to everyone at the same time. After we tell Hester, I want to discuss Lucy's meals and see if a possibility exists where a particular food is implicated."

Cavelle ignores the apology. "Do the police think Lucy ate poison here at home?"

"We will note the incidences when she didn't dine here. Poisoning could have occurred somewhere else, Cavelle. We have no evidence." For effect, she adds, "Toxicology can't test for possibilities. We must make suggestions."

"Was Lucy poisoned? She threw up in my room." Hester rounds the corner into the kitchen with Opal at her heels. "It smelled, but not the same as when Mama died."

"Come sit here beside me, Hester." Stella focuses to calm her voice. "The lab people think Lucy ingested a toxin. We aren't sure if she consumed something bad by accident, or if a person gave her poison because they intended to hurt her. Let's discuss the food you know she ate in the days leading up to her death."

Hester smirks, leans back against the oak chair, and closes her eyes. "My dog was poisoned by accident. People and dogs are alike."

Stella retrieves a paper calendar and a pen from her handbag. She starts at November 4, 1980. "Let's begin two weeks before she died and see what comes to mind, okay?"

"We cooked stew that day. It was Tuesday. Opal made biscuits, and I helped."

"Wow! Your memory is excellent, Hester. Do you recall other meals?"

"I remember every supper, Stella. I told you, I am very smart." She opens her eyes and meets Stella's. "I know what Lucy ate here at home. I can recite a list. You take notes." She wags her index finger in the vague direction of the calendar on the table in front of Stella. "She made lunches to take to work. Often, she included a slice of Opal's homemade bread. Lucy spooned peanut butter into a Mason jar and grabbed an apple or a pear from downstairs. She didn't favour breakfast, so drank coffee and orange juice."

Cavelle's expression reveals her shock at Hester's revelations. Opal, hands clasped in her lap, keeps her eyes directed toward her teacup. Stella hesitates, unconvinced anyone could remember such detail.

Hester's tone is impatient. "Shall we start?"

The process consumes an hour, but Hester rattles off every meal cooked in the Painter household. She tells Stella the meat, the vegetables, and the dessert. She states who was present at the table. If a member of the family was not home, she reveals whether a plate was left for them. Stella writes as fast as she can manage. She notes two nights when Lucy did not eat at the farm. Once, she and Jacob were invited to the Smithers' for Sunday dinner, and once the young couple ate at the Purple Tulip in Port Ephron before they returned to attend a community theatre production in Shale Harbour.

Stella checks with both Opal and Cavelle. "Do either of you disagree with Hester's assessment?"

Cavelle whispers, "I understand she possesses an exceptional memory, but the detail is unbelievable!"

"And you, Opal?"

"Oh, I know, don't I, Hester?" Stella notices the fondness with which she gazes at her youngest sister. "I always understood you are very, very smart."

"I want to return upstairs now. I am at an important part in my book." Before anyone replies, she slides off the chair and turns.

"You may go, Hester. Thanks for your help. I hope to see you again soon." The younger woman does not turn to acknowledge Stella.

Back in the car, Stella can't wait to return home and review Hester's information. She counted four meals which included mushrooms served the week before Lucy died. *I need to clarify why Lucy, alone, suffered ill-effects.*

She and Aiden planned to discuss their interviews tonight. She wonders how Jacob reacted to the idea his wife was poisoned less than three months after their marriage.

Chapter 13

It's Difficult to Point a Finger

"Jacob is obsessed with William Sylvester. He's convinced beyond the shadow of a doubt that William participated in Lucy's death."

"What was his response to the report and the likelihood she was poisoned?"

"He said William must have given her poison when she made home visits to see Mrs. Sylvester." A heavy exhale precedes Aiden's answer. "To him, the possibility she ingested poison at the farm is out of the question."

"Was he shocked? Angry? At a loss for words? What was his immediate response?"

"When I told him the toxicology report indicates his wife was poisoned, I didn't mention mushrooms or amatoxins. He nodded and then said he figured Cat was our perpetrator. Cat blabbed to friends how he and Lucy were a couple. The guy went on being convinced, despite Lucy's clarification of their status. Then he wanted an invitation to the wedding, and this worried Jacob."

"Jacob considers William's attitude points to motive? Was he afraid the guy would disrupt their wedding?"

"Correct. He refused to entertain alternative possibilities. How did you do?"

"I managed a measure of success, Aiden. I'll tell you each sister's response before I discuss the food."

"Did you discover information on a few meals?"

"Hold your horses, but yes...I discovered *all* the meal information."

"Go on. What did you find out?"

Stella takes a deep breath. "To begin, I never said we expected a particular toxin. Cavelle was annoyed at the possibility Lucy might have been poisoned under the Painter roof. She took the suggestion as a personal affront, even though I was clear that an accidental poisoning is a distinct possibility. Despite her melodrama, she's believable. Opal was reluctant to include Hester in our initial discussion and refused to allow her downstairs until after I revealed the contents of the report.

"You agreed?"

"Yes. She told me they need to be able to predict Hester's reaction by hearing details regarding any topic first."

"Their approach is fair given the circumstances."

"Opal's face was a blank canvas as we reviewed the toxicology report. She kept her eyes focused on her teacup. Then she trudged upstairs to retrieve Hester."

"How did Hester react?"

"Here's the wild part. She mentioned the terrier she owned when she was younger. She suspects he was poisoned. She said people are no different from dogs. What happened next was extraordinary—she was able to list for me every meal in the house from November 4 until Lucy died. Four contained mushrooms. They were evening meals. Opal and Hester were always present. Jacob was absent on occasion. Lucy ate outside the residence twice, and Cavelle was not around much, although Opal oftentimes left her a plate in the warming oven."

"Let me get the story straight. Hester recited every supper the family ate from November 4 to 18, like a menu in a restaurant?"

"She listed the choices Lucy packed for her lunches and described her breakfast routine, too." Stella hears Aiden's breath catch in his throat before she launches into the details.

"Remember, Hester hates mushrooms. She claims they are fungi, and she refuses to eat a fungus under any conditions. On one particular evening, Opal concocted a chicken stir fry with dried mushrooms. She separated portions before adding the mushrooms. Hester said she didn't see which one Opal or Jacob ate. Opal shrugged her shoulders when asked and said she can't remember. Another night she made soup, again with dried mushrooms. Hester fetched them from the stash in the cellar and then made herself a tuna sandwich while everyone who was home for supper had the soup."

"Were specific varieties of the dried mushrooms poisonous and others safe? Was Hester controlling who consumed what?"

Stella remains anxious and noncommittal. "They enjoyed a roast beef dinner one evening. Opal made gravy with mushrooms and gravy without. Opal avoided gravy and Hester, of course, chose the gravy without. She did not notice Cavelle's choice, and Jacob was at a meeting. Lucy ate mushrooms. She praised Opal saying how good the gravy tasted. There were mixed frozen vegetables one night. Under normal circumstances, Opal never added dried mushrooms to frozen veggies, but Lucy loved the mushrooms so much earlier that Opal offered to mix them into her serving. Lucy was thrilled."

"After your descriptions—and excellent job, by the way—it's difficult to point a finger at either Hester or Opal. Agreed?"

"If Hester gave dried mushrooms from their stores to Opal, and she used them in total ignorance of what type they were, then Hester is the murderer. If Opal chose the contents and manipulated the meals—except for the one where Hester retrieved dried mushrooms, then she's the culprit. They could also be in cahoots. They decided they wanted Lucy gone, and the least suspicious way to accomplish the task was to poison her. Since Hester doesn't eat *'fungi'*, as she often points out, the choice of the non-poisonous dish makes any circumstance less obvious."

"And Cavelle?"

"Cavelle isn't involved in Lucy's murder." Stella is blunt in her response. "She's been disengaged from the family for a considerable time."

"Okay. I guess I need a way to interview Hester without Opal around to interfere. Any ideas?"

"As a matter of fact, Eve Trembly, one of my workers who happens to be Del's granddaughter, is home for a few days. I expect a call from her to arrange a get-together here at my house. She'll tell Opal she wants to take Hester out for an afternoon with Del, and they'll come here instead. Care to join us?"

****

Eve, as predicted, telephones Stella early Saturday morning.

"How's school? Have your courses taught you enough to help with the park accounts next summer—less time for you on the mower?" Eve is a hard worker. She's committed and never has to be supervised. Stella wants her to stick around for as long as possible.

"Oh, Stella. You may trust me not to screw up your paperwork, but I'm probably better as the toilet cleaner instead of the bill payer for another couple of years." She giggles.

"We'll make plans before the season starts, okay? Now, what's the story with you and your grandmother?"

"I visited her after I arrived home yesterday. She wants me to drive her and Hester out to see you and we wondered if Sunday afternoon—tomorrow—is convenient."

"Perfect. Do you remember Detective North from last summer? He'll be here, as well."

"Sounds serious. What's up? Gramma refused to say a word."

"Detective North wants to take advantage of your second cousin's remarkable memory." Stella avoids further details.

"Does Gramma know you invited the detective?"

"No. Will you tell her when you pick her up?"

"Sure. I expect we'll get to the park by two o'clock."

****

Stella has the tea prepared except for boiling the water. She places a dozen store-bought cookies on an old green glass plate, another relic found at the back of a cupboard before they painted. Nick is in the living room. He decided to rearrange the chairs closer to the fire. The sub-zero chill outside has succeeded in crawling through the walls. Stella's afraid both Del and Hester will find it chilly.

With the snow packed hard on the gravel in the driveway, she doesn't hear the car approach. "I'll get the door," Nick shouts to her. She makes her way from the kitchen.

"Hey, Aiden. Great to see you. Come in out of the wind."

She's relieved. She wanted Aiden to arrive early, and he hasn't disappointed.

"Nick, hi! Stella, I hope this proves to be a fruitful afternoon."

Nerves are setting in. "We need Hester to be talkative. Here, let me take your coat, and there's a boot tray closer to the fireplace." She meets Nick's eyes. "Oftentimes, it seems my feet will never warm up." She complains her toes are freezing on a regular basis. Dry foot gear helps. Nick understands.

Aiden isn't interested in boots. "Our visit with Hester today has gotten me trying to find a way to use her without arresting her, Stella." He takes a seat in a chair positioned to give a clear line of sight to each of the other potential participants. "I can title her our subject-matter-expert, our confidential informant of sorts. She understands plants, and we need expertise. Part of her role will be to avoid discussion of the topic with anyone outside this room."

"I don't know. With Eve, Nick, and Del here, her information isn't very private."

Nick, who has tended to the fire during their exchange, turns toward them. "When you give me the sign, I'll usher Del and Eve into the kitchen and close the door. We'll organize the timing and be out of the way to drink our tea so you three can talk. Good idea?"

"Great, Nick." Aiden settles into the upholstered side chair and crosses his legs. "I want to learn the mushroom drying process at the house, and how much Hester participates."

"We need to get a more detailed idea of how meals are prepared at home," Stella adds. "She told me she helped with biscuits one night. There may be other times."

A significant rap on the old door startles Stella. She jumps to attention. Upon opening, she sees Del and Eve huddled on the threshold. Hester remains fixed on the bottom step. "Come in out of the weather, you three. Welcome. Hester."

Hester stays rooted to her spot. Her voice is quiet. "I visited here before—many years ago. I saw flowers."

Stella wraps her cardigan around her torso and wriggles past her guests out onto the veranda. The icy cold of the floorboards seeps through the bottoms of her slippers. She creeps down the frosty stairs to Hester as fast as she's able, jumping from one foot to the other so neither touches the frigid wood for long. "I'm pleased to see you, Hester. Come in out of the cold. Nick built a cozy fire. It's teatime." Stella hugs the woman, snuggled in a parka large enough for a good-sized man. Hester's knitted hat is pulled tight around her ears and touches her collar. She has a multicoloured pink crocheted scarf made of angora, wrapped around her nose, which has turned red. "My poor feet will freeze soon. Let's go inside," Stella adds for extra encouragement.

"You are outside in slippers and a sweater, Stella. You'll catch your death." Hester keeps her eyes straight ahead as she climbs up to the veranda.

Once the door is closed and secured, Stella sees Del and Eve comfortable on the sofa. They're engaged in an animated conversation focused on the unreliability of television weather forecasters.

Without further prompting, Hester removes her outer garments as well as her ancient galoshes. She places them on the tray with the others. She holds her coat, hat, and scarf out to Stella, who bounces from one foot to the other in an attempt to get warm. With quiet composure, she chooses the leather chair opposite Aiden and near the fire. Nick jumps to retrieve the clothes from Stella and carries them to the alcove off the main living room.

"Why are you here, Detective North? My Aunt Del and second cousin once removed, Eve, told me we were invited to Shale Cliffs RV Park for tea."

Hester's expression, as she directs her remarks toward Aiden, is curious but remains open. Stella knows she's capable of closing off any direct communication. She hopes such a circumstance can be avoided.

Before she has an opportunity to explain, Aiden begins. "I came here today to talk with you, Hester. I am told you possess a remarkable memory as well as a wealth of knowledge relative to local flora. The police want to ask you to be our subject-matter-expert as we investigate your sister-in-law's death."

Hester's response is demure. Stella has never seen such behaviour in Hester before. This shy and meek version has clearly succumbed to Aiden's attempt at flattery.

"You are correct regarding my memory, Detective North, and I'm more familiar with local plants than anyone in the area. I will be your subject-matter-expert and help you in any way I'm able."

Stella observes both Del and Eve. Eve's expression is full of pride, but Del looks at Aiden as if he's out of his mind. "Nick, why don't you take Eve and Del out to the kitchen for tea. I'll bring a tray in here shortly. I hope our arrangement is suitable for everyone." Before her guests formulate an answer, she approaches Del, reaches for her arm, and assists her off the sofa.

Once in the other room, Stella addresses Del's expression of confusion which is highlighted by an element of annoyance. She beckons the group closer. "Aiden and I decided to encourage Hester to keep our visit secret." Stella's voice hisses when she whispers, "The discussion is to be in strictest confidence, so she won't repeat details to Opal, Cavelle, or anyone else. We want her convinced she's a subject-matter-expert and a witness, not a potential suspect, while we put the puzzle pieces together. No one can be charged. We have no evidence."

Eve gasps. "Hester isn't capable, Stella. You must be wrong."

Del turns to her granddaughter. "I, on the other hand, am certain she killed Lucy and maybe her father. Let the police, along with Stella, do their work." Del's Breton hat remains planted firmly over her permed curls. The rolled brim vibrates periodically.

Stella returns to the living room with her tray of three cups of tea, cream, sugar, spoons, napkins, and the green glass plate with a few cookies. The warmth of the fire wraps around her as she gets closer. She regrets how drafty the kitchen, with the door closed, is in comparison; sorry Nick, Del, and Eve are relegated to a cooler part of the house. "Here we go; warm tea on a blustery day."

Hester reaches for a cup and saucer. She tucks a napkin under the cup and adds two cream-filled wafer cookies to the saucer. "The sweets look yummy, Stella. Opal makes cookies, but they're never perfect and the same size the way these are." She munches on a wafer.

Aiden shakes his head as Stella passes the plate in his direction. He crosses one leg over the other, holds his tea against his knee, and leans toward Hester. "Can we talk, now, Hester? I need more information regarding meals consumed at your home before Lucy died."

"We may, Detective North."

"Can we keep our discussions between the three of us?"

"I can keep a secret. Right, Stella?"

Recalling the occasion when she broke a glass in the kitchen at the Painter's house, she nods. Hester helped her clean up and dispose of the shards in the rubbish dump behind the house and never told anyone.

"Okay. You reported four evening meals in which we are interested. Will you tell me how they were prepared, and every detail related to who did what? Are you able to remember?"

She takes a sip of her tea and picks a wafer crumb off her navy wool skirt which Stella observes to be clean and likely worn for the first time since its last wash.

"Of course, if you are specific."

Stella leans back into the leather couch cushions to observe Aiden ask Hester for more details regarding any meals which contained mushrooms. Hester reminds Aiden on numerous occasions how she hates fungi and refuses to eat them. She describes picking mushrooms with Opal, so she can be sure no poisonous versions find their way into the basket. Destroying angel mushrooms grow everywhere, she explains.

When she mentions the destroying angel, she peeks up at Aiden from under her lashes. Stella expects, at this exact moment, Hester has determined the crux of the investigation.

After they return home from foraging, she explains how they slice their harvest very thin, put them on baking sheets, and dry them in the oven. They place their product in jars to store in the basement. They eat what they don't sell after their vegetable stand opens.

"If I may summarize, Hester, the one meal for which you accessed the mushrooms for your sister, Opal, was when she made soup."

"Correct. She sometimes assembles the ingredients and asks me to assist with mixing or shaping. I want to participate, but she permits me to do very little."

"Why do you suppose she won't let you help more, Hester?"

"I am very smart—as you know." She regards Aiden with an expression clearly indicating the lack of wisdom in challenging her statement. "I suggest options, different ingredients, other methods to enhance efficiency. Opal objects. She generously taught me what she knows, but forgets I learn from books and other people; not her alone."

Stella focuses on her empty teacup. The conversation has dragged on for over an hour. She hopes Nick has discovered a way to entertain Eve and Del.

"We're finished for today, Hester. You are an informative and helpful subject-matter-expert. I hope I'll be able to call on you again in the future."

"Of course, Detective North." She turns her attention to Stella. "You may invite me here whenever you see fit. You can pick me up in your father's old Jeep or Jacob will drop me off. I hope we can be friends again, like when we were girls. Please fetch my coat now. It's time I go home, or Opal will worry unnecessarily. Thank you for the tea. If you have more wafers, I want to take a couple with me."

Chapter 14

You People Have Missed the Point

Stella thumps down the stairs from her private apartment. She fiddles with the last couple of buttons on Nick's shirt she borrowed without permission before she clears the corner leading to the kitchen.

"You dressed up this morning."

She peers at the shirt. "The plaid called to me from the hanger. I couldn't help myself, so I helped myself." She giggles.

Nick chuckles along with her. "I imagine my old flannel shirt is much happier on you. If I make waffles, are you in?"

"Yup. I have time before I'm due at the manor. Want to come with me and visit with Dad?" Nick's hair falls over one eye when he turns toward her. She melts at the expression of concern reflected.

"Of course, I'll go. I'd love to talk with Norbert for a few minutes. You need to meet with Del?"

"Yes. Aiden wants me to debrief her and ensure she understands not to discuss our conversations with Opal or Cavelle."

She opens the fridge to retrieve the juice. "Del's sure Hester killed Lucy, and perhaps even Leon, but we can't let her blab her theories to the whole world. Not yet."

"Not ever, would be my assessment, Stella. Poor Hester. She has social or psychological issues, or whatever, but she's no psychotic murderer."

"You're right of course." She extends her torso enough to be able to plant a kiss on his temple. "Hester is a weird duck, though, and I, for one, have no clue what ideas flit unharnessed inside her brain." She shrugs. "Del, on the other hand, is convinced she can read the girl's mind."

Harbour Manor never changes—except for the ebb and flow of residents.

Stella walks beside Nick until they reach her father's door. He gives a light tap to the frame before he enters.

As Norbert recognizes Nick, the joy in his voice is unmistakable. An odd mixture of pleasure and pain overwhelms her. She trudges on.

Del's door is ajar. Stella pushes it open but remains at the entrance. "What's up, Del?" The old lady is standing at the edge of the bed and sorting through the contents of her upturned purse. She doesn't turn around.

"I put my wallet inside my purse. I always do." Stella can hear a tinge of panic mixed with frustration in her voice.

"Let me assist, Del. What's happened?" Stella sidles into the room and toward the television, which blares an episode of "The Phil Donahue Show." "May I turn the television off?"

"Come help me find my wallet." Her curls vibrate. "I always put it in my purse."

Stella scans the room, and in a matter of seconds locates Del's wallet perched on the edge of her nightstand. "Here you go."

Del grabs Stella's find and stuffs it, along with the other paraphernalia piled on the chenille bedspread, back into her black leather handbag. "Thank God." She acknowledges Stella for the first time. "I figured someone stole my wallet."

Her eyes become slits. "The staff in here aren't reliable. I thought my money was gone for sure. Help me over to my chair, will you?"

Holding Stella's arm, Del shuffles toward her recliner. She drops into the seat and stuffs her bag deep into the folds between her pudgy leg and the overstuffed arm. "Thank you. Your message said you wanted to debrief me? Is it Hester? She's not talkative, as a rule. I don't imagine Detective North learned much."

The old lady leans forward and the distaste in her voice is hard to miss. "She's a sly one, though. I expect she wrapped the poor old detective around her little finger."

Lacking another option, Stella seats herself on the side of the hospital bed. Del did not see fit to ask for an additional chair to be brought in. "Detective North wanted me to share details regarding his interview, Del. He also requested I make sure you understand the information is confidential. He does not want you to review any of our discussions with the Painter siblings. Do you agree?"

"I am not nuts. I suspect foul play at the farm. Hester is involved—or all three of them—or some combination—and they disposed of their parents and then Lucy was next." Her tightly curled hair, unimpeded by her customary Breton, quivers with her disapproval. "I am incensed and do not require a lesson on confidentiality."

Stella swallows. Del is ornery today. "Protocol, Del. The police want to keep information in the community to a minimum until they're sure they have uncovered the whole story. The request isn't personal, okay?" Although, in fact, it is.

With slumped shoulders, she smooths the jacket of her ruby-red tracksuit and meets Stella's eyes with reluctance. "Now, tell me what happened."

Aiden's discussion with Hester is shared, including the idea that they will consider her a subject-matter-expert. She explains how Hester recited meal details to Aiden, which proved very helpful; and how Hester understands the police are reporting Lucy was poisoned but they aren't sure how, or why others in the house weren't sick as well.

"And the deaths of Leon and Velma?" Del's voice has begun to rise again, and she starts to fidget in her chair.

"First off, Del, Hester was ten years old when her mother died in childbirth. She hemorrhaged, correct?"

"Yes. I didn't see for myself, though," Del sniffs.

"Of course not. You weren't there."

"Hester could have poisoned Leon. My brother was a healthy man. She was eighteen when he died and well involved with her plants and poisons. Her dog died around the same time."

"I have no idea, Del, but both Cavelle and Paulina McAdams told me Leon's death was as the result of a cardiac event—a heart attack or stroke."

"I'm quite familiar with the story." Del stares at the wall past Stella's right shoulder. "You people have missed the point. It's possible Leon was poisoned. Maybe Velma's death was natural causes, but Hester could have tried out poison on her little rat terrier first, before Leon. Hester has problems. She's a sicko."

****

The next day, on their way to have another talk with William, Stella states what's on her mind. "Aiden, William Sylvester could not have killed Lucy Painter."

"You are probably correct, but before the police can lay charges, all possibilities have to be examined. William is one of those."

As they pull into the Sylvester driveway, Stella's stomach churns. "There might be a problem, Aiden. His battered Chevette isn't here."

"Is today the day he does his errands, and the nurse is with Mrs. Sylvester?"

Stella uses her arm to push the door open as she explains. "He said he did errands on Thursdays and if a nurse was here, we'd see a car. Come on."

Stella knocks as loud as she's able. When there's no answer, she opens the unlocked and flimsy wooden door. They enter the tiny foyer. "Mrs. Sylvester, Detective North and Stella Kirk. We're on our way inside, alright?"

She rounds the corner. She can see the wheelchair on its side. She hears William's mother moan. The chair rests on one of her legs. Before Stella manages to get on her knees beside the woman, Aiden is on his radio requesting an ambulance.

"Are you okay?" She takes Miriam's hand.

Miriam provides Stella with a watery grimace as she tries to shake her head. "No." Her voice is raspy. She pushes air with the word.

"Don't talk. We'll wait for help." Sirens sound in the distance.

Once the paramedics have her assessed and loaded her into the ambulance, Aiden turns to Stella. His controlled rage spits out. "I could charge William Sylvester with negligence, or abuse. Let's go find him. Lucky we arrived when we did."

William's car is parked in front of the Harbour Hotel. Stella struggles with the concept he's inside drinking, in the middle of the day, after leaving his disabled mother alone. Nevertheless, there he is, straddled on a bar stool, body lolled to one side, and nonsense slurring from his chapped lips.

Stella stands back as Aiden approaches, taking a position on the stool beside William. "Decided to take a break and leave your mother to fend for herself, did you?"

The sound of a voice close to his face startles William. He blinks his eyes and attempts to sit up straighter. "What do you care, mister? I can go wherever I want *whenever* I want."

"We came to see you today, but you aren't fit to have a conversation."

"I told you two a long time ago I had nothing to do with Lucy's death." His voice becomes a whine and blends with the sound of the bar stool as he attempts to swivel and focus on Stella. He loses his balance in the process.

Aiden reaches out a hand, but he shrugs off the touch. "Hey, now! We found your mother on the floor with her chair on top of her. She's been taken to the hospital in Port Ephron."

He sways on his perch.

"Steady on, Cat. Can't have you fall and get hurt. Who will care for your mom if you take a tumble?"

William slams both elbows hard on the bar. Stella suspects he will regret the veracity of his response by tomorrow morning. "Not me. Nope." His shaky denials result in strands of greasy hair dragging down over one eye. "Somebody else can do the work. Home is no better than jail. Only my friends can call me Cat, and you're not friends," he adds as an afterthought.

Stella, frustration and annoyance bubbling inside her, decides to take a seat on the other side of their drunken suspect. "Your mom may have broken her hip, William."

"Don't care. She should be in a home. She can go to the manor."

"Have you talked to her about admission to the manor?"

William's chin drops to his chest. "Nope."

"I bet your mother expects you to be the one to help her forever." Aiden's tone has mellowed slightly.

He peers at Aiden with hooded eyes. "She wants me to be her nursemaid for the rest of her life. Well, she's wrong." He motions the bartender for another beer.

Aiden declines with a raised hand. "You're finished, my friend. I will take you home. You can walk back to the hotel tomorrow to get your car."

They leave him in the front room of the little house. On the way out, he perks up enough to ask, "Why were you after me, anyway?"

Stopping for a moment, Aiden turns. "We came to report Lucy Painter was poisoned."

William straightens in the chair, his eyes bleary and sad. "I told you I didn't kill her. No way I would hurt Lucy. I don't know nothin' bout poison." He starts to blubber. "I loved her."

Back in the car, Aiden and Stella sit a moment. Stella is the first to put her concerns into words. "I'm not sure we've progressed very far, Aiden. I also think Del Trembly has begun to lose her grip. Her information might not be the most reliable. I caught her yesterday in search of her wallet which was on the bedside table right at her elbow. She was frazzled."

"I understand, but we have loose ends left to tie before we begin a strict focus on the Painter family."

"Do you need my help?"

"Yes, if you're able. Another set of ears is an advantage."

"I'll come by after lunch. Okay?"

****

Stella arrives at the RCMP station at one-fifteen on Wednesday, not sure where they will go, whom they will interview, or when she might get home. Nick struggled not to show his disapproval, and she sensed his discomfort. She and Aiden have spent considerable time together on the Painter case. *Focus. Nick will be fine.*

The days have gotten colder. The roads are icy, and the wind whips off the water with a vengeance. She snuggles further into her parka before she reaches the entryway.

Sergeant Moyer is manning the front desk. She prefers the office when Moyer's on duty. It's comfortable; she's part of the team. "I'll call Detective North and tell him you're here. Not gettin' any warmer, eh?"

"Not one degree, Sergeant. Has this winter been colder than normal, or what? There were those two warm days, but we've burned more wood so far than in the whole of last year."

"Me, too. Heating is sure a challenge in the temperatures we've experienced lately." He returns his attention to the telephone. "Okay, sir. I'll send her in." He peers at her from the elevated desk. "He says to go right back. You can find your way, right?"

Stella nods and starts to make her way along the dreary hallway to Aiden's office.

"Glad you're here. I want to discuss our adventure for today." His head is tilted to the side, which is usually the case, and his teeth twinkle, even in the glow of yellowed ceiling fixtures.

"Nick asked, and I told him you're looking at specific details." She settles in a wooden chair with straight arms—no doubt used in another building before the current place existed.

"I hope it's okay that I've pulled you away again, Stella. He doesn't get jealous, does he? Is he aware we dated in high school?"

It was way more than dating, if my memory serves me. "Oh yes, he knows.

No, no jealousy; more in the realm of curiosity, I guess. He says we're too focused on Hester, though."

"Do you agree, Stella?"

"No, I don't. She has your standard motive and opportunity. She possesses the skills."

"True, but since we have no direct evidence which points toward her, or any member of the Painter household, eliminating other options becomes the chore. We have an appointment with the Smithers in," he glances up at the clock on the wall behind Stella, "thirty minutes. We'd better be on our way. We're scheduled for a mid-afternoon meeting with the owner of the Purple Tulip."

"Our search is for mushrooms on the menu, right?"

"Absolutely, but for now, we'll reveal only that the reports states there's a likelihood she was poisoned, and we need a list of items she ate or drank for the two weeks prior to her death. I want you to watch body language and facial expressions. I can't seem to focus on the nuances."

"Trouble at home? Is Rosemary okay?"

Aiden shuts his eyes for a moment. "I could spout the stock answer, but I'll be honest. She's off the rails. She needs to be placed for a few months, but her sisters pressure me not to give up." He puts on his coat while he talks. "Mary Jo even threatened to move Rosie to her house, but location with another family member won't make any difference." His expression is defeated. "I try to stay in the present. It's a challenge."

Sympathy seems inadequate. She doesn't know what to say.

Bitsy Smithers has written down every detail of the meal she prepared for the family the night Jacob and Lucy were guests. On her foolscap list, she's noted the spices, as well as any liquids. She included the recipe for her lasagna, the salad dressing, and her homemade tomato sauce. Dessert was pie. She documented the recipe for the pie, too. "I prepared dinner with no help. Glenn set the table and Reid poured the wine. Lucy was sweet. She cleaned up and loaded the dishwasher."

She begins to blubber, holding a pathetic excuse for a hankie. "I'm sorry. I still cry every day. Reid says I'll get better as time goes by, but I'm positive I'll be grieving until I'm an old lady." She snivels. "My beautiful little Lucy will be twenty-one forever." Her blubbers turn to soft choking sobs before she finishes.

Aiden shakes hands with Reid when they depart. "We appreciate you seeing us today. We want no stone left unturned."

"Lucy was poisoned for sure, Detective North?" Reid tries to contain his emotions by biting his lower lip.

"We are quite certain, sir, but cause of death is only one step. We'll keep the family informed."

The Purple Tulip is on a side street in Port Ephron. The establishment is impossible to find if you don't have an idea where to search. The restaurant is in an old and renovated single-story home which served as the doctor's office and surgery over a century ago. There is a veranda-style deck across the front, with a trellis roof for trim. Outside seating isn't an option today.

Stella leads the way into the gloomy interior. Every wall is painted the same deep charcoal grey. A tall, thin young man with a Clark Gable mustache greets them. "Hello. My name is Mitchell. Are you Detective North?"

Aiden nods.

"Our manager, Marni Webb, is waiting for you at the far end table. Supper service begins in an hour."

"Thanks, Mitchell. I hope we'll be able to spend a few moments with Ms. Webb before she gets busy." As they follow Mitchell, Aiden whispers to Stella, "I never told them our victim was poisoned. I said we are investigating cause of death."

The interior is designed to reflect a modern industrial look, decorated with metal chandeliers made from cheese graters. Black circular tables are mounted on chrome pedestals. Most of the seating is red basket lawn chairs, and the polished floors are cement. Conversations of the servers preparing the venue have a hushed and hollow quality.

Marni comes across as efficient and impatient. She has anticipated their requests and provides them with a copy of the register receipt for the night Lucy and Jacob ate dinner at the Purple Tulip. She has a list of items they were served, and the ingredients used for each dish.

"I am attempting not to be offended, but I imagine you suspect Mrs. Painter was poisoned and I can assure you our establishment will not be implicated." Marni sweeps blond hair, cut to a razor-sharp edge an inch above her shoulders, away from her face. "Any other details you might want?"

Aiden picks up the sheet of letterhead with the list of foods. The sales receipt is attached by a paper clip. "Your information is in order. If we have any questions, I'll give you a call."

On the way out, Stella ponders the restaurant as the perfect place for a romantic dinner with Nick. Expensive, but romantic. None of the recipes noted by Marni contain mushrooms.

Chapter 15

I Burned a Few Bridges

Icy drafts drift through the downstairs kitchen as Stella assembles coffee mugs and serviettes. The house is quiet. Nick has gone to Port Ephron to organize the delivery of more wood. She flips on the radio as a CBC announcer starts to read the news.

Trixie will arrive any moment. Today is the last banking day in January, and she's on her way to pick up her cheque.

A noise in the yard piques her curiosity. She trots through the cavernous living room to check. Sure enough, she sees Trixie's VW Microbus slide to a stop within a few inches of the veranda stairs. Trixie, wrapped in a pink bunny-fur jacket, alights with a wiggle and a bounce. Stella wonders how she manages in her heeled boots and hopes the coat is faux.

"It's frigid out here. Hope you have a fire lit."

"If you wore more clothes, you might fare better." Stella fails to keep the humour out of her tone or the smirk off her face. Her sister will never change. "There's a fire built, thanks to Nick. Coffee's made as well."

She tiptoes up the icy steps. "Cheque?"

Stella groans. "Yes, I have your money. The summer was good. We're in fair shape, financially, as long as you or Nick don't need a buyout."

"Great, because I hate the times when we muddle through our little money talks." She gazes at her fashion boots. They lace up the front. "Do I need to go to the trouble of taking these off?"

"No, you're fine. The old floorboards have seen worse. Come on in. I'll get our coffee and your cheque. I have a favour to ask."

"Favour?" In a sudden change of tone, Trixie becomes suspicious. "Do you need me to manage the place while you and your teenage boyfriend go away on a winter vacation? Any information you haven't shared?"

"What? No! What do you mean?"

"I wondered if you two want to take off somewhere warm and tie the knot." She sounds contrite.

With her brain focused on murder and little else over the last weeks, Stella struggles with interpretation.

"Trixie! Nick and I are happy with the status quo. No! I need you to talk with Cavelle. Here's your coffee...and your cheque."

"Thanks for both, but I refuse to talk with Cavelle if the topic is expected to be Lucy's death."

Stella appeals to Trixie's curious side. "You were very helpful when we gathered information at Ruby Wilson's house before we knew she killed Lorraine." She raises her eyebrows as she studies her sister. "Being part of an investigation again might be fun."

"Cavelle is my friend. Ruby was not. Besides, why won't you talk to her?"

"I burned a few bridges the last time. She's cross with me because I suggested Lucy ate a meal at home and whatever was in the food killed her. I visited on Friday. Aiden asked me to try to review the meals she ate. I'm not permitted to reveal details, Trixie, but I want to rule Cavelle out of the equation. I'm certain she wasn't involved. Nevertheless, the woman is very angry with me."

"Maybe Lucy was poisoned when she was somewhere else. What has convinced you the deed was carried out at home? I can understand why Cavelle is miffed."

"She's well past miffed. To answer your question, we suspect food Lucy ate at the farm contained poison. Hester, with her miracle memory, knows every morsel she consumed until her death, and we spoke with the restaurant and Lucy's family specifically regarding the two meals she and Jacob ate away from the farm. Besides, it could well have been an accident and not a 'deed'."

Trixie's expression softens.

"Will you please talk to Cavelle? Find out her assessment. She might reveal a suspicion she avoided telling me. At least try?" She forces the whine from seeping into her voice.

"Okay, okay. I'll organize a lunch date. Work is slow for both of us right now. Oh. Oh." She starts to bounce while still seated. "I almost forgot. Are you and Nick able to come for supper at Russ' cottage a week from Sunday? I promised to ask. He organizes his schedule well in advance, but his plans often change because of job demands."

"I don't see any problem with the time. We'll be flexible if he's called away." Stella is curious, and an opportunity to get a peek inside the cottage Russ Harrison bought and renovated last summer sounds interesting. She knows Trixie is smitten, but the guy often stands her up because of work. "No need to wait and check with Nick. I know we have no plans. An evening out will be fun."

"Great! He said he'll cook Italian. Says he's a connoisseur." She giggles. "He told me he'll even make bread to go with dinner. I'm assigned dessert." She stands to leave. "Thanks, Stella. I want Russ and I to do more stuff as a couple. Right now, we eat out somewhere quiet and then it's back to his place." In an uncharacteristic burst, she puts her arms around Stella and gives her a squeeze.

Stella, surprised by Trixie's overt demonstration of affection, is at a loss for words.

"No cooking for you or Nick, although Russ liked that local brew Nick served the last time we were here." She hauls on her coat and makes her way to the door.

"Don't forget to talk to Cavelle. Your help means a great deal to me."

"It may take a while for us to get together, but I'll do my best." She turns to descend the stairs as the RV park pickup, normally relegated to duties on the grounds, trundles into the yard with its box full of firewood.

"Bye, Trixie. I guess we won't freeze to death in the foreseeable future." She waves as Nick rounds the corner to the side of the house.

****

The following Thursday, Stella is curled up in front of the fire to relish a few moments of solitude before their dinner guests arrive. Nick is busy in the kitchen. She hears him pull buns out of the oven. The sudden bleat of the telephone invades her space. "I'll get it." She dashes into the office and picks up the extension.

"Shale Cliffs RV Park."

"I'm afraid we're going to be late. Rosie's in the middle of a huge argument with herself. She's undecided as to what to wear." His voice drops to a whisper.

"She's not good, Stella. I'm concerned we shouldn't come out to the park."

"Don't be silly. There's only the four of us. We'll be fine. She can dress however she wants, but the old place is drafty in spots. We set the table in front of the fire. The evening will be okay."

"Our tardiness won't ruin your efforts?"

"First off, they're Nick's efforts. Macaroni casserole, buns, and salad keep. See you soon."

"Okay."

She places the receiver back in the cradle as Nick materializes at the office door. "Problems?"

"No." She tries not to let her concern show, but it's impossible to disguise the strain in her voice. "Aiden called to say they'll be late because Rosemary is still struggling with what to wear." She winces. "He says she's erratic. I told him we'd be fine. I hope I was right."

Nick throws the tea towel over his shoulder. "Rosemary is Rosemary. How bad can she be? The woman's a hoot."

"We'll soon see."

Their entrance is chaotic, even for the Norths. It's obvious to Stella that they argued before their arrival. Rosemary is annoyed and not afraid to show her emotions. She marches into the living room without removing her footwear. Taking them off is not an option. She's chosen bright-yellow backless patent leather pumps with little bows on each toe. Her feet must be frozen.

She tosses her swing coat to Nick and sashays across the room with one arm bent and her hand raised. "Can't anybody offer a girl a drink?"

Aiden's voice is soft. "The doctor said no alcohol with your medication, Rosie." Stella is reminded of someone trying to cajole a mean dog.

Rosemary turns to him with an expression of pure hatred in her eyes. "Keep your mouth shut, mister, and call me by my proper name in front of people. I will have whatever I choose, and little Miss Sweet-On-You can damned well fetch it for me."

Stella is speechless for the second time in three days, an unusual state of affairs because the circumstances relate to the same person. Rosemary is dressed in skin-tight cigarette pants most popular in the 1960s, and a white blouse with a stand-up collar and wide cuffs rolled up above her wrists. She links her arm in Nick's and pilots him toward the kitchen. Stella is thankful for Rosemary's obvious change in preference.

Aiden has taken a seat in one of the leather chairs normally nearer the fire but pulled away to make room for the table. "She took an hour to tie a perfect bow in the orange sash around her waist. There could be no visit without that sash."

"Well, she has 1960s fashion nailed, if appearance is any consolation." Stella graces him with a weak smile. "She'll be fine."

"Nope. I know her, Stella. We are in for a very long night."

Stella's expression is watery. "Miss Sweet-On-You?"

At that moment, Nick and Rosemary appear from the kitchen, arm-in-arm. Nick's face is a dull rosy shade and his shirt is rumpled. "Stella, please help me serve supper. Rosemary has her drink."

He locks his eyes with Stella's in such a way she has no choice but to interpret his expression as an emergency. "Sure. Rosemary, you have a seat by the fire. Aiden, a glass of wine, too?"

He nods.

"What is wrong, Nick?" She whispers once they get into the kitchen, even though the door is closed.

"Rosemary tried to take my shirt off, Stella. She made a huge pass at me!" He tucks his shirt back in.

"You're kidding, right?"

"No." His voice rasps out a hushed bark. "Here. Help me. We can serve the bread and salad first. She said you and Aiden were 'getting it on' so she and I should do the same. Man, Stella. I must be out of practice. I was shocked. I didn't know what to do!"

They understand Rosemary isn't well. She tries to tease; to calm him. "You're all flustered. I think I'll rip your shirt off more often."

Nick, usually the cool one, remains blank-faced. "This situation isn't cute. She's out of control. Rosemary wasn't here. Some other person took her place. There's been flirting before, but tonight is way worse."

"Okay." No more teasing. "Don't take her behaviour personally. We'll try to support Aiden. Let's give them supper and make the best of the evening. I'll tell Aiden, but not tonight."

Supper was scrumptious. Rosemary did not behave. Throughout dinner, she often touched Nick's hand, guffawed at his jokes, and rubbed her foot against his ankle under the table. Stella saw her antics. Each time she made a move, Nick turned a bleached-out purple colour.

The Norths did not linger for tea after supper. Aiden apologized at the door before they left.

****

"Daddy died on October 10, 1959. I was eighteen." Hester's voice is flat—devoid of emotion.

"When did your little dog die?" Stella focuses on her tone—conversational and quiet. When she called Opal on Monday and requested an interview, she explained how Hester is now considered a subject-matter-expert in the field of local flora. Her primary focus, at this moment, is not plants, although they have spent the last half an hour in an intense discussion of the characteristics of monkshood, or wolfsbane as it is commonly called. Hester has elaborated on the consequences to animals or people after ingestion. She has described various locations where it can be found.

"Stamen died April 2, the same year as Daddy."

"You asked me if you could come over here to talk plants with Hester. You said she was an important part of your investigation." Opal sounds incensed. "The focus of your visit is not local weeds, is it Stella?"

Her eyes hold a challenge. Stella tries to explain. "Hester has been very helpful, Opal. Her information regarding poisonous plants is invaluable. Hester told me weeks ago how her rat terrier died because he ate monkshood."

"Which is unrelated to the death of our father. He collapsed in the barn—a 'cardiac event', in the doctor's opinion." She wiggles her fingers in the air to put imaginary quotation marks around the words. "He did not eat monkshood."

Stella notices Hester squirm in her chair. Opal turns toward her with annoyance. "Hester, what is wrong with you? Do you need to go to the bathroom?" She questions her sister as one reprimands a six-year-old who won't sit still.

Hester flushes. "No, Opal." She scrapes oily bangs away from her forehead. "I want to go and get the samples I put aside for Stella. I felt sure they might come in handy."

Opal's eyes narrow. "What samples, Hester?"

Her expression is secretive. "Curiosity killed the cat."

Once the thud of her shoes can be heard on the hallway stairs, Opal sits up straight and glares at Stella. "I should ask you to leave. Why must you turn up at my home and torment my sister? She has no additional information you can't read in a book or find out from a scientist. I'm sure the police have access to countless experts." Her face turns red. She puffs—a barnyard rooster defending its territory. "Do not, and I repeat, do not discuss the death of our father," she hisses.

"Sorry." Stella tries to sound contrite but is more interested in Opal's extreme reaction. Hester is a thirty-nine-year-old woman. She may have social issues, but Stella isn't convinced she needs to be guarded to this extent—unless Opal knows she poisoned members of the family and Stella is witnessing her attempt at protection.

"You people have already decided Hester killed Lucy. You tell her she's needed as your expert, so you can question her without a lawyer around. Cavelle said we should have a lawyer present when you talk to our sister." She sticks her chin out and scowls across at Stella.

"I don't want to be taken advantage of." Hester stands in the doorway and Stella isn't sure how much she overheard. She walks toward her chair with her nose in the air and refuses to make eye contact with either woman seated in the room. She sits, arranges her grubby skirt around her, and proceeds to sort the contents of a small cloth satchel placed on her lap.

The mantle clock ticks, and the north wind rattles the old windowpanes. Stella breaks the silence. "Hester, please don't be offended." She tries to appeal to the younger woman's intelligence. "As you know, if the police have a suspect, they arrest the person, and the accused hires a lawyer. We must research and learn. The police call it...."

"An investigation, Stella. I know."

"You are an expert on poisonous plants, and we need to talk with you. We're interested in your knowledge even if the case happens to be unrelated to you. The police could well contact you again if similar circumstances arise."

Hester keeps her eyes focused on the contents of the bag in her lap.

Opal sips her tea and watches her sister.

"I do not want to be taken advantage of, Stella," she repeats. "As you know, I am exceedingly smart, but I miss social cues. The doctor says I am not the only person who doesn't recognize when they are teased or used. When we were children, you understood. Have you changed?"

Stella is shocked at Hester's insight into her awkwardness and enhanced intelligence; even more shocked she has discussed her personality traits with the doctor. "We were always friends when we were children. I have admired you, Hester." She struggles to find the right words. To squander Hester's trust at this juncture would be a critical error. "Your sister is very protective, but you have a mountain of information. We want to learn from you. The police have no suspects to arrest." She's flustered. Her connection to Hester could easily slip away.

"Your words are true." Hester's voice is soft but firm.

"Hester be careful. These people," Opal glares at Stella, "are out to get you."

As if none of the previous conversation happened, Hester adds. "I have information for you." She pulls out two small plastic bags, each labeled with Latin names. "These are dried samples of wolfsbane and cowbane from my personal collection. You may keep them." She reaches into the black canvas bag once more, replacing the samples and rummaging for something else.

"Thank you, Hester. I'm sure your contribution will help the police scientists."

"Yes, they will. I have three books for you to borrow. Two are pamphlets. You saw them when I researched the banes several weeks ago. I took a long time to return from upstairs because my book by L. H. Pammel was misfiled." She holds the volume in her hand and stares at the cover. "There is no logical reason for Pammel to be out of place in my library. It is said memory lapses occur with aging. I hoped to avoid such an affliction." She points her finger. "The books are not for you to keep. I expect them back when your investigation is over, Stella."

Stella does not reveal that she read many of the references in the previous days. "Thank you, Hester. I will take very good care of them. I know how important books are to you."

Hester hands over the canvas sack which holds her offerings. "You may keep the bag until you return my books. Now, if you don't mind, I will go back to my room for a while." Her eyes dart toward Opal before she stands.

Chapter 16

If I Go Under a Bus

She pokes her nose out from under the covers. Nick's side of the bed is empty. The air is consumed by a damp chill as sleet taps with fierce persistence against the old windowpanes. A shiver ripples through her naked body. She sits, still protected by the comforter, and reaches for the top of her two-piece tracksuit crumpled on the floor. She smiles as the combined smells of fire and coffee tickle her senses. It's hard to fight contentment, despite her constant anxiety he'll cut and run.

"Good morning, sleepyhead." Nick looks up from his kneeling position in front of the fireplace. The soft glow reflects pinkish tones on his stubbled cheeks. "Coffee's ready."

The sudden flush as she recalls the night before results in her weak response of "Okay."

In the kitchen, away from his puzzled eyes, she worries. She wants to trust he'll be beside her for the long haul. Nick answered her ad for a park manager almost three years ago and stayed. He inherited money when his aunt died, so now works by choice. She wishes for a future free from uneasiness, so she can embrace their unconventional alliance.

Stella shakes off her trepidations and returns to the big living room with their coffee. She sets his mug on the table in front of the sofa before she curls up in one corner of the leather couch. She pulls her mother's old crazy quilt off the back and lets the multi-coloured fabric fall over her chilled bare toes. The pottery warms her hands.

"Tomorrow night, we go to Trixie's boyfriend's cottage for supper—Sunday, right?" Nick stands, retrieves his coffee, and cuddles in beside her. Bob Dylan's *Slow Train Coming* plays in the cassette deck.

"Russ Harrison is nice enough compared to other guys Trixie has brought around, but I still don't feel as if I know him. Dinner together will be an opportunity to get better acquainted."

"Good. That's settled, so now I have a number of propositions for you." Nick's tone becomes business-like, but he wiggles his eyebrows at her and snickers.

"I'm propositioned by you on a regular basis, guy." She leans over to sneak a quick kiss. "On the other hand, what do you have in mind?"

"First off, shall we have scrambled eggs and buns for breakfast? I put a stash of rolls in the freezer after I made them last Friday."

She nods, game for any meal he plans to cook for her.

"My other idea is more complicated. Hear me out, okay?"

She nods again. Butterflies awaken in her gut. He hasn't mentioned Florida in a while.

"We've finished the kitchen and chosen to use it every day since I've taken up residence here with you. We haven't even made coffee in the little kitchenette upstairs."

"Correct. The upstairs has become our bedroom and bathroom...and privacy when the lower floor is busy."

"Yes, exactly, so here's my idea." His words come out in a flood. "Let's tear apart the upper apartment and turn the whole space into a master bedroom, a new bathroom with a big shower, and maybe a small sitting area near the veranda door. We can replace the appliances in the manager's residence with the ones upstairs and rent the cottage to tourists in the summer. Good plan?"

Her mouth is open, and her eyes are saucers. Her reaction is unpreventable, having assumed he understood their financial challenges when he paid for the water system improvements.

"Money's your concern, Stella, but this renovation will be on me."

He's read her face.

"I have the money. Allow me to contribute. We can upgrade our living quarters. Any cottage rental means extra income for the park and we'll have our own spacious retreat upstairs. No strings. I want to do the project for you."

Despite her lack of confidence, she smiles through tears. "Why?"

"You aren't one to share your heart's deepest secrets, but I'm smitten by you, Stella Kirk. I am head over heels." He reaches for her hand.

"At ten years your senior, I'll soon be an old lady—emphasis on senior."

She omits how she worries he will meet a younger woman and leave her, or simply get tired of her and go. "I have a demented father, a rundown RV park, and a sister who refuses to contribute except to pick up her cheque once a month."

Nick frowns. "None of those details matter, Stella. I want to build a life here with you. To prove my intentions, let me create a retreat for us."

"And opportunities in Florida?"

"There'll be no trip this year. I told Dad. When I spend this inheritance, it will be here...with you, not on some cockamamie investment idea my father scares up."

In a sudden change of heart, she realizes surrender is her best option. "Okay. Who am I to argue? What's your plan?" She settles further into the sofa and retrieves her coffee from the table. She lowers her guard and embraces a possible life with him for now—another step with this sweet man, although her hesitation is silent—one day at a time.

"I have measurements and a few ideas on paper." He can't contain the excitement in his voice. He glances over at the living room windows away from the veranda. The rhythm of sleet is steady against the panes. "Let's have breakfast and you can review my drawings afterward."

"Okay. We need to have a conversation about Rosemary North, too."

He gets up from the sofa and stretches out his hand to assist her. "I understand she's sick, Stella. Her behaviour caught me by surprise." His expression is sheepish. "It's not very often I'm at a loss the way I was Thursday night." He blushes.

"Aiden needs to be aware. I'll tell him on Monday."

Nick's eyes are dark with emotion. "Oh, he knows. I bet he won't be surprised in the least."

****

The drive to Russ' home takes no more than five minutes. "Will we reveal our plans to renovate, Stella?" His face is shadowed by the glow of lights from the dashboard when he steals a glance across the front seat of the Jeep.

He's excited. "Let's wait until Trixie comes out to the park. Tonight, she wants to show off her new love. Besides, if you want to throw more money into Shale Cliffs, we'll need to make a formal arrangement. I don't want her reaping the benefit if a catastrophe were to befall me."

She giggles at his shocked expression. "I appreciate the idea sounds ominous, but if your renovation project costs you twenty thousand dollars and then I die, Trixie stands to be the net gainer. My forty-five percent goes to Brigitte and you're left with ten."

"Fair enough. Let's carve out an addendum to the owners' agreement which states the value of the changes are mine before any sale is contemplated."

After leaning nearer, she pats his shoulder. The weather's warmed up a few degrees, but she finds she's chilled to the bone, nonetheless. "Good idea. If I go under a bus, I want you protected over and above your ten percent we've already contracted."

"There are no buses in Shale Harbour." He nudges her. "Once we have the plans laid out, and the budget determined, we can meet with Trixie and instruct the lawyer to write a rider for our ownership agreement. Okay, we're in the right place." He turns off the gravel road into a grassed driveway littered with icy patches and small ruts. Trixie's Microbus is parked askew on the frozen lawn.

Stella assesses the cottage through the velvet greys of early evening. When the government leader's retreat was built in the 1920s, the Craftsman style architecture and the wide expanse of beach complimented one another to perfection. The front veranda is balanced by circular support columns. Stella recalls the version before Russ' purchase was painted chestnut brown, but he has decided the cedar shingles will be a foggy grey with green undertones paired with darker trim and ivory pillars. The house is stunning by any measure even if the light provided by two antique wrought-iron pendants hanging from the porch ceiling is muted.

Trixie, dressed to the nines in a long black skirt and red silk blouse, throws open the windowed oak door. She has a half-dozen strands of twinkling crystal beads around her neck. As is often the case, the formality of the evening overwhelms Stella and she smothers a sigh.

"I'm glad you're here." Trixie gushes as she trots onto the veranda in backless pumps. "Come in. Let me take your coats. Russ is in the kitchen. He told me I couldn't help." She thrusts her bottom lip out in a contrived pout. The effect is overly dramatic and childlike.

The front foyer of the Craftsman is flanked on one side by a set of stairs and on the other by the living room entry and a hallway leading to what Stella presumes is the kitchen. As she follows Trixie into the living room, the dining room along the back of the house becomes visible. The home's architectural beauty is dramatized by the solid oak woodwork throughout.

"Didn't Russ do a professional job? Later in the evening, he said he'd let me give you a tour of his place." Trixie leans over to whisper in Stella's ear. "Soon to be mine, too, I hope."

Russ pops around the corner. "Welcome to my humble abode, you guys. What can I get you to drink?"

"We've been admiring your great renovation. 'Humble' is not the right word." Nick nods to their host. "I brought my favourite brew. Shall I help with the drinks?"

Requests are obtained. Nick scurries through the dining room to the kitchen and returns with wine for the women and a beer for himself. Russ joins them with a beer of his own. The chatter focuses on the converted cottage—the refinished floors and woodwork, the new kitchen, the traditional colours, and the stained-glass transom windows.

After a fabulous supper of lasagna, salad, and homemade bread, followed by a fluffy lemon pudding contributed by Trixie, the men clear away the dishes while Stella and her sister retire to a small study off the entrance and behind the stairs. Stella is impatient to hear Trixie's feedback regarding her latest talk with Cavelle.

"Yes, we met for lunch. Honest to God, Stella, she's really annoyed with both you and her Aunt Del. She told me the police investigated because you two refused to keep your noses out of their business."

Stella nods. "She could be right, but the fact is Lucy was likely poisoned before she fell. If someone intended to hurt her, they might have gotten away with murder if we hadn't started to dig."

"Well, you still haven't identified a suspect." Trixie points out the obvious. "By the way she spoke, I'm sure Cavelle wasn't involved. She assumes Hester is the guilty party. She says the investigation is a waste of time because if Hester were to confess she killed Lucy, what could anybody do?"

"She's right. Hester would never go to trial for a crime, even murder." Stella doesn't mention how Cavelle first made the point back on December 12. "Her sister could be institutionalized though. The notion of a mental hospital is no doubt the source of Cavelle's angst."

On the short drive home, Stella and Nick discuss Trixie's boyfriend. "To me, Russ is still the mystery he was before we visited. Did you learn anything new regarding the terribly vague Russ Harrison while you were on cleanup duty?"

"Honest answer? Very little. He's nice enough but distant; unattached. I expected he might want the scoop on how you and Trixie get along, but not a peep. He was preoccupied, except for one momentous remark."

"What did he say?"

"He said he wants to make a life with Trixie but can't get out of his job yet."

****

Stella wraps both hands around her coffee cup and drums her fingers against its sides while she waits for Aiden to appear in the doorway of Cocoa and Café. He needs to be aware his wife is more troubled than he realizes, but her insides knot at the idea of offending him. Her goal is to assist with investigations as often as possible, and further their friendship. Her stomach twitches.

The bells sound above the door and a cool draft puffs toward her table when he arrives, stamps his feet on the rope mat, and turns in her direction. She waves. He nods at the waitress and makes his way over. Stella has chosen the back corner for a modicum of privacy, but a Monday morning in February isn't busy.

"Hi. Glad you picked this spot. We need to talk in private." He removes his overcoat before he sits.

Patience.

"I want to apologize for Rosie's behaviour on Thursday. The minute her wardrobe became the focus and she got cross with me for no reason, I should have canceled."

She opens her mouth to interject.

"Let me go on."

He needs to speak what's on his mind, so she remains silent.

"My wife must understand you and I are friends. You have a partner it's obvious you adore."

Stella blushes despite the truth of his statement.

"Our ancient history need not influence us socializing today. The circumstances are even more difficult because she copes with her problems by living in the past."

He leans aside as his coffee is delivered. "Thanks." After they are left alone, he puts both elbows on the table. "Stella, Rosemary is very sick. She's in hospital."

"What?" Stella is dumbfounded. "Is she okay?"

His shoulders slump. "She is far from okay. Let me tell you what happened. Don't be shocked." His tone is that of a man defeated.

"You can share with me whatever you want, Aiden." No longer compelled to reveal Rosemary's behaviour with Nick, she sips her coffee and studies his face.

"Friday morning, she appeared to be as angry as when we went to bed. She moved into the guest room in the middle of the night. I was surprised she was still in the house when I woke up. This isn't the first time she's left." He stops to study her for a moment. "Are you prepared to hear the sordid details? We planned to meet and review suspects in the Painter investigation."

Stella concentrates on making her voice soft. "I am happy to focus on whatever topic you want, Aiden. If I can help with Rosemary, you realize I will lend a hand."

"The long and short of the story is she marched off in the cold, in slippers, yelling she was moving to Toni's. Her sister lives a half a mile away. I let her go and called Toni, but Rosie never turned up. One of the Port Ephron patrol cars found her across town, transported her to the station, and telephoned me." His chest heaves, punctuating his distress. "She screamed when I walked into the office, so I contacted Toni again. She arrived soon after and drove Rosemary straight to the psych ward."

"Such a difficult decision for you."

"Oh, I didn't commit her. She was out in below-zero temperatures in her slippers, was disoriented, refused assistance from family despite efforts, and is convinced I sleep with every woman I meet. They have admitted her for a thirty-day assessment because she is a danger to herself."

"And her sisters? How did they react?"

"Toni is very pragmatic. She's always been stern, almost motherly, with Rosie. Mary Jo is the pushover. She would have put her in the car and taken off, but fortunately, Rosemary accepted Toni's help when she was in the hands of authorities."

"What happens now?"

"Counseling, medication—same old stuff. The psychiatrist on call said she has clinical depression exacerbated by anxiety and a delusional disorder.

Her delusions revolve around her need to live in high school as well as her extreme jealousy of any woman she assesses as a threat to our marriage. Right now, you are in her sights."

Stella's smile is softened by understanding. "Her behaviour at my house was a good example, I assume."

"Yes. She made a pass at Nick, too."

"You figured that out?"

"Thursday wasn't unique. Other friends have experienced Rosie's indiscretions." He clears his throat. "Besides, his shirt was no longer tucked in and he was flustered. I'm not sure I've ever seen Nick flustered." He purses his lips while peering at her over nonexistent reading glasses. "You understand I'm a detective, correct?"

Her tension begins to ebb away. "Yes, you're right. She's getting the help she needs. We won't dwell on what happened at our house. Remember, whatever you might need from me, say the word, okay?"

"Of course. Shall we discuss the case now?"

She nods and motions to the waitress for refills.

On her drive back to the park, Stella reviews their discussion regarding the case. They re-evaluated various suspects, or non-suspects, in what they are sure is a murder. Stella reported on her interview with Hester and Opal the previous week. She gave him the dried flower samples and books Hester loaned her. They realized one or all the Painter siblings could have taken part, either directly or indirectly, in Lucy's death.

Aiden decided he wanted to meet once again with each relevant person outside the Painter household. Stella silently felt it to be a waste of their time. She didn't express her opinion. He is the detective, not her. She agreed to accompany him to visit the various players—William Sylvester, Maeve Cavannah, and Ardith Holland—to make sure no detail was missed. They also determined it would be advantageous to interview the four Painter siblings as well as the Smithers family, together out at the farm by the first of next week. The purpose will be an attempt to force possible cracks in their inter-relationships.

Chapter 17

What Does She Want?

Hot water rushes across her arms and back. Nick let her oversleep. She woke when she heard the rumble of the truck leave the yard. The sun forces its way through the frosted glass of the bathroom window. As she reaches for her towel, cool air caresses pink skin.

Warmth from the fire he obviously banked before he left for the lumberyard, to obtain quotes on materials and fixtures, drifts up the stairs. Last night he told her how anxious he is to get started. He's bound and determined to renovate their quarters before spring and the new camping season. Her mind skips through various subjects and tasks. The tax assessment arrived yesterday—higher than expected, of course. Trixie must be kept informed. Inquiries regarding reservations for the summer have been brisk and most of the seasonal fees are paid. No need to worry yet.

Did I hear the door? She knows she overslept, but she heard Nick leave. Maybe he forgot his wallet or his drawings. After wrapping herself in a cotton robe, she runs a towel over damp hair and trots, albeit with trepidation, down the stairs. She hates to be startled.

"Hello. Nick, are you back? Did you forget something?"

She peeks into the kitchen. Empty. She rounds the corner into the living room, subdued by the veranda despite the rarity of a sunny day, and sees a shadowed form rigid on the mat. "Hello, Stella. I hope I didn't startle you. I knocked. When no one came, I tried the door—which was open." Opal's appearance is sinister. She wears a black felt cloche, bereft of any adornment. The upturned bowl structure is pulled tight over her grey hair. Her cloth coat is charcoal with a shiny fur collar. The hem brushes her clear plastic galoshes, which are folded in the front and fastened with elastics to buttons on each side.

Dorothy Kirk wore overshoes like those thirty years ago. "Opal! You came into my home when no one answered your knock!" An image of Opal pulling back the shower curtain crosses her mind. Her heart beats faster and her stomach lurches.

"Your house is always open to the public, Stella. People come and go here like it's Grand Central Station." Opal remains resolute at the door.

"In the summer that's true, but we're in the dead of winter, Opal. What do you want?" She ignores her manners and doesn't invite the woman in.

Undeterred, Opal bends to undo the loops which secure her boots. "I came here to discuss Hester and Jacob, but predominantly Hester." She does not make eye contact. Once her galoshes are removed, she opens her coat and takes the liberty of crossing the floor to a chair near the fire.

Stella is struck by a sudden awareness. She is afraid of Opal. She concentrates, to prevent nervousness from seeping into her tone. "Are you assuming Nick isn't here, Opal?"

"I saw him on the road when I came into the park. You're alone."

Her statement sounds calculated. *Was she waiting on the road? No one knew where Nick was going. What does she want?* Stella's manners kick in. She'll try to play for time until Nick returns. "Coffee? Tea?"

"No thank you." She adjusts her coat around her shoulders and her fingers touch her hat for a second.

"You never come out to Shale Cliffs to socialize, Opal. Why didn't you call me?"

"I've been angry since your visit last week. Hester was unnecessarily disturbed by the conversation." Opal stares at Stella, not acknowledging the question. "Hester requires supervision as well as communication as if she were a child, despite her thirty-nine years. She is a genius but inept in the social sense. I'm sure you understand."

Stella, seated now across from her guest, nods. "I have appreciated Hester's challenges since we were children, but she holds the key to the mystery of who killed Lucy." Despite Stella's concern Opal may be implicated, she adds, "Hester knows more than she's revealed. You and Cavelle continue to protect her as always."

Opal remains mute. Her expression is stern.

She makes another attempt. "What's Jacob's opinion on how his wife was poisoned?"

Her squirm is barely perceptible before she speaks, but Stella has a keen eye. "You are convinced a member of my household killed my sister-in-law?"

"Yes." Stella tries another tack as she recalls Opal's reaction upon learning Lucy was pregnant. "Was Hester upset when she discovered Lucy was having a baby?"

Opal's eyes flash. She blinks. "Hester wasn't aware Lucy was pregnant. None of us were. How can you begin to consider she was killed to avoid the addition of a baby to the family?" Her voice quiets and takes on a wistful tone. "A baby is a joy. A baby is a miracle. We were unaware, Stella. Hester was oblivious."

"There are examples of men harming their wives during a pregnancy."

Opal's eyes widen.

"They're jealous at the prospect of competition." Her mouth is dry. This approach is risky.

"Are you suggesting Jacob poisoned his wife of three months because she was expecting a baby? Unbelievable!" She huffs her exasperation.

Stella backs off; goal accomplished. Opal is on the defensive. "A family member poisoned Lucy. The police are certain, Opal. Detective North will find out who is responsible in due course."

Opal rises and begins to button her coat. "I want you to leave Hester alone. She isn't competent. She is easily upset, and I refuse to permit you to ask her more questions."

"Don't be surprised if Detective North wants a family meeting soon. You cannot prevent the authorities from interviewing Hester, or anyone else. The investigation won't stop."

She watches as Opal struggles into her old-fashioned boots. A dull hatred is reflected in her former friend's gaze.

Compelled to add, "Hester's condition does not excuse her," Stella waits with arms crossed. "A murder will be solved despite her challenges."

Damp breezes rush through the screen when Opal opens the inside door. "You'll regret your interference. Mark my words."

The threat hangs in the air while she watches Opal gingerly traverse the veranda stairs and then stride across the lot to her rusted Pontiac parked on the other side.

****

"I found her in the living room when I came downstairs after my shower."

"Where the hell was Nick?" Aiden's voice is anxious and angry.

"Nick left for town to get estimates on our renovation. I expect him back anytime. He didn't lock the door." Self-annoyance is reflected in her tone. "Under normal circumstances, security isn't an issue in the winter."

"Well, security will be an issue now. Her visit was an obvious attempt to intimidate you."

"Without a doubt. She wants us to stop investigating because Hester isn't competent. She reminded me how Hester is bright but inept around people. Opal's goal was to scare me. I admit I was uncomfortable."

"You can withdraw, Stella. There's no need for you to be involved but I admit I'll take much longer to figure the Painter family out if you step aside. I don't want you to be in any danger though."

"Might I be in danger? From Opal? Or Hester? You're not suggesting one of the family would try to hurt me, are you?"

"My advice is that you not eat at their farm or buy food from them." She detects a muted chuckle. "Police humour. Sorry. On a serious note, Stella, we need to start to work together instead of separately, to be on the safe side. If you want to help me, no more private interviews, okay?"

"Deal. Now, what's next?"

"Will you come in to the Shale Harbour office tomorrow afternoon for another chat with Jacob? I'm sure he wasn't involved but I'm curious to see if he'll point the finger at one of his sisters. Then I want to schedule a big family get-together with the four Painters as well as the three Smithers. I'll return Hester's books when I go back. I copied a number of reference pages."

"What time tomorrow?"

"I've set our meeting up with Jacob for two o'clock."

"See you then."

"Describe your visit from Opal to Nick. Make sure he knows the doors need to be locked, at least until we figure out who killed Lucy."

Most of the afternoon is spent in her office while Nick sits at the kitchen table completing the estimate for their project and supervising the simmering chili.

"Are you okay? I figured out prices and timelines if you want a tea break so we can talk reno plans."

She glances up from her paperwork, none of which has been urgent, although the mail has succeeded in making her appear to be busy. His eyes are full of concern. "I'm fine." Aiden's directions niggle her. "Yes. Tea sounds wonderful." When she reaches the doorway, he puts his arm around her. She leans into his side while she walks.

The kitchen smells heavenly. She plunks into a ladder-back while Nick fills the kettle and plugs it in. He turns toward her. "Okay. Give. What's on your mind, my dear? You have been holed up in your office most of the afternoon and there isn't enough work this time of the year to occupy an hour in the day, let alone three."

"Let's put the tea in our travel mugs, Nick." She attempts enthusiasm. "We can bundle up and take a walk around since the road has clear patches, and the sun is out. We'll be back in the gloom again soon enough."

He approaches the table and leans over. His nose touches hers. "We can walk the park with our tea but be prepared to talk to me." His eyes cloud. "Did I upset you?"

"No. No, Nick." She rushes to clarify. "I'm troubled by the Lucy Painter case. Let's go and I'll tell you as long as you promise not to get angry."

Worried eyes follow her as they prepare for their trek.

Dressed in warm gear, insulated mugs in hand, they trudge from the main house toward the water. The sun has melted lingering snow after the last time Nick plowed. Stella hasn't been this close to the ocean in days. The weather has been miserable, both cold and stormy. Today is a treat.

"I took a spin around yesterday and no trailers show visible damage so far, Stella. I hope we're through the worst of the storms."

"Not likely. We always end up with a blizzard in late March or early April." She loves these days. The air is crisp. The light is brilliant. The water looks blanketed by diamonds reflected from the blue of the sky. The wind swirls around them. She sips hot blueberry tea and snuggles into Nick's arm. "My morning took an interesting turn." She keeps her eyes focused on the ground.

He squeezes her shoulder. "Did you enjoy your sleep in and the fire I made?"

"Very much, although it was a surprise to find Opal Painter poised on the doormat in my living room when I came downstairs."

With an abrupt halt, he releases her, turns his back to the cliffs, and studies her expression. "What? How did she get in?"

Before she has a chance to explain, he pales. "My God, Stella, I didn't lock the door. I was focused on my drawings and getting the quotes. I forgot."

"Her visit was benign, but she scared me half to death at first. She said the door was open, and she decided to come in. Her purpose was to warn me off the investigation. She accused me of tormenting Hester when I interviewed them, and she insisted I stop."

Nick's voice morphs from shock to calm. "You need to get uninvolved, Stella. Did you call Aiden?"

"Oh yes. Right away. He told me I could withdraw, but we're close to a resolution and this is what propelled her to turn up. He said we'll conduct future interviews together, and to ensure you are aware."

"He wants me to remember to lock the door." Nick puts his arm around her again and pulls her close before they resume their trip around the park.

"I guess we're forced to be more careful, at least for the time being. I'll join him tomorrow to talk to Jacob one more time before a family interview. He thinks Jacob is withholding information. Jacob hasn't a clue, but Aiden's the detective." She leans into his shoulder. She smells the scent of him mixed with the salt air. "When we get back, let's review your plans for upstairs. I'll share an idea or two of my own." She snatches a glance up at him and grins.

****

The next afternoon, she climbs into her Jeep and makes the short trip into town and the Shale Harbour police station. Aiden meets her at the entrance.

"Jacob is in the conference room. I decided to wait out here for you. Still able to help me, or did you change your mind?"

His remarks are meant to tease. She can tell by his expression. "At least I locked the door when I left today. Nick will be safe and sound." Then she becomes serious. "How do you prefer to handle the session? There are a few questions I'd like to ask once you've gathered the information you need."

"Sure, Stella. I need to determine once and for all whether he has pertinent details which point toward one of his sisters as a more likely suspect."

"Okay. I'm ready when you are."

His back is toward the door when they enter. "Good morning, Jacob. I asked Stella to join me because she knows your family and we hope she might be able to help."

"No problem, Detective." He swivels his chair. "But Opal is tired of

Stella's questions to Hester." He turns toward Stella. "I gather Opal was over to the park yesterday. She said she startled you."

"Indeed." Stella tries to relax. "We had a discussion."

Aiden interrupts. "We determined Lucy was poisoned at the family home. Did one of your sisters possess motive to kill Lucy?"

Stella focuses on Jacob's demeanour. He's distracted; silently exploring options. He was sure William Sylvester hurt his wife. She suspects the challenge has been for him to face the fact she was killed by his family.

"I've racked my brain and talked to my sisters. No one can account for what happened. Hester has been funny though—odder than normal. She wants a dog, and continually harps that she won't let her puppy be hurt; she'll protect her pet, so it won't end up like Lucy."

"Did she poison her other dog accidentally or on purpose?"

He appears shocked by Aiden's bluntness. "She claims she did neither. She says her dog ate monkshood. Did she poison her dog?" His eyes dart from one of them to the other. "Really?"

Aiden turns to Stella and ignores Jacob's question. "Do you want to speak with Jacob, Stella?"

"I do."

Jacob runs his fingers through his hair and takes a sip of his water. "You guys scare me. You think my sisters killed my wife?"

Stella starts with a simple question. "Who most concerned you regarding Lucy's safety—Hester or Opal?"

"Hester, of course. She's always into plant information I don't understand. I know grain. My limit is grain." He takes another sip of water. "If you've decided she killed her dog...well, you're entitled to your opinion." His voice starts to shake. "She's not violent, but people change. We all do."

Maintaining a level tone takes concentration. "Who welcomed her the least when she moved to your home—Opal or Cavelle?"

"None of them welcomed her. They weren't happy when I started to date. What did they expect? Did they want me to end up like them? With no one? Cavelle was indifferent. She bothered me the most. She couldn't give Lucy the time of day."

"Did Lucy tell you she was more uncomfortable around Cavelle or around Hester?"

"Damn it, Stella. Lucy was kind to Hester. She understood Hester—

the same as you. She didn't care that Hester's different." He rubs both hands through his hair now. In a much quieter voice, he adds, "Lucy was uncomfortable around Cavelle. She said Cavelle made her feel inadequate, whatever the hell that means."

"One final question, Jacob, and I'm sorry if I've upset you. I told Opal yesterday that Detective North and I want to resolve the question of Lucy's murder for her sake, and yours, of course. Now, who was most distressed you and Lucy were building a house—Cavelle or Opal?"

Jacob moves forward slightly. "That's easy, Stella. Opal was crazy mad when we began house construction. She worked herself into a real fit one night and said she expected her children—imagine, she called us her children—to live under the same roof." He leans back, breathless. "Opal has sacrificed the most for our family. Mom died when I was born and Dad when I was eight." His tone becomes more forceful. "She was a mother to me, but she's not my mother."

Stella is reminded of Cavelle's admiration for her older sister and how she acknowledged Opal devoted her life to her siblings.

"We want to make arrangements to visit with the whole family on Monday. Can you ensure the four of you are available right after lunch on Monday, February 16?"

"I will take care of it, Detective."

After Jacob's departure, Stella and Aiden linger for a few minutes to discuss the interview. Their consensus is Jacob has come to terms with the idea that one or a combination of his sisters had a hand in the murder of his wife. There is no doubt he attempted to cast suspicion in the direction of Cavelle to protect Hester, in much the same way Opal has tried on numerous occasions to shield their youngest sister.

As the weather begins to close in and the predicted snowstorm ramps up in earnest, Stella starts what is most often a short excursion back home to the park.

Chapter 18

I Forced Him to Compare

Darkness is abrupt. Heavy flakes crowd out the illumination from her headlights. She crouches over the wheel in a futile attempt to improve her visibility. The centre line is obscured by snow. Tire tracks from her Jeep recede in her rear-view mirror as she creeps toward home. *What if something happens to me and I've never told him?* The normally short trip becomes interminable. When she makes the turn onto the road leading into the park and to the house, she's thankful Nick was out with the truck and spread a thin layer of sand on the driveway in anticipation of her approach. There's no place she'd rather be at this moment.

She skirts a blue dumpster sitting in the parking lot. It resembles an abandoned shipping container. She leaves the Jeep near the veranda and plods up the stairs to find a stack of lumber covered in a brown tarp. The building materials could be a pile of bodies. She shudders. Too much time discussing murder. "I'm back! Thanks for the sand. I managed to stay between the ditches."

Nick rounds the corner, a tea towel in one hand and a generous glass of white wine in the other. "Boy, I'm glad you're here. The radio says tonight's storm will get way worse before the weather gets better."

Nodding, she tosses her coat on the arm of the chair closest to her while she reaches for the drink. "What smells so good? I'm starved. The trip home was exhausting."

"Chicken stew. We need a warm supper in case we lose the power and are forced to live on peanut butter and egg salad for a few days. We're supposed to get fifty centimeters, Stella. Fifty! I filled up water jugs and cooked a half-dozen eggs."

With her arm firmly around his waist, they walk toward the kitchen. "Who would take care of me if not for you? Thanks, Nick." Inclement weather is of no concern if Nick is here with her. "I gather you accepted deliveries while I was gone." Her tone teases and his response is boyish at best.

"The municipality dropped off the dumpster and the lumberyard delivered the supplies. I won't start any demolition until after the storm, but I have the work planned." He vibrates with enthusiasm. "I'll put cardboard over the floors. Sawdust shouldn't be a problem."

Stella sits at the kitchen table and savours a sip of her wine. "Don't worry. I'm in, Nick. Do what you need to do. There'll be no complaints from me." She doesn't want to sound tired, but she's done in. "Shall we make up the great room alcove into a bedroom before the day's over?"

"Sure. We can move downstairs as soon as the weather clears, and I get started. Now...." He turns on his heel and runs around the corner to the small pantry which houses the freezer. He returns with two plastic bags. "Buns or biscuits?"

After supper, they curl up together on the sofa by the fire. Gale force winds rattle the glass. The wooden screen door vibrates as gusts whistle through the porch eaves. Stella gets up long enough to make tea and peer out the living room window which faces the parking lot. The yard light reveals the truth of the storm's severity. Snow swirls and dances in the glow as if the particles will never reach the ground. Drifts pile up against the stairs. She expects tons to shovel in the morning.

Turning toward Nick, she studies his chiseled jaw and unruly brown hair, the sweatshirt with the Mount Allison University logo, and the corduroys with the hole in the knee. His handsome face is flushed because of his proximity to the fire. The lights flicker but remain on. Her heart beats faster in anticipation of the words she wants to say.

"How did the interview go with Jacob this afternoon? You never said." He pauses and then raises his hand in stop-sign fashion. "Never mind, Stella. If you can't discuss what went on, I understand."

"Not at all, Nick, although Jacob might have learned more than we did. I asked him questions where he was forced to choose between his sisters."

His expression is puzzled. "Can you explain?"

"Well, for example: 'Who was more upset when you and Lucy decided to build a house—Cavelle or Opal?' He needed to examine their individual attitudes and behaviour to answer. If I asked who was most distressed, he could have said no one. I forced him to compare his sisters—to choose."

"Did you and Aiden figure out which sister actually killed Lucy?"

"Not yet, but we've given Jacob food for thought so he'll be more inclined to cooperate. Today, he shed a light on Cavelle as his way to take the heat off Hester. Jacob knows more, although he doesn't fully comprehend the various interactions."

Nick moves closer to her on the couch. "Of course. Your analysis makes perfect sense to you and Aiden, I'm sure. I think Jacob knows the truth, but he won't incriminate anybody directly, except Sylvester."

She meets his gaze, ignoring his last response. Her brain will soon explode if she remains silent. She begins to sweat and hopes her flush can be excused by the fire. "Nick." Her voice is gravelly.

As if he understands her desperate struggle to share her thoughts, he leans across the space between them and kisses her cheek.

"You are my love. You understand, right?"

He kisses her again, on the lips this time. She can't tell if the wind is roaring outside or if the noise is the rush inside her ears. "You are my love, too, Stella." He gives her upper arm a tiny shove. "Was it the biscuits? I bet it was the biscuits."

She smacks him on the shoulder. "Emotion talks are hard for me, Nick Cochran. Give a girl a break. I was *not* influenced by the biscuits." She graces him with a wink before she settles in against his body. "Maybe the stew, though."

****

Most of Thursday is spent in cleanup after the storm. Nick begins to shovel the veranda and stairs. He will use their truck and plow for the parking lot and the road through the park. Although their liability insurance does not necessitate the effort, the roads to the seasonal trailers will receive attention as well in case of fire. Services are disconnected for the winter, but one can never be too careful. Stella tackles the walk which leads to the office door. She doesn't expect guests, of course, but they always try to keep both exits open after such weather systems barrel through. Drifts are high and cumbersome, but the snow is light. She grits her teeth when the wind blows her efforts back into her face. Icy crystals creep inside her parka.

As she leans her shovel against the old shingles by the veranda door and takes a break to make coffee, she hears the phone bleat. "Shale Cliffs RV Park. Stella Kirk here."

"Hi. Are you cleaned up after the storm?"

"We're trying, Aiden." She's still breathless from her trot across the living room to the office. "What's up?"

"You don't have triskaidekaphobia, do you?"

"What? Friday the thirteenth? No. Oh, tomorrow is Friday the thirteenth." She snickers into the receiver. "Why? Do you?"

"No, but I wanted to check. Will you come with me to see Maeve Cavannah, Ardith Holland, and our friend Cat Sylvester one more time?"

"Of course, but to what end?" Realizing her error, she adds, "Sorry, Aiden. You're the detective. I shouldn't have questioned your methods."

"I'm not offended, Stella. We're convinced one or a combination of the sisters was involved in Lucy's death. The next step in the process is to eliminate any previously potential suspects or witnesses with whom we've had discussions. Are you in? I know I shouldn't keep asking for your help, but I appreciate your insights."

"Where and when?"

"We are to meet Maeve Cavannah at Cocoa and Café near ten-thirty tomorrow morning. We'll catch her between home visits, she told me. We'll go to Ardith Holland's office at lunchtime and visit William in the afternoon."

"Will he be sober?"

"I hope so. He said his mother is content at Harbour Manor, but he has no money. He plans to sell the house. He sounds worked up."

"Maybe he regrets his behaviour. It was necessary to place Miriam Sylvester because of his negligence. I imagine she's better for the decision, though. I'll be interested to hear what he has to say later today. Coffee shop at ten?"

"Perfect. See you tomorrow."

The next morning, Stella and Nick are up and on the go before seven o'clock. With the yard cleared and blue skies for a few days, Nick intends to start demolition of the upstairs while she's in Shale Harbour. Tomorrow, Duke, and no doubt Kiki, will pop over in the morning to help Nick move the appliances to the cottage. Duke has a friend with a cabin and the old appliances from the manager's cottage will be picked up by him. At least they won't be thrown in a dumpster.

Aiden is nursing a cup of coffee. His expression is forlorn when Stella breezes into Cocoa and Café to meet him. The waitress arrives with a mug of hazelnut-flavoured brew. Stella nods her thanks.

"You appear to be a man with a troubled mind, Aiden." She has a hunch and follows through. "How is Rosemary? Not home, yet, I assume. You haven't said."

His smile is watery. "I plan to take her to dinner tomorrow night for Valentine's Day. She specifically requested the Purple Tulip. Although we interviewed them in terms of the investigation, I figured we could eat wherever she wants."

"Sounds wonderful. The place is very posh. What's the problem?"

"She's not good." His words are blunt, with no emphasis on the positive. "I asked Toni and Mary Jo to come along, but both her sisters are reluctant. They said February 14 is for lovers and we need to go out together alone. I'm worried she'll make a scene."

Stella silently argues with herself. She wonders if she and Nick should cancel their much-anticipated dinner at the hotel to join the Norths in Port Ephron. Despite Aiden's indication he might appreciate company, she remains quiet.

Maeve Cavannah falls in the door. She has tripped on the threshold because of her unsecured boots and fights to keep her balance as she flails toward them. "I need a big cup of coffee and the sooner the better," she exclaims across the open space to the waitress working behind the counter. She throws her coat over an empty chair at a nearby table, drops her bag with a thud, and collapses in a gust of air which has the vague scent of antiseptic. She reaches for her coffee before the young woman has an opportunity to set the mug in front of her, gulps a mouthful, and blurts, "I'm pleased you called, because I was thinking I needed to call you."

Aiden remains nonreactive while Stella struggles to maintain her composure.

"What did you want to speak with me about, Maeve?" Aiden's tone is professional. No element of curiosity has crept into his voice.

"Have you spoken to Jacob Painter lately?" Her voice projects an element of challenge.

"We have contact with Jacob as a result of our investigation."

"Well, he showed up at my house last Wednesday, later in the day; after work. He expected me to provide a report on Lucy's opinions of Hester." She leans over. Stella smells the coffee on her breath. "He *demanded* to hear if Lucy ever felt threatened by Hester." With her cup held tightly in both hands, she sits back in her chair. "I'm not afraid to tell you I was uncomfortable. I cope with crazy issues in my work, but the husband of a dead friend, wild because of information he assumes I possess, has never come up before."

"You were convinced, when we talked earlier in the investigation, that Jacob might have hurt Lucy. Have you changed your mind?" Aiden ignores any emotion or hyperbole originating from Maeve.

"I'm sure he's decided Hester is the killer, but I told him Lucy loved and trusted Hester. To answer your question, he didn't kill her, although you need to watch him in case he decides to take the law into his own hands."

****

When Aiden and Stella arrive at Ardith Holland's office, she's seated behind her sprawling desk with a sandwich wrapped in wax paper and a cup of tea in a chipped white mug. She glances up, wipes her smeared lipstick with a napkin, and motions for them to enter. "Glad you're here. Have a seat." She waves her hand in the general direction of the chairs placed in front of her workspace.

"Thanks for your time, Ardith. The purpose of our visit is to tie up any loose ends at this stage of the investigation." Aiden, as with Maeve, presents himself as benign.

Ardith chomps as she talks. Her corseted figure is poised to burst through the seams of her navy pantsuit. "You have one loose end who needs to be tied up and his name is Jacob Painter."

"How so, Ardith?" Stella suspects she knows the answer.

"He showed up here at my office—when staff were still in the coffee room—and accused me. He said Lucy was pregnant and I didn't tell him."

"What was your reply?" Aiden asks the specific question whereas Stella wants to hear every word of the complete conversation.

"I told him I suspected, although Lucy did not discuss her status. I went on to say I was sure Lucy had no clue, and furthermore, if she had confided in me, her secret was secure. He was very angry."

"You didn't call the police, Ardith."

"No, Detective, I did not. My behaviour was likely unwise, but I see him as distraught and bereft, as are many spouses who have suffered a loss." Her voice sounds supervisory—dictated by her role. "He blew off steam, heard the truth from me, and left. I assumed the police would get wind of Jacob's independent investigation sooner or later."

"Independent investigation?"

"He talked to Maeve, too. I assume he's prowled around and accosted everyone involved with Lucy in some way or another."

"Did he give you any indication he suspects one of his sisters, Ardith?" Stella worries Jacob will decide who is culpable and take matters into his own hands.

"His only comment related to his family was that Hester might know details but is oblivious. I wasn't sure exactly what he meant. I told him to leave the sleuthing to you."

****

Stella climbs into Aiden's police-issue sedan to go over to the Sylvester house. She leaves her car parked up the street from At-Home Care Services, to be picked up later.

"I guess a serious conversation with Jacob Painter is in my future. He wants to do my job for me."

"My either/or questions probably precipitated his visits to the people in Lucy's life. He ran around after our interview. I wonder if he landed on William's doorstep as well?"

"We'll soon find out. We don't suspect William anymore, but I want to follow up, regardless. He may have information he doesn't realize is relevant. Here we are." He parks in front of the shabby home. The pathway to the door has not been shoveled. The car, hidden under snow in the driveway, is an abominable lump. The property shows no sign of life.

Despite the abandoned facade, William opens the door before they have a chance to knock. His crow-like features and stringy black hair have not improved since their last encounter although he appears to be sober.

"Come on in. I expected you earlier. I made coffee."

"Great, Cat. Don't mind if I do. Black for me. Stella?" Aiden peels off his topcoat and graces Stella with a wide-eyed expression William is unable to see.

"Not for me, thanks. I never drink coffee in the afternoon. I'm good." They stamp and then remove boots before muddling into the living room. Stella first notices the adjoining space now resembles a dining room. The furniture is rearranged and the hospital bed in the corner is gone. "I see you've removed the hospital bed. Will your mother stay on at Harbour Manor, William?" Stella has been given to understand Miriam Sylvester is now a permanent resident at the nursing home, but she's curious how William will present the decision.

"Mom wants to live there." He twitches on the chair, as if the upholstery itches his bottom. "I told her she could come back, but they take good care of her."

"How are finances, Cat? I imagine most of your mother's money goes to the manor."

The question suggests Aiden doesn't want William involved in any unconventional means of earning a living.

"Oh, I can tell you good news in the job department. Glenn Smithers' dad offered me work at the car dealership in Port Ephron—clearing snow and dirt off cars, or parking for owners. It's a shit job, but Glenn says it's better than a kick in the arse. Besides, once I sell the house, I'll have money for an emergency."

"You still plan to let go of the house, regardless of the new job?"

Aiden's voice sounds surprised to Stella. William was probably living on his mother's savings, but now her pension cheques will help pay for her care.

"Yeah. I've been to talk with Cavelle at Grey Cottage Realtors. Cavelle Painter is why I'm glad you came by today."

"Go on."

"Jacob stopped me on the street, the day of the big storm, and asked me why I was talkin' to his sister. He said he saw me comin' out of her office; got all huffy sayin' Cavelle and me had somethin' to do with Lucy's death." William starts to wiggle in the chair again as his anxiety level rises. "I tried to explain I'm gonna' sell my house and I need a realtor."

"Did Jacob accept your explanation?"

"I doubt it. He said he was watchin' me because he's suspected me of hurtin' Lucy from the start. I told him I could never hurt her. Alls I want to do is dump this place and move to Port Ephron."

On the drive back to deliver Stella to her car, Aiden shares his thoughts.

"Our Mr. Painter has crossed the line into serious meddling. I'll talk to him before the day is over and we can confirm our family meeting. Are you still good with Monday?"

"No problem, Aiden. I hope your evening goes well with Rosemary tomorrow." As she returns to the Jeep, she's happy they won't have any interviews the next day. She has been invited to lunch with Paulina McAdams at Yellow House.

Chapter 19

Where Did You Get the Samples?

"Happy Valentine's Day, lovers."

Stella rounds the corner from the kitchen as Duke and Kiki struggle through the veranda doors and onto the inside mat.

"Where's our contractor? Ready to move the appliances?"

Duke is unique but trustworthy. The park provides him a free lot with a view in exchange for his security duties.

"Hi, Duke. Is Kiki along for the ride?" Kiki remains tucked under Duke's arm. Despite a white quilted winter coat matching Duke's, her pink sequined collar twinkles.

"She loves to go in any vehicle." Nick rounds the corner. "There you are, Nick."

"Good morning, Duke. Is your cousin out in the truck?"

"Yeah, Merle's here and ready to go." He drops his John Wayne persona long enough to add, "I appreciate you givin' the stuff to him. He needs any help he can get."

"No problem. The cottage appliances still work. They might as well be put to some use. Tell Merle to come in. We can load the fridge and stove from upstairs and move them to the deck at the cottage. We can get his appliances on the truck and then lug the newer ones in. Shouldn't take long."

"Kiki, do you want to have a visit with Auntie Stella while we work?"

"Can't help, Duke. Off to town. I have a lunch date." Kiki spends hours in the house with Alice in the summer, and she and Nick dog-sit on occasion, but Stella is reluctant to leave Kiki to her own devices. "It'll be truck guarding today, I'm afraid. At least the temperature isn't freezing."

Duke nods as he turns toward the door on his way to returning his

Pomeranian to Merle's truck and telling his cousin to come in.

Stella grabs her coat and hurries out to the Jeep, happy to be away from the house for a while. Lunch with Paulina will be a welcome break from the chaos of Duke, Kiki, and appliances on the move.

Paulina McAdams opens her front door with a flourish. Her attire, unlike her usual slacks and sweater sets, is a red plaid flannel dress. The design is high-waisted and resembles a nightie in which one might curl up beside the fire.

"Paulina. Thanks for the luncheon invitation. I'm happy to escape the house since I've renovations starting today."

"Come in. Come in. I can't make up my mind if the weather is cold, or damp, or both." She touches the side of her dress. "Hence the cozy attire." Her eyes drift to the bag in Stella's hand. "Are those the books I loaned you?"

"They were an immense help. They're also part of the reason I wanted to have a visit with you today. Aiden's narrowed the scope of the investigation, but we want to hear more history from you."

"No problem. I'm happy to provide a little assistance." She swishes through the library and miniature bookstore on her way toward her kitchen and sitting room in the back of her home. Stella follows. "I hope you're fond of tomato bisque. I made bread to accompany the soup and I have apple tarts for dessert."

"Sounds wonderful. It wasn't necessary to go to any bother, you know."

She turns from the stove. "I don't receive guests in the winter, whereas my house is busy most of the summer, like yours. I think I mentioned my 'interest' but our 'affaire du coeur' is very hush-hush. To have company for luncheon is a pleasant distraction."

The table is set. Stella helps her with the soup plates and the bread. She waits with contrived patience until they're seated. She's finally able to pose the question related to the most troubling facet of the investigation for her.

"Paulina. Did Leon ever discuss Velma's death?"

"You never cease to amaze me. Such an odd inquiry!" She nibbles on the crusty edge of her slice of bread. Her eyes indicate more curiosity than surprise.

"I can't share my reasons, but you've been terribly helpful with my research of local poisonous plants. I hope you can enlighten me on this topic as well."

Sitting up straighter in her chair, she begins. "I will try, but only because I'm fond of you. Unlike your plant research, these questions are quite personal. Leon, as you can imagine, discussed Velma very little when he was with me." Her expression is wistful. "I was young. He wanted to get married, but Opal resisted the idea of another woman in the house. I was happy to have him stay with me a few nights a week." She views Stella over her wire-framed glasses. "Such an arrangement suited me. He always felt he needed to go home because circumstances became difficult if he left the farm unattended."

"Lunch is great." Stella pauses to finish the last of her soup and mask her disappointment. "He never discussed his wife's death?"

"Oh yes. He told me what happened. I don't suppose anybody cares who knows how she died now."

Stella mumbles, "Whatever you're comfortable sharing." She wants to encourage but not appear anxious.

"Velma birthed Jacob." She shivers. "The delivery was difficult, but the doctor expected improvement within a week or two with lots of support. After she was up and around, she would be fine."

"What happened? I understand she died in childbirth. Del said she hemorrhaged."

Paulina begins to clear the table. "Del Trembly's recollection of events is not entirely accurate. Her death was because of complications from childbirth but occurred three days later. Opal found her upstairs in her blood-soaked bed. Velma was already cold. Opal cleaned up the mess before she called for help from Leon or the doctor. When Leon saw Velma, she was dressed in a clean nightie, with the covers pulled tight to her chin, and an expression of complete peace on her face."

"Do you recall if he discussed events afterward?"

"Oh yes. The physician arrived, and Opal reported what she assumed happened. Jacob's crib was moved into Opal's room, and, for the record," her eyes peer over the top of her glasses once more, "Leon's recovery after Velma's death took almost a year. He told me he couldn't recall how Opal coped. At the ripe old age of sixteen, she never went back to school and took over operation of the Painter farm until Leon managed to pull himself together." She serves apple tarts the size of saucers. "I didn't meet Leon until much later."

"Is there any possible reason Velma's death might have been suspicious?"

"How could I ever question how Velma Painter died, Stella? I understand the nature of the investigation into Lucy's unfortunate demise, but Velma? What? Leon most certainly did not kill his wife." She leans back in her chair, huffs, and dabs at the corners of her mouth with her paper serviette. "Preposterous, Stella. Preposterous!"

Stella munches on her tart. "Your pie crust is perfection, Paulina."

Paulina's lips are an annoyed line as she forces a nod and acknowledgment of the compliment. "Listen, Stella. I was young when I was involved with Leon. Our affair took place over twenty years ago. If I were given that time to live over again, I would not permit an entanglement with a man twice my age, with three daughters and a baby boy. Are the daughters a little strange? Why yes, but I find it difficult to imagine any one of them hurt their sister-in-law. And as for their parents, you are so far out in left field, my dear, you aren't even in the ballpark anymore. Tea?"

"Thanks, tea sounds great." Stella decides not to pursue her theory with Paulina although now she is sure she knows who killed Lucy. The family meeting on Monday may help sort out ways and means.

****

A satisfied expression remains planted with firm insistence on her face. Stella is curled up on the couch in front of the fire early on the Sunday morning, the day after Valentine's Day. They feasted on a fabulous meal at the Harbour Hotel last night. No doubt the occasion is their biggest draw in the winter, but Nick secured them a quiet table in the back room where only one other couple vied for the attention of the server. The hotel prepared a shared pork tenderloin dinner where the complete meal was served on a platter and they could help themselves or eat together off the serving dish. Leonard Cohen tunes on the tape deck, and their hushed conversation competed with a wind that howled at the crevices of the old three-storey structure. The windows rattled. Their evening was romantic and perfect.

She snuggles further into the cushions and blushes as she sips her coffee. The sudden realization of their relationship's transformation startles her. They are more than lovers and more than in love. She and Nick love one another. They have the same goals and agree on how to reach them. She has come to appreciate her life in the RV park because of his presence. They are a team. Contentment and hope for the future wash over her.

The pocket doors which separate the alcove from the main living room rumble as Nick slides them back. He stands in the partial opening in boxer shorts and a T-shirt with mustard stains on the front. His hair is tousled. His knees are bony.

Unbridled guffaws fly out of her mouth when she sees him. "You're damned lucky somebody loves you, mister, because the way you appear right now will most certainly not win the ladies over."

He surveys his attire and leers at her. "Maybe I need pants?"

In search of more coffee, she ambles toward the kitchen. She suspects he'll cook her breakfast. She peers out the window and assesses the weather. A walk around the park might be in order because Monday will be a long day.

Aiden calls at ten past ten. "I've confirmed our meeting with the Painter family, along with the Smithers, tomorrow after lunch, Stella. I want to reveal the mushroom information and see what happens."

Before she shares her hunch with Aiden, she asks, "How did your evening with Rosemary go at the Purple Tulip?"

The silence before his response speaks volumes. "I felt forced to take her right back to the hospital. The whole experience was a challenge."

"What happened?"

"Do you remember Marni Webb, the owner? We spoke with her when we suspected mushrooms?"

"Of course. She was very cooperative."

"Well, she paid personal attention to us, I assume as a favour, and Rosemary became completely unglued. Within seconds she decided Marni and I were involved in an affair. She screamed and cursed." He stops for a moment to catch his breath. "She threw dishes, Stella. I whisked her out of the restaurant as fast as I could. I told Marni to expect me in today to settle up the bill which is sure to include significant damages."

"Have you spoken to her sisters?"

"Not yet. If the hospital doesn't get her medication regulated soon, I don't know what I'll do." He coughs and changes the subject. "Back to the task at hand. When we go to the Painter farm tomorrow, I want you to focus on Hester. Perhaps we can encourage her to describe what she's done."

Stella understands Aiden prefers not to discuss his wife further. Instead she responds to his request. "Of course. This get-together may prove invaluable. Besides, Aiden. I'm sure I know who killed Lucy. If my suspicion is correct, it wasn't their first murder."

****

The Smithers are at the farm when Aiden and Stella roll in. A Buick demonstrator, parked in front of the walk which leads up to the closed-in veranda, is their clue. Jacob answers the door.

"Glad you made it. The air is tense in the living room. Here, let me take your coats."

"I try to arrive right on the dot." Aiden is nonplussed by overt anxiety.

Stella pats Jacob on the shoulder and thanks him as he places her coat across his arm. "Don't worry." She says the words but fully appreciates how life at the Painter farm will change forever if her hunch proves to be correct.

They make their way to the front parlour which shares one side of the house with the dining room. Hester is once again wedged into the bow window seat.

Cavelle is perched on a low rose-coloured slipper chair. She has a binder and papers spread out on the floor space near her feet. "Didn't want to waste a complete Monday, so I brought work home. Hope you don't mind."

Aiden tilts his head. "Of course not."

Opal, on the couch beside Bitsy, nods to them both.

"How have you been, Bitsy?"

A crumpled piece of tissue and a muffled blubber answer Stella's question. "I made lemon squares," she mumbles from behind her hand.

Jacob has dragged several dining room chairs into the space. Glenn and his father, Reid, have each chosen one. Jacob places two for Stella and Aiden to enable them to face the group. He then sits on the floor at Opal's feet.

"Could Hester join us, please?" Aiden directs his question toward Jacob. Opal starts to shake her head.

"I'll go get her, Detective." Stella jumps up and works her way past the furniture into the dining room.

"Hester, will you sit with everyone? You have been a big help to the investigation and we very much appreciate your presence."

"You think I killed Lucy." Stella leans in to hear her whisper. "I don't want to talk."

"You're wrong, Hester. Come with me. No one will accuse you in Lucy's death. She was your friend. I understand. Trust me."

Hester unfolds her lean frame from the confines of the window seat and follows a vaguely surprised Stella. When she stops to grab another chair, Hester pulls on her sleeve. "I'll sit on the floor by you," she whispers.

Once the group is settled, Aiden begins. "An exhaustive investigation into the sudden death of Lucy Painter has been conducted." He pauses. "Everyone has been interviewed over the last few days. I am here now to tell you Lucy was killed because she ingested a poisonous mushroom known as destroying angel. We believe she was given the poison, and her fall was the result of her precarious condition. The poison would have caused her death within a few days if the fall had not occurred." He waits a moment for the gasps and exclamations of disbelief to dissipate. "I will not give you details." He turns to Hester and smiles. "Thanks to Hester and others in the community, we know every mushroom Lucy ate in the two weeks which led up to her death. In addition, we are certain the poisonous mushrooms were consumed in this household."

His tone has become more forthright and formal. "I may have to execute a search warrant of the property if the family chooses not to cooperate. Opal, are you willing to volunteer samples of your dried mushrooms for us to test? We have a theory."

"Your theory is my sister poisoned Lucy's food, Detective?"

Stella notices how Jacob has started to lean against Opal's leg as if she requires protection. Maybe he wonders if Opal is a murderer.

"A possible explanation is that a few examples of the destroying angel variety became mixed up in a batch as the family harvested and dried wild mushrooms. Her death would be classified as a case of accidental poisoning. As a result, I hope to take samples of dried mushrooms back to our lab for analysis."

Jacob turns to examine his sister's face. "Do you have any left, Opal? There could have been a mistake; an accident."

Opal focuses on the painting of a shipwreck which hangs on the opposite wall. "A poisoning accident—a mushroom mix-up—is unforgivable, Jacob." She huffs while she readjusts her skirt. "Besides, we have no mushrooms left. We've eaten our harvest and each of us is fine." She focuses her bright blue eyes, which snap with black hatred, toward Aiden. "Your fancy police lab is outta luck."

Reid Smithers interjects. "Detective, are you sayin' my Lucy was fed poison mushrooms by people and bad mushrooms is how she died? Are you sayin' she was murdered by one of the Painters?" Bitsy's blubbers are as loud as Reid's voice.

"Mr. Smithers. We know Lucy was poisoned by destroying angel mushrooms and any mushrooms she ate, to the best of our knowledge, came from within the confines of this house. We also know the fall killed her and expect the reason for her fall was her reaction to those mushrooms. Whether by accident or on purpose, she was killed because of mushrooms she ate here."

Hester has remained quiet at Stella's feet until now. Without a word, she stands, leaves the room, and Stella can hear her footfalls on each tread as she makes her way upstairs. The group is silenced by her departure. Hester returns as Stella asks Aiden if she should follow and retrieve her. Hester walks over to Aiden and presents him with two plastic envelopes. One is marked "Dried Wild Mushrooms." The other is labeled "Destroying Angel Mushrooms. Do not eat."

"Thank you, Hester. Where did you get the samples?"

"They are not samples. They are from our supplies in the basement. I hid them after I visited Stella's and we discussed fungi. I assumed examples might be important in the future." Her expression is sweet and innocent as if she doesn't understand the consequences of her behaviour.

Cavelle, Opal, and Jacob remain dumbfounded. Bitsy bawls. Reid stands and gestures to his son. They are leaving, and no explanation is required.

CHAPTER 20

Are You Done, Yet?

Kiki's ears flatten when another resounding crash from upstairs rattles the house. The morning has dragged.

Duke arrived while it was still dark, dressed for work in blue jeans, a plaid shirt, and a suede tool apron designed for a man with significantly more height than her security guard. A shiny new hammer, hung from a metal hook at his hip, dangled below his knee. Stella imagined Duke would have a huge bruise by day's end because it would bounce against the bone.

She must have given Nick a quizzical look because he whispered in her ear, "He volunteered. I couldn't say no."

Duke placed Kiki on the floor and told her she must promise to behave herself.

"What? Duke, I never committed to watching your dog."

She was then confronted with the Duke version of a pout. "Aw, Stella, she's a good little girl; no trouble. Here, I brought her water dish." He hauled a silver bowl out of his back pocket. She relented.

The day before, she covered the furniture with sheets. Nick taped cardboard on the hardwood floors. The threadbare rug was rolled up.

Duke and Nick rip the old plaster off the walls and lug pails of scraps through the living room, past the kitchen entrance, and out to the dumpster in the parking lot.

The noise is merciless. Kiki is no happier than she is. Braving the dust, she opens her office door and makes her way to the kitchen to scare up lunch for the three of them. She hopes Duke has a morsel for the dog. Kiki's nails click a steady rhythm as she trots, sporting her pale cream fisherman's knit sweater created by a lady friend of Duke's, toward the kitchen.

Stella pulls egg salad, along with carrot and celery sticks, all prepared earlier to save time, from the fridge. She assembles sandwiches on store-bought whole wheat bread. She arranges the vegetables on a plate with a bowl of cream cheese dip. She boils the kettle for a pot of tea and retrieves a plastic container of chocolate chip cookies from the freezer. She pours three glasses of ice water before opening the door which leads upstairs, and shouts, "Lunch is ready, you two. Take a break."

"On the way." Her yell proves unnecessary. Nick is at the top of the stairs.

Both men thunder down the narrow staircase. Duke retrieves his jacket where he's stashed a small bag of kibble for Kiki. Without a courteous pause to ask permission, he strolls over to a cupboard, finds a candy dish, and prepares a snack for his dog. He glances up. "You don't mind, do you?"

"No problem, but you might as well provide me with both food and water dishes when you're here for the day."

Nonplussed by the suggestion, he sits with a thud and digs into his sandwich. "Okay. Food's great." His mouth is full.

"Want a report? We're makin' progress." Nick grins, but his eyes say sorry—she assumes for Duke's presence—but his apologetic expression could also be because of the noise and disruption.

"A report sounds great. Are you done, yet?"

Duke's open mouth sprays egg salad across her table when he jumps in with, "Are you serious? We could be weeks, right Nick?" He leans down, picks up the hopping fluff which is Kiki, and feeds her tiny bits of sandwich.

"Not weeks, in the sense of *many* weeks, but perhaps a few weeks."

Stella knows the frown on her face reveals her thoughts.

"Let me give you the facts." Nick glances over at Duke. "The demo is officially completed. We'll finish framing the new bathroom before today is over. Tonight, you and I can mark out placement for electrical plugs, plus vanity and ceiling lights. We'll draw lines where the plumbing fixtures are to be set. I want you to see actual positioning in the space, not just drawings on a blueprint."

"Okay. What's next?"

"The plumbers and electricians are here tomorrow to do rough-ins. While they're here, we can drive to town and choose lights and tiles. We'll pick up a new toilet, sink, and faucets. Are you up for a shopping trip?"

She understands Nick hopes the act of choosing finishing products will distract her from the mess. She decides cooperation trumps agitation and reaches for a cookie. "Fun times. Did you line up the guy to refinish the pine floors?" The old soft woods are a prized possession. They could have replaced them with new, but she didn't have the heart.

"Oh, yeah. After the guys complete the rough-in, Duke and I will install the drywall and tape. Then the floors can be sanded. We can handle the paint if you pick the colour. Once the tilers build the shower, the plumbers and electricians come back to finish, and the glass door gets hung last. See? Not long." His eyes remain transfixed on the three chocolate chip cookies he's placed on his plate.

"Is your shopping suggestion an attempt to pacify me?"

"Well, maybe. Anyway," he sits up straighter in his chair, "we'll have a good time."

"I've never seen two people get along the way you lovebirds do. When are ya gonna tie the knot; make it legal?"

Catching Nick's eye for a moment, she takes a breath. "Nick and I are happy, Duke. A piece of paper doesn't help a relationship work any better. How many times have you been married, since you brought the subject up?"

"Gotta take the dog out before we go upstairs. Good lunch, Stella."

She smirks at his back as he exits the kitchen with Kiki wedged under his arm. "There's chili for supper. You're welcome to stay," she sings out toward the closing door. She turns to Nick and without a sound she raises her eyebrows and three fingers.

He makes a half-hearted attempt to muffle a snicker.

****

Imaginary check marks fill the air. "We have a vanity light, a ceiling light with an exhaust fan to be installed near the shower, a ceiling fan with a light included for the bedroom, and a new outside light for the balcony. Are we finished, Nick? I have bedside lamps and a table lamp already for the sitting area."

His expression is indulgent. "Choose new lamps, if you prefer. I told you the project is my gift. Whatever you want."

Nick's generosity creates unsettled, kept, beholden feelings—unaccustomed emotions. "The lamps we use now will be fine." She's overwhelmed by the prices. Her previous renovation experiences consisted of painting and repairs.

"Okay, if you're pleased with our choices here, we can drive back to the lumberyard to make decisions on the vanity basin, a toilet, taps, and the countertop. Then off we go to Port Ephron Flooring to choose tile for the bathroom walls and the shower. How are we for time?"

Stella pulls on her coat sleeve to get a peek at her watch. "We're good. Visitation at the hospital doesn't start until eleven. We have another hour. The lighting boxes are big, but they should fit in the back of the Jeep." She catches the attention of the clerk. "I guess we've made our choices. We'll take them with us today."

Over at the lumberyard, they decide between a limited number of vanities and toilets. The process is surprisingly quick. The taps are plain. Stella is satisfied. A Formica countertop is another matter. There must be over a hundred colours. "Pick a colour. There will be lots of tile options in Port Ephron."

"I'll need a sample to take with me."

"Oh, they give out samples. Is there one you prefer?" He sounds supportive and helpful.

She's engulfed by perceived pressure. "Let's have marble-coloured ceramic and keep the bathroom plain, okay? No crazy stuff." She frowns. She'll leave the extravagant and trendy décor to Trixie.

They finalize their order and travel to Port Ephron for tile. They'll visit with Rosemary North at the hospital when they're finished. Stella is on a mission.

Rosemary was not in the patient lounge. The nurse suggested they try her room. When she peers through the doorway of Room 222, Stella's breath catches at the sight of her—not in the chair with a book or with eyes fixated on the television but reclined on a half-dozen pillows in the bed. Her recently dyed and very dark hair is drawn behind her head, rolled in a perfect chignon, and tied with a pink ribbon—an exact match to her crocheted bed jacket. The sheet is pulled tight and smooth. Her hands are clasped in front of her and she's staring straight ahead at the blank wall.

"Hi." Stella keeps her voice soft and accompanies her salutation with a gentle knock. "Nick and I have come for a quick visit."

With the force of a person who has been revived from drowning or awakened from a terrible nightmare, Rosemary arouses from what appears to be a trance. "What? Stella? Why are you here? Is Aiden all right? Where's Toni?" She starts to struggle with the sheets and becomes tangled immediately.

Stella rushes over to the side of the bed and reaches for her hand. "Here, let me help. Aiden is fine. I came today with Nick to visit you; to tell you how we miss you and hope you get well soon." Stella can sense Rosemary start to relax.

Ignoring Stella, she simpers at Nick. She bats her eyes and mews, "Hi, Nick. You came to Port Ephron to visit little ol' me?"

The desire to have a conversation fades before it starts. Rosemary is in no state to understand.

"Stella and I came to see you." Nick makes brief eye contact with Stella and works his way to the side of the bed. He puts his arm, with possessive firmness, around Stella's shoulders.

Rosemary scowls as she assesses his behaviour. "You two are terribly cozy. You and Aiden were classmates in high school. You dated. He loved you." Her statements bubble with accusation.

Rosemary's overt knowledge of her history with Aiden renders Stella silent.

Despite Stella's reluctance to do more than exchange pleasantries, Nick plows ahead. "Stella and Aiden's relationship is in the past, Rosemary. Stella and I are lovers. We love one another and are best friends."

Rosemary's face starts to crumple. Given Nick's direct approach, Stella's afraid she'll go to pieces as well. He has not parsed his words.

"Furthermore, Aiden adores you. Through his eyes, you are wonderful and gorgeous. He loves you more than you imagine."

"Mary Jo and Toni tell me Aiden loves me, but I always worry they're lying."

"Not true, Rosemary. Aiden worships you."

Stella leans over and touches Rosemary's arm. The yarn of the bed jacket is silky soft.

By the time they leave the hospital, noon is upon them.

"She isn't in a good place, Nick. For a minute, I was concerned she wouldn't cope with what you said."

"I realize she has challenges, Stella, but I want to avoid another episode. The past couple of times we socialized with them were brutal. I just tried to reason with her. I hope I didn't make matters worse."

"I'm not sure about Rosemary, but to me, you were great." She sputters to get the words out. Her voice catches in her throat.

****

On the road to the park, they pass the electricians. Nick stops the Jeep long enough to determine they're finished the rough-in and will wait for a call to return and install fixtures. The plumbers are tidying up. One of the two men is out in the parking lot packing tools into a van.

"I'll make tea," Stella states as Nick opens the rear lift to retrieve the boxes of lights. Stella meets the second plumber, a burly man in his forties whom Stella often sees when she's in town, as he tramps toward the door.

"Inspect the job, Miss Kirk. I'm sure we did what you wanted. If something isn't right, call us. If not, we'll come set the toilet and finish up once the tile's hung." He shifts the extension cord used for the work light fastened to the end. He has draped the coils over his shoulder for the trip to the van.

"No problem. You guys made good time." She's impressed. She didn't need to stay and serve coffee or sandwiches. Both contractors assured her they could manage without the customer underfoot.

Voice murmurings tell her Nick is reviewing the tasks completed with the men. He'll be anxious to run upstairs and measure each rough-in and every plug to make sure both trades followed his plans to the letter.

She checks the answering machine. No messages. *Should the lab require more than two or three days to test for Amanita toxins in dried mushrooms?* When the phone finally jangles, she jumps as if she's never heard the sound before. "Shale Cliffs RV Park."

"Can we talk for a moment?"

"Of course, Aiden. We arrived home a few minutes ago. I've put the kettle on. Want to come out for tea?" Describing their visit with Rosemary face to face with Aiden is her preference.

"Can't today, but I wanted to tell you the lab results."

"Okay. Were the mushrooms poisonous?"

"The bag marked 'Destroying Angel Mushrooms: Do not eat' were without doubt correctly described. The lab report says: *Extremely toxic. Eaten in small doses will cause vomiting and diarrhea. Eating destroying angel mushrooms as a side dish could put an adult into liver and kidney failure within a matter of hours."*

"And the other samples?"

"Common species consumed on a regular basis. No problems. I want to interview Hester again. Why did she have samples of poisonous mushrooms in her possession?"

"Is it possible to put off an interview with Hester for a few days, Aiden? I have a hunch and I need to talk with Trixie as well as Del Trembly again. Then, serious one-on-one interviews will be necessary."

"Hester isn't going anywhere, but today is Wednesday, Stella. I can't delay my response to the toxicity report past early next week."

"Aiden, I'm sure I know why Lucy was killed...and if I'm correct, the matter goes much deeper than we first imagined. There are a few pieces of information to organize, but I promise we can hold interviews on Monday, or sooner."

"Tell me what you think, Stella. I don't need you putting yourself at risk again like when you went to visit Ruby Wilson without me."

"Please let me talk to Del and Trixie, okay?"

"Fine, but do not, and I repeat, do not put yourself at risk."

"Del and Trixie are hardly risky." She smiles into the receiver. "Before you go, Aiden, Nick and I went to see Rosemary today."

"I heard."

"Oh. She called you?"

"We visit at lunchtime, if I'm able to get away from work. She was anxious to report how in love you and Nick are."

Silence. His breath is steady. "Nick wanted her to be aware, in no uncertain terms, how we are a couple and she need never be concerned when it comes to you and me."

"So it seems."

"Are you upset we talked to her, Aiden?" She hears the panic in her voice. "We want to be able to get together and be friends without any worry she might be triggered by you and me in the same room. Nick was forceful. He made his point."

"Rosemary told me he was very romantic, and she said you're lucky, in light of the fact you are much older."

There's the barest hint of a tease in his voice. "Listen, mister. You manage Rosemary and I'll keep track of Nick." She giggles. "Age is but a number. Didn't somebody say that once? Seriously, though, we understand Rosemary's condition and how you've struggled to convince her you're not out gallivanting. Nonetheless, Nick and I want to be in your company without precipitating another meltdown."

"Well, we'll see. The truth is not necessarily your friend when you get embroiled in Rosemary's delusions. Call me after your conversations with Trixie and Mrs. Trembly."

Stella remains preoccupied. Her conversation with Aiden rattles her mind while she carries two cups of tea up the stairs to meet Nick. He's mumbling to himself. A receptacle was mistakenly installed a half an inch higher than the designated spot.

Chapter 21

Don't Search Me for Answers

"She was only ten years old when her mother died. If Aiden is correct, and Hester poisoned Lucy with destroying angel mushrooms—and my instincts indicate the evidence points to the poisoning of Velma and Leon Painter as well—then the conclusion must be multiple murderers are involved. Another family member, or two, has taken advantage of Hester's knowledge and skill."

Nick places cups of blackcurrant tea on the coffee table, then sits beside Stella on the sofa. They snuggle into their post-supper spots in front of the fire, interested in the company of one another. Television, radio, and personal pursuits are secondary.

"Hester's a terrifyingly smart person, but poisoning her mother?"

"At ten," Stella blows on her tea, then tastes the tartness on her tongue, "was she experimenting with poisons? Opal has always claimed Velma hemorrhaged after childbirth. Paulina said it was three days later and no one attended Velma until the room was cleaned. If Hester poisoned Mrs. Painter, did Opal cover for her younger sister to protect her from potential discovery? Did she again shield her when their father died, and now once more with Lucy's death?"

"Don't search me for answers. The whole concept is troubling. The Painter sisters are in cahoots and killed their parents, followed by their sister-in-law? Why, for God's sake, Stella?"

Stella's voice is soft. She holds her mug with both hands and stares at the contents. "If I'm correct, they wanted baby Jacob. Later, their goal was to prevent Jacob from being sent to school or avoid Hester's institutionalization. Since Leon sent Jacob to public school, my money is on the latter." She refocuses her attention on Nick. "Lucy was targeted because she took Jacob away from them."

"To a house in the dooryard? Come on, Stella. Nobody gets killed because they married your brother and moved next door. What a crazy idea."

Her theory sounds preposterous when phrased Nick's way. "You might be right." She settles back into the old leather couch. "Aiden's focused on the fact that Hester has issues; that she murdered Lucy because Jacob redirected his affections from her toward his girlfriend and then wife. Hester mentioned to me how Jacob was moving away." She meets Nick's gaze. "Yes. The house was in the yard but in Hester's mind, the structure probably felt distant at best. Her world revolves around the farmhouse and the garden; her books and her plants."

"What else?"

She winces. She won't reveal her thoughts too soon. "I need to talk to Del Trembly, as well as Trixie, one more time. Trixie said she'd come out for lunch tomorrow, so I'll visit Del on Friday. I promised Aiden we could interview suspects on Monday at the latest."

"Shall I stop in and see Norbert while you talk with Del?"

"You are very thoughtful, but no, I'll pop in." She can tell by his expression he's worried. "I'm okay. I'll tell Norbert I stopped to say hello because you're busy with renovations at the house."

"He might be interested in the changes, Stella. He often mentions this old place." Nick refocuses back to the discussion at hand. "Why Trixie and Del? What do you expect them to contribute, above what they've already said?"

"First, I want Trixie to help me study Cavelle. She and Trixie are good friends. Trixie is adamant Cavelle is uninvolved. I need to understand her reasons. What has convinced Trixie Cavelle's not part of a cover-up? There's also the possibility she murdered Lucy to get the house from Jacob."

"If you want an honest assessment, your theory is exceedingly lame, my girl." He pauses to sip his tea. "No one kills a young woman for a house. Cavelle sells houses, for God's sake. She has access to any property she wants. You're reaching." He takes a long sip of his tea. His eyes are kind although he's emphasized his point.

"Okay, okay, but Cavelle's certainly capable of covering for Opal or Hester; or ignoring the obvious. I want Trixie to describe her emotional capabilities; what she might do if pushed to the limit."

By the frown on his face, Stella knows she's failed to convince him of the possibility.

"What do you want to discuss with Del Trembly? The last time you visited her, you came home with the idea she's started to lose her grip."

Stella appreciates his doubts. "Del is sure Hester killed her parents and Lucy. She has given her theory consideration for years. I want to explore her rationale."

"That sounds logical."

"In addition, Aiden's assumption is Hester killed Lucy and the Painter parents died of natural causes. If Hester was involved in any capacity, she wasn't alone."

"How will you ever obtain evidence related to the deaths of Leon and Velma Painter? Weren't any possible clues buried with them?"

"There's no way besides conversation and confession, Nick. We need a confession, or we'll never find the truth. Right now, my biggest concern is that Opal and Cavelle have conspired to pin murders they committed on their sister. I'm sure I've missed a clue or a motive along the line, but I intend to figure it out." She purses her lips in self-doubt. "Trixie will be here tomorrow. I'll get as much information as I can from her before I go to the manor on Friday." She stares into her empty cup after reconfirming her plans, and wishes for answers to emerge from the bottom.

"Tomorrow, it will be bedlam here. I expect Duke. I'm never bored when Duke or Trixie are around. Do you need me to help?"

Gratitude is reflected in her expression, but his job is to complete the reno. "We can take a few minutes to give Trixie a tour. She'll be anxious to criticize what you've done." She giggles. "Let's go to bed."

****

Trixie arrives at ten o'clock the next morning. Neither her curls nor her emotions are contained as she tosses her creamy leather jacket on a living-room chair and prances through to the kitchen before Stella has a chance to dry her hands.

"I'm excited you invited me to lunch, Stella. I am in possession of fabulous news." She focuses dark-blue shadowed eyes on the coffeepot, scampers over, reaches for a mug, and helps herself to the fresh brew. Nick and Duke returned upstairs right after retrieving theirs a few minutes earlier.

Stella is nonplussed. She has learned to take her sister's invasiveness in stride. "You let yourself in." She states the obvious.

"No need for you to run across the house for me." Trixie tilts her face to the ceiling. "Could they be noisier, do you think? Shale Harbour needs to hear them, too."

"Drywall today." She exhales. *Patience.* "Despite my hesitation, with Duke's help they've managed to move the project along at a respectable pace. Now," she bends and picks up Kiki, who sports a yellow sweater with a leopard-print collar, "to find a more suitable option for Kiki instead of under my feet."

Trixie roars. "I didn't even notice the little insect! Good grief! Is she your penance for Duke's assistance? Why don't you help Nick yourself?"

"Aiden and I are at a critical point in the investigation. I wanted to talk with you today and Del Trembly tomorrow." She lowers her voice, as if she needs to reveal confidential information. "I'm certain I've figured out who our murderer is, but I need more answers from you, as well as Del."

"What can you possibly want from me? I can't tell you much. My friendship is with Cavelle, and she didn't kill anyone."

"Fill me in on your news first and then I'll give you a tour of our progress upstairs. After lunch, we'll talk, okay?"

Without further preamble, Trixie jumps into her story. "Russ has asked me to go to Florida with him for a week—the first of next month! My God, Stella, he may be serious. I'm wound up and flustered. He suggested I shop at the underwear and cruise-wear store in Port Ephron—I can't remember their name—Somebody's Finery. He instructed me to go shopping to buy new clothes and he'll foot the bill. Quite the guy, right?"

Stella studies the joy, laced with an element of competition, on her sister's beautiful face. Let Trixie bask in her glory. "A vacation sounds wonderful. Which part of Florida?"

"Not a clue. He said the destination is a surprise but to make sure I pack my dancing shoes." She plunks her elbows on the table and her chin in her hands. Her dramatic moan fills the kitchen. "I'm in love, Stella. Russ is the real deal."

Additional convincing will be required. Every boyfriend since high school has been the one. Russ Harrison's commitment remains to be seen. "He'd better treat you well." She smiles, recalling Russ' remark to Nick and adds, "maybe he'll settle down once he retires and doesn't have to travel so much. Let's make the trek upstairs. I'll show you samples of the finishes, too."

Their tour took only fifteen minutes. Trixie wasn't impressed with Stella's classic choices. She insisted the space needed more colour; more pizazz. Nick stole quick glances at Stella. She was heartened by his obvious understanding. Prompted by Kiki, who started to bark at the foot of the stairs, they retreated to the kitchen to prepare lunches.

With lunch over, Nick and Duke back to work, and the dishes cleared, Stella decides the time has come to discuss Cavelle. "In your opinion, is Cavelle capable of murdering Lucy Painter?" She raises her hand to interrupt before Trixie has an opportunity to answer. "Examine Cavelle in the light of 'anyone has the ability to commit murder under the right circumstances', before you answer."

"Before I answer," she glares at Stella as if her sister is insane, "what exactly is her motive?"

"The house? Or was Lucy the centre of too much attention from Jacob? Was the family disrupted in ways I might not understand?"

"Okay. Next question, Stella. Explain to me how Lucy was poisoned. She ate some sort of food that killed her. Cavelle has been told more, but she hasn't revealed details to me."

"They were instructed to avoid gossip and not to theorize but the police determined Lucy died from the consumption of destroying angel mushrooms. They came from the Painter farm since no other location where Lucy ate in the two weeks prior to her death served mushrooms of any kind. Hester produced samples of different dried varieties kept in the house and they included a specific poisonous batch."

"Why isn't Hester a suspect?"

"Each of the three sisters, and even Jacob, are suspects." She detects the exasperation in her own voice. "Aiden is sure Hester killed Lucy because she was jealous, but my gut tells me more than one Painter has been murdered."

Trixie's perfectly symmetrical plucked eyebrows lift.

"I can't discuss my theory yet. I have to have more personality details to be sure."

"Okay. Okay. You've convinced me. God knows why. Here's my point of view, for what it's worth. Cavelle doesn't cook. If she killed a person, she would need to lob them over the head or drown them in a pond. Cavelle wouldn't be able to hard boil an egg, Stella. If she lived in the house next door, she'd still be going across the yard for meals and expecting Opal to leave her dinner in the warming oven."

"Perhaps supportive involvement without cooking?"

Trixie squints as she focuses on the blue sky through the kitchen window. "You can imagine Cavelle pushed her off the wall, but I'm doubtful. If a sibling conspiracy exists at the Painter family farm, I bet my trip to Florida any murder doesn't involve Cavelle."

****

Voices echo as she approaches her father's room at Harbour Manor. "I think there's people who handle my money matters, Jack. I'm pretty sure a woman goes to the bank for me."

Stella wiggles through the space where the door stands ajar, compelled to intervene. "Good morning, Norbert." She turns to the volunteer attendant she recalls from one of her visits to Del's. "Jack Lawson, correct?"

The volunteer nods and starts to shuffle toward Stella and the door. Stella glares. "Mr. Kirk has family members who assist him with the management of his affairs, Jack. He is well cared for. He has a family."

Norbert jumps up from his recliner. Stella assesses her father to be spry for his seventy-three years. "There's my daughter Trixie. She comes to visit." His words are shouted and breathless. "And a granddaughter, Brigitte. She helps me, too."

Her demented father has carved one daughter out of the family picture in his troubled mind.

"And Stella, here, is married to my friend Nick Cochran. He runs my RV park." He points an arthritic index finger at Jack, who hovers in the entryway. "Last year was good for the business." He cackles and waves toward Jack again. "I don't need no help for sure." His expression is self-satisfied as Jack closes the door when she leaves.

"Well said, Norbert. Does Jack offer to assist other residents with their affairs?"

He shrugs his shoulders. "How's Nick? Why didn't he come in today?"

Stella is relieved to retreat to what she hopes will be neutral territory. She'll remember to ask more about Jack later. "Nick is at home in the middle of a big renovation on the upstairs apartment."

Norbert seems to feign interest. "Oh, yeah?" *Is there a possibility a person with dementia can pretend to be engaged in a topic of conversation?*

"Want me to tell you what we're up to?"

"Never liked upstairs after we put in the apartment. The place was better when there were three bedrooms, and everyone used the toilet off the kitchen." He sounds grumpy, resembling her true father instead of her pretend husband's business partner.

"Well, you might appreciate the space more, now. The whole floor is being transformed into our master bedroom with a bathroom and sitting area." Stella tries her best to sound jovial and upbeat.

He stares at her for a moment before he returns his attention to the television, which has murmured all the while she's been in the room. "Good for you. Nick is on the ball. Did he send me a message?" His eyes remain focused on the program.

Stella relents. "Nick asked me to stop in to say hello and tell you the park is great. He'll be by one afternoon after he gets the reno done."

"Okay, bye." A withered hand flutters and Stella returns to the hall.

Unlike her father, Del Trembly is thrilled Stella has popped by. She wiggles with satisfaction, snuggled into a bright-red velour tracksuit and spread out in her recliner. "Come in. Sit. Jack brought me another chair. Is it cold out? Did you visit Norbert?"

After dragging the stackable chair nearer to Del, she puts her hand gently on the woman's leg. "Hold on, Del. Let me take my coat off. The temperature is mild, and I visited my father, but as Mrs. Nick Cochran. He likes her, as opposed to his daughter, Stella Kirk."

Del huffs and presses her bum further into her chair. "Well, in my opinion, you should be Mrs. Nick Cochran and the sooner the better. Not to change the subject, but I'm gonna change the subject. Are you hirin' Eve again this summer? She called me last night at the nurses' desk and said she hoped you were. You want her to do bookwork, too? You will hire her, won't you?"

The date on the calendar is past mid-February, and she hasn't sent out offers to her favourite staff. "My God, Del, you are a lifesaver. What with Lucy Painter's murder investigation and now the upstairs renovations on the old house, I guess I'm neglecting my business. I'll send contract letters to Eve, as well as Alice and Paul Morgan, before the day is over. If Eve calls again, she's hired!"

"Polite niceties and questions aside, are you here to dissect my relations?"

"I am indeed, Del. Here's my big question for you. What are the reasons you are certain Hester killed her parents, her dog, and Lucy? Why Hester and not Opal, for example?"

"The answer is easy, Stella. Opal and I are close. I understand how her mind works, and I've been very fond of both her and Cavelle since they were little girls."

Obviously, Opal and Cavelle don't harbour the same fondness for their Aunt Del.

"Opal has a fierce loyalty to the family," Del explains. "She did what was needed to assist Leon in raising both Hester and Jacob. She ran the farm after Leon died. Hester is an odd duck. She's a stranger compared to the other two." She wipes the back of her hand across her nose. "The girl is a social cripple with the mind of a genius. She was perfectly capable of preparing a concoction for her mother when she was ten years old. The child was talented, and into lots of weird experiments at the time. Killing the dog for practice before killing her father is a logical step. Leon wanted to send her away to attend a special school. If Hester found out.... As for Lucy, Hester has always been jealous of anyone who comes near Jacob. Poor little Lucy became the person in her way."

One piece of information, although understated, is pivotal. Del never took the opportunity to understand Hester. It's easier to condemn the person about whom you care the least.

Chapter 22

Accidents Happen, Right?

A flash of bright salmon catches Stella's attention as she speeds through town following her visit with Del. The Shale Harbour Savings and Loan stands proud in the brilliant late morning sun. She planned to stop and make a withdrawal, but almost forgot. With an expertise she rarely acknowledges, she spins the Jeep around and into a parking spot in front of the square two-story building, historically a posh sea captain's home and now the bank.

She races up the stairs and into the familiar lobby with its stone floors and three wickets. Memories of Lorraine Young and Ruby Wilson roll through her mind. Eight months ago, Ruby killed Lorraine, a teller, because Lorraine uncovered an embezzlement scheme cooked up by Ruby, who was the manager and in cahoots with her convict brother.

Stella spots Terri Price at her station and trots over to take a place in her line-up. Then the door opens and Opal Painter strides in. She approaches the queue beside Stella. An opportunity has presented itself. Aiden will be furious, but she'll follow her instincts.

"Opal. How are you?"

"Good morning, Stella." Her eyes remain fixed in front of her.

Opal is dressed in the exact attire she wore on the day she walked uninvited into the living room at the park. Perhaps the black cloche is pulled lower around her ears if such an act is possible.

Stella takes her turn with Terri and nods recognition. "I need a hundred dollars out of the company account. Here's the withdrawal slip. How are you?"

Terri, nervous and nondescript, whispers her response as if the whole world might hear her say, "Fine, Stella. Everyone tries to manage." She counts out five twenty-dollar bills. "Here you are. Nice to see you."

"Thanks. You, too." She turns her attention to Opal, who has chosen a slower line with a teller Stella has never met. "Opal. Time for coffee and a muffin over at the café before we both go home to whatever the afternoon holds?"

"What? Coffee at the café? With you?"

"Yes. A little change in schedule?"

Opal watches as the man in front of her counts his cash and prepares to turn around. "Is our meeting part of the investigation? My brother and sisters and I decided we won't talk to you or Detective North again unless two of us are present."

Stella is surprised but not deterred. "No problem, Opal. We're old friends. We can have a friendly chat and a cup of coffee without witnesses. I'll wait for you by the door." Her biggest concern is how she'll elicit answers without a promised casual encounter becoming an interrogation.

They walk in uncomfortable silence. The café isn't busy this late in the morning. It's still too early for the lunch crowd. Stella chooses a table for two near the back. Opal stares straight ahead, and Stella senses the woman's reluctance.

Once they've ordered and their homemade cranberry and lemon muffins are delivered, Stella overcomes her nervousness and leaves the niceties of weather and restaurant décor behind. Opal can refuse to answer her questions. She has a choice. "Opal, you must appreciate Hester's expertise when you collect mushrooms and dry them for sale. After what we discovered concerning Lucy's death, accidents happen, right?"

She sits poker straight in the tiny bistro chair. Opal has not unbuttoned her charcoal wool coat. Her stiff and structured black handbag is poised on her knees. She has taken one sip of her coffee but has not touched the muffin. "Stella, I said no investigation-related discussions. You aren't to be trusted."

Stella's heart thumps in her chest. "Opal, I'm not asking about the investigation. I'm impressed with how intelligent Hester is. I expect she helps at home a lot more than I thought she could. Does she help you with the harvest? Did she teach you how to identify different types of mushrooms?"

"Well, yes, in the past she has assisted me. Her supervision is not necessary anymore. I am perfectly capable. I can differentiate species on my own." She picks a piece of muffin off the top edge near the paper holder and pops the crusty morsel into her mouth. "She isn't the only smart one in the family."

"Oh, people give her too much credit, right?"

Opal's eyes lock with Stella's. "I taught Hester at home from the time she was ten and our mother died. I *taught* her. She tells everyone she learns from books, but she learned from me."

The day Hester loaned her plant references and had trouble locating one title, deciding it was "misfiled," crosses Stella's mind. "I imagine your expert knowledge has come from the very volumes Hester treasures now."

"Of course. It was through my efforts she obtained her library of resources. Paulina McAdams was very good to her, but their interactions were at my urging."

"Hester must have been hysterical when your father suggested he might send her away to a special school—or even to public school. She wanted to stay at home with you as her teacher." Stella holds her breath. Opal may become defensive and her informal interview will end in a moment.

"Did Del tell you Hester was informed? Del pestered Dad to put Hester in an institution. Dad understood his children. She was not to be sent away. Hester, to my knowledge, was never aware of the discussions." She picks up another morsel. "My muffin is good. I'm surprised." Her hand flutters. "In any event, I've tried, to the best of my ability, to protect Hester from such issues. You understand only too well how self-involved she can be."

"I admire Hester. We remain friends. I hope you understand my goal is not to upset her."

On the way home, Stella reviews the reasons she's convinced that Hester is not a party to murder. First, she was clear in her description of the meals prepared at the house and her own participation. Second, she provided the mushroom samples which included an example of destroying angel. Third, she noticed her book by L. H. Pammel was misplaced. There's a good chance another person availed themselves of Hester's library without her knowledge. Fourth, during the family interview when Lucy's episode of throwing up was mentioned, Hester added her observation that the odour was different when her mother died. Finally, she had no inkling there was any possibility she might be sent away to school. Therefore, a motive for her to kill any one of the three victims remains unclear.

****

Stella trudges up the veranda stairs, vaguely aware she neglected to call Nick to tell him she was stopping at the café. She assumes, since her chat with Opal lasted later than expected, he managed Duke with no problem. He doesn't need her assistance to put together lunch. Still preoccupied by her interaction with Opal, she's startled by the stacks of plumbing fixture boxes when she opens the door. Her living room is now a storage facility.

"Hi. Anybody home?" The sound of the din from above makes the question redundant.

"Hard at work. Where have you been?" Nick's voice gets closer as he approaches from the floor above. "I worried. Are you okay?" He kisses her forehead and takes her coat while she struggles with her scarf.

"I'm sorry I didn't call. I ran into Opal at the bank after I saw Del. We went for coffee and a muffin. I was distracted. Did you and Duke manage to scare up a sandwich?"

"No problem, Stella. I was worried, and now I have a reason since you were with Opal." His eyes search hers for an explanation she isn't ready to share while Duke is in the house.

"I learned a lot and I'll tell you later."

"Okay. Come upstairs and scope out the finished drywall." He leans over and whispers in her ear. "Duke is proud he's been able to help."

"We should pay him, Nick. Where's Kiki? Did he leave her home?"

Nick's expression is difficult for her to read. "I agree. We should give Duke some money. As for Kiki...." He pushes open the door to their downstairs temporary bedroom. "If you wondered what Her Highness Princess Kiki has done to occupy her day...."

Kiki, in her glory, is wrapped in her fuchsia doggie blanket and curled up with her damp nose on Stella's pillow. Stella studies Nick to determine if he has more to add. "She's spent the morning here, perfectly content and out of the way."

"Come on, Miss Dogface. Nap time is over." She tries to appear stern but her frown crumples to a giggle when she walks over to the bed. Kiki stands, stretches, and waits for Stella to put out her arms. She jumps up. "We'll go for a pee and be upstairs afterward. Okay?"

His face relaxes. "I'll tell Duke the inspector is on her way. I took a casserole out of the freezer for supper."

Aiden calls before the afternoon is over. She and Kiki have been in her office assembling offer letters for returning staff. The park is in good shape—much better compared to this time last year, thanks to Nick and the loan from the bank.

"Hi. I'm glad you called. Are you willing, or able, to ask Opal to come to the station for an interview?"

"Yes, but why Opal, Stella? What did Trixie and Del Trembly tell you?"

"Trixie told me Cavelle can't cook. Del has imagined Hester as the murderer of both her parents and Lucy because she has no relationship with Hester. She never had an opportunity to know her because first Velma and later Opal prevented it. Opal made sure Hester never went to Paulina McAdams again after Leon's death, too. She isolated Hester."

Until now, Aiden has remained quiet. "Del has focused her accusations toward Hester because they have never been close? The old lady blames Hester for an additional two deaths which are likely natural causes?"

Stella ignores Aiden's tone. "The final piece of information I learned related to proper schools. Hester was unaware of any discussions to send her away." She falls over her words, much to her own annoyance. "If the motive for her to kill her father was to avoid formal schooling, as Del suggested, the concept has no rationale because Opal insisted the poor girl was never told."

"You want to interview Opal because your theory is she killed their parents as well as Lucy? Stella, you can't be serious."

"I am, but I want to review the information I've assembled on poisons, and we should have a discussion with Opal away from the farm. It's important to see what happens when she's not in control of her siblings or her environment. Then we'll know for sure."

Aiden relents. "Fine. I'll request Opal come to the station Sunday afternoon. The sooner we get our questions answered, the better. Rosemary will be home by midweek." His voice sounds flat; his emotions blunt.

"An interview over the weekend isn't necessary. It's okay to wait until Rosemary settles in. The Painters won't run. Whichever one of them killed Lucy, and their parents," she can't help but add for emphasis, "is convinced they got away with their crimes."

"Listen, Stella." He sounds frustrated and out of patience. His tone more likely reflects his concerns for Rosemary and not Stella or the investigation. "We need to drive our inquiry to a conclusion. We disagree as to whether the murderer is Hester or another Painter. We have no real evidence except the mushrooms," he mutters. "Let's start with Opal. I'll make the arrangements for two o'clock Sunday afternoon."

****

"Why are you up this early in the morning?" Nick has found her at the kitchen table before seven with her notes and summaries referencing local poisonous plants spread out around her.

"I'm reviewing the research I've done on the case, and any clue which might have been dropped inadvertently while we investigated. I need to find out whatever I can before tomorrow afternoon."

"Breakfast? I can't be much help, except to make you waffles."

She lifts her eyes to meet his gaze. His expression is full of patience and love. He deserves significantly better than he gets from her. Although not the least bit hungry, and reluctant to take a pause from the task at hand, she acquiesces. "Waffles sound fabulous."

As Nick assembles ingredients for the batter, she starts to gather her information based on the specific deaths. She begins with the easiest. *Lucy was killed by a fall. She was also poisoned with destroying angel mushrooms. The toxicology tests are proof. The autopsy showed liver and kidney damage. Hester possessed samples. Amanita causes nausea, vomiting, and diarrhea. Hester reported how Lucy threw up in her room although her pregnancy was an additional complication.*

"Got anything to share?" He has his back to her.

For a moment, she watches his body move as he whisks eggs and milk before he adds the flour, vanilla, salt, baking powder, and sugar. She leaves the table long enough to go to the pantry and fetch the waffle iron. "Here you are. I want to figure out each murder before the interview with Opal tomorrow. I'm looking for methods and motives. I'll ask, if I need a sounding board." She smiles at him before resuming her task. His crestfallen expression is unmistakable, but she's sure he would deny the emotion if asked.

"Fine with me. After breakfast I'm upstairs with the sander. The drywall mud won't smooth out on its own."

Hester and Lucy were friends. They shared secrets, for example when Lucy hurled on Hester's floor. Was her motive related to the fact Lucy was going to ultimately take Jacob to live next door? Conversations indicate Lucy included Hester in her plans. Cavelle was indifferent and didn't cook. She wasn't capable of using destroying angel mushrooms without help. Opal may have wanted to keep Jacob at home. Hester's possible motives for Lucy's death are lame. No one suspected she was pregnant, not even Lucy, herself. Jacob was definitely not enraged by her pregnancy. Was she pushed or did she fall because of complications from the poison?*

Contradictory theories and competing arguments swirl.

"Nick, those smell heavenly."

"Let's add the stewed blueberries you cooked. When we freeze them in the fall, I forget how good they'll taste come February." He bustles around, sets the other end of the table, warms up the berries, and checks the waffles. "Another ten minutes, okay?"

"Perfect." *Hester said she detected a funny odour after her mother died. My research determined water hemlock possesses a strong scent resembling parsnip. Did the tea reek of parsnips or does the smell only occur if you handle the plant? Tea consumption might take more than a day or two to cause repressed respiration and death. If Hester gave her mother water hemlock tea, then why did she mention a funny smell in front of everyone? Cavelle might have made her mother the tea, but why? Did Opal make the tea because she wanted Jacob for herself? Did Opal poison Lucy for the same reason? She's stated on more than one occasion that Cavelle, Hester, and Jacob are like her children.*

She peers up from her paperwork as Nick sets two generous plates of waffles on the table. In a rush, she's ravenous. "You are a miracle worker. Breakfast looks scrumptious." She moves from one chair to another as he hands her a fresh cup of coffee.

"We aim to please, my dear."

They eat in companionable silence. She glances up from her food to catch him when he smiles at her. "What?"

"You are very intense." He puts his fork on his plate and his elbows on the table. "I won't pressure you into sharing your thoughts, but I understand that look. You have the Painter murder figured out, don't you?"

"Painter murders, and no but almost. I'm sure I will before we interview Opal tomorrow afternoon though."

Following breakfast, she ruminates once more. *Hester reported that her dog, Stamen, died the same year as her father; that he stumbled into monkshood—wolfsbane. The doctor suggested Leon Painter suffered a cardiac event. Monkshood paralyzes nerves, lowers blood pressure, and eventually stops the heart. Was Stamen used for practice? Who had motive?*

Hester didn't understand, according to Opal, the possibility of being sent away to school. Or did she? It's possible she practiced with the plant on her dog before she slipped root bits into her father's food. Maybe Opal performed the same task.

Hester told me her L. H. Pammel book was misfiled in her room. She has been very forthcoming. Did she concoct the misplacement story? I'm convinced one of her siblings took her book for reference purposes or tried to put the pieces together in the same manner as I am now. The question is Jacob. He's run hot and cold. First, he denied the possibility of murder, period. Later, he ran around town and accused William Sylvester. He visited her boss as well as her closest friend. Did he move Hester's book when he searched for answers of his own?

After another hour of deliberations and study, Stella sits back against the rungs of the kitchen chair, satisfied with her completed assignment. Tomorrow afternoon they will explore poisons with Opal.

Chapter 23

Lots I Want to Understand

Late. She hates to be late and blushes despite the icy gale whipping around the front of the police station. *How did I manage to let Sunday morning slip away?* She clutches her file folder of research and manhandles the heavy plate-glass door, wedging it between her body and the wind. She sees Aiden leaning against the reception desk, deep in conversation with an unfamiliar young constable.

"Hi. I was beginning to wonder."

"Sorry, Aiden. I wanted to be here early but was waylaid." Despite an aggressive shower in the old downstairs stall, barely thirty inches square, she fears he'll sniff out her excuse from across the room. The pleasure of her morning remains wrapped around her.

"Well, no matter. She isn't here yet. I suspect she won't show up and we'll end up out at the farm again." They turn toward the interview room. "I can't force any of the family to talk unless I arrest one or more of them. They can prevent us from going to the house without an invitation. I hope they haven't retained a lawyer."

"Me, too." She settles in a chair near the corner of the conference table. Her location creates a clear line of sight toward Aiden as well as Opal, and whoever else arrives. "She'll meet us here at the station, Aiden, but I'm positive Jacob will be with her. She told me on Friday how she, Cavelle, Hester, and Jacob made a pact. None of them will talk to either of us alone again. She will have company."

"As long as they don't engage a lawyer too soon." He purses his lips. "Once a lawyer tells the Painters not to talk, we're screwed. We can't prove who gave Lucy the mushrooms." He sounds sullen; impatient.

Stella suspects Rosemary occupies most of the space in his troubled mind right now. She resolves to carry the interview, despite any attitudes from the Painter siblings. "Lots I want to understand, Aiden."

"Tell me the nature of your questions, Stella. Do you expect to focus on choices in the way you did with Jacob?"

"I hope we can discuss poisons. She told me on Friday she's an expert as well as Hester. She sounded jealous." Stella shuffles her documents as she talks. "She said Hester tells people she's learned from books, but Opal insists she was the teacher. I'm not convinced. Hester hasn't obtained her extensive knowledge from a woman who quit school when she was sixteen to care for a baby. No doubt information has been exchanged the other way around. Hester's mind is exceptional. Her skills are limited in a social sense, but extraordinary in her areas of expertise. Opal has revised history to ensure a place of importance."

The expression of admiration on Aiden's face is encouraging.

"You'll have the floor, Stella. If Opal wants to talk, I'll take a backseat and intervene when or if I see a question requiring follow up. Are you ready? I hear the constable approaching, and he's not alone."

She gives him a sharp nod as the young officer throws open the door. Opal and Cavelle march into the room.

****

Detective North directs the women to seats on the opposite side of the table. "Good morning, Opal. Thank you for coming. Cavelle, you've accompanied your sister. Nice to see you both."

Cavelle removes her coat and tosses the burgundy wool, cut to perfection, over the chair beside her. "We decided, as a group, none of us will talk to either of you by ourselves. We've considered hiring a lawyer." She turns toward Stella. "Is an interview necessary now? On Sunday afternoon?"

Aiden intervenes. "The time was my idea and I apologize for the inconvenience. We wanted to have a private conversation, away from the farm and your various responsibilities."

Opal remains quiet in her chair, reminding Stella of their time spent at Cocoa and Café on Friday. She clutches her purse on her lap. Her knees and ankles must be in perfect parallel to enhance her square and rigid posture.

Stella assumes the lead as they decided before the Painters' arrival. "Opal, first off, I want to apologize in advance if my questions uncover painful memories, but we need to clarify contradictory information." She doesn't wait for permission of any kind. "I'm sure you understand."

"I will try, Stella. Lucy's death has been a horrible ordeal, and the family needs a resolution."

"Horrible is a good word, Opal. Tell Detective North and me, to the best of your recollection, how your mother died and what were the circumstances from your viewpoint."

"Our mother? How in God's name does our mother's death relate to Lucy Smithers?"

"Painter." Stella corrects Cavelle's outburst in a quiet voice. "Please, Opal, be as detailed as possible."

Opal stares at the opposite wall of the office, as if she's watching a movie. "Jacob was born January 10, 1951. Mom was in labour for hours. The doctor took far too long to drive out to the farm. The weather was frigid. We were surprised her labour was difficult because she'd birthed the three of us, but Hester was born eight years earlier, which must have made the difference."

She glances around the table, as if in a trance. Stella isn't convinced Opal has managed to focus on either Aiden or herself.

"The doctor arrived after a very long time. The delivery took another couple of hours. Our father was no help. He sat downstairs with Hester and never came near." She turns to Cavelle. "You weren't home, as I recall. You were at a friend's house and their car froze up, so they couldn't bring you back to the farm. Dad didn't want to leave to fetch you." She shivers, despite the warmth of the interview room and the fact she has not removed her wool coat. "I helped the doctor by myself."

Cavelle and Stella briefly make eye contact.

"Jacob was a beautiful baby. I held him in my arms and cried. Mom was too tired to hold him. I took care of him until she decided he needed to be fed." Opal frowns as she shares her story of Jacob's initial hours of life.

"Was your mother happy following Jacob's birth?"

Opal's face goes blank. "Any mother is happy to give birth to her first son, even if the delivery is hard, and she's exhausted. Of course, she was happy. Dad was overcome with the joy of finally having a son."

"What happened after Jacob was born? When did Velma die?"

"You are aware of the answer. Our mother died three days later. She hemorrhaged."

Stella keeps her voice level and nonthreatening. She doesn't want to spook Opal early in the process. "Yes. The big picture is clear, but not the details. Please tell us what happened and what you did."

"First off," Opal huffs, "I did whatever was necessary. I helped Dad with chores in the barn. I cooked, I cleaned, I waited on Mom, I took care of Hester. She was barely ten." She turns toward Cavelle. "My sister, here, stayed in her room."

"There were tests at school. I needed to study."

"Tests which I missed." Opal's tone takes on an accusatory quality. "I never went back to school."

Cavelle's voice becomes elevated. "If Mom had lived, she would never have let you quit. Dad was upset. He didn't care for us, the farm, or even the baby."

"Your life's goal was to get away, Cavelle."

The younger woman crosses her legs and folds her arms. "Fat lot of good my goals did me."

Stella intervenes. "Tell us how your mother died."

"I did everything for Jacob," she insists. "Mom sat up in bed long enough to feed him, but not much more. Understand, I managed the house and the farm. She didn't ask if I wanted to go to school. She slept and let Dad come in to hold her hand. The doctor said she should rest for a week; that she would be right as rain." She turns to Cavelle. "That was the expression the doctor used. 'Right as rain'."

Cavelle nods.

"On the third day, I took Jacob downstairs for a bath in the kitchen sink." Opal has resumed her fixation on the wall behind Aiden. "He was fussy most of the morning. He settled after a warm bath. When I carried him upstairs for Mom to feed him, the bed was covered in blood and she was cool to the touch." Her voice becomes virtually inaudible.

To better hear her, Stella needs to lean forward.

"My mother's face reminded me of the snow when the sky is bright blue—a mix of blue and white. I stood beside her dead body with Jacob in my arms. He was warm against my chest. I worried that the baby was hungry."

"What did you do?"

"The doctor told us to get store-bought formula in case Mom couldn't breastfeed him." She turns toward Stella as if surprised by her presence. "I fed the baby. I fed Jacob."

"And where were your sisters and your father, Opal?"

She turns to Cavelle. "You were in school. Hester was in her room wrapped up in a book. Dad was in town. I don't remember why."

"When did you call the doctor?"

"After I fed Jacob, I snuggled him in his bassinet—in my room and away from Mom. I cleaned up the mess. I changed the sheets on the bed. I washed her, put her in a clean nightie, combed her hair, closed her eyes, and waited for Dad to come home. I went downstairs. I didn't want to disturb Jacob. Dad called the doctor."

"You waited until after the room was clean and tidy, and your father came home before you called the doctor? Why?"

Opal expels a gust of air in obvious frustration. "My mother never permitted anyone to see her when not at her best. The doctor arrived, and I told him what happened. He said he was surprised, but the circumstances weren't unheard of. Dad called the undertaker. I don't remember much afterward. I took care of Jacob. I stayed in my room when the undertaker came and took her away. Dad told me to keep Hester with me and I did."

"Where were you, Cavelle?"

"Around. Shocked. To be honest, I don't remember much of those days either. I stayed near Dad, but he was a mess. Opal made meals and managed the kids. I dove into schoolwork." Her smile is watery. "Not the best way to handle the death of your mother. I see, now, how her loss damaged me."

"How did her death impact you, Cavelle?" Stella did not intend to interview Cavelle, but since she's here, her thoughts and impressions could be important, and she has already volunteered information.

"I'm distant. I don't make close attachments—Trixie is the exception." She acknowledges Stella. "I can't discover a way to leave home, despite my financial circumstances being secure. I have a responsibility to stay because Opal is stuck. I guess you could consider me independently dependent." She presses her lips together. "Sad, eh?"

Aiden takes the opportunity to add, "No, Cavelle. Your reactions to the death of your mother, and later your father, are not unusual for a young person. Carry on, Stella."

"What did you do with the sheets, Opal?"

"Sheets? What sheets?"

"The bloody bed clothes and nightie after Velma died, Opal. What did you do with them?"

Her pause is imperceptible to the casual observer. Stella watches her swallow. "I don't remember details. I burned them in the woodstove. In January, the fire would be roaring." She gives her head a tiny nod. "Correct. I burned everything in the stove."

"Do you recall, Cavelle?"

"No." Her response is blunt; a cut-off to the conversation.

Stella changes the subject. "Opal, did you teach Hester the dangers of water hemlock?"

Opal's pupils dilate. She purses her lips and directs her gaze toward Stella. "We reviewed Hester's education on Friday, Stella. I explained to you I was her teacher. She learned a great deal from books, but I taught her much of what she knows. Most people are familiar with the fact that water hemlock is one of the most poisonous plants around. Don't the dying choose to use hemlock tea to commit suicide? Won't a single piece of root cause convulsions and kill a person?"

"Did Hester appreciate the characteristics of water hemlock poisoning?"

"Why? Do you think Hester gave our mother hemlock tea? Honestly?" She smothers a guffaw.

Stella ignores the outburst. "Can you describe Hester's behaviour before and after Jacob was born?"

"To be honest, Mom couldn't control Hester's behaviour and often avoided intervention of any kind. She didn't have a firm hand. Hester needs structure and requires her curiosities to be satisfied. Mom left her to her own devices. One silver lining in the death of our mother is I took over responsibility for Hester's management and her problems. She is a better person now, and no longer the wild and crazy child she was before." Opal leans back into her chair with satisfaction plastered across her face.

Cavelle's mouth is open in a perfect circle. "Opal, I cannot believe you have told Stella and Detective North how poor Hester has been better off over the years without a mother!" Cavelle's voice shakes in what Stella interprets as shock and anger.

Opal doesn't address her sister face to face but stares into space. "I didn't say she was better off without a mother, Cavelle. I said she was better off with me as her mother."

"Let's change the subject for a moment, Opal." Anxious to have another conversation, focused on monkshood this time, she asks, "Did you and Hester learn to identify monkshood together and pick the plant to dry for a specimen collection, or did Hester harvest the wolfsbane on her own?"

Opal's demeanour changes. "She may have studied monkshood on her own. She was reading about her banes one time when you were visiting. I can't see any reason to want such a plant in the house. Didn't she give you samples of monkshood? She might have collected the stuff without my help."

Stella is alert to the attitude adjustment which has moved from protecting Hester to verging on the implication of her younger sister. She needs to hear no more, and now wants to talk with Hester alone. "We've managed to tie up a few loose ends. Opal? Cavelle? Do you have any questions?"

Cavelle is the first to speak. "Again, what do your inquiries have to do with Lucy? You said she was poisoned by mushrooms Hester happened to have in the house. Are you two still chasing after ideas planted by Aunt Del?" Her eyes hold challenge. "She's a crazy old woman. We were close to her once, but not for years. After Dad died, she abandoned us. I expected her to come around more often, but she stayed away."

Opal's voice is quiet but stern. "I didn't want her in the house. She tried to convince Dad to send Hester away and then asked some distant relation to raise Jacob. I remember what I told Dad. I said if he listened to Aunt Del, I planned to take off with the baby and Hester. I think I scared him. Dad avoided Del afterward."

"Mrs. Trembly has implicated Hester in the deaths of your parents because she has been disenfranchised by her brother's family?" Aiden cannot prevent shock from seeping into his tone. His eyes meet Stella's.

"I wasn't aware Opal threatened Dad until right now, but Del can be vindictive." Cavelle pats Opal's hand. "In retrospect, Opal exhibited significant courage for a sixteen-year-old, standing up for what she considered was best for her sisters and brother." She reaches for her coat. "If Hester had any part in the deaths of our parents, I want to go on the record to say no charges—not one charge—will come from her actions." She points her finger at Aiden. "Hester isn't competent, and our parents died years ago. Even if she's responsible for Lucy's death, she will never see the inside of a courtroom. You are both as aware of the circumstances as we are." She turns to Opal. "Are you ready? Time for us to leave."

****

They sit in Aiden's office for a few minutes before Stella prepares to go home. "You were certainly thorough, my friend." Aiden's voice holds a hint of admiration.

"Not done yet. I want to get out to the farm and talk to Hester without Opal or Cavelle present. We need to go tomorrow morning. Hester was ten when her mother died. Her recollections of Velma's death are important. We have never discussed this with her, except for dates and times."

"Hester is not going to tell us she murdered her mother."

"If she didn't poison Velma Painter, she might reveal what she saw in the room. The poor woman didn't hemorrhage. There were no bloody sheets burned in the woodstove. The smell is unmistakable and lingers for hours. We've missed a piece of information and I'm certain Hester has more to share." Stella pants her assertions.

"What about Leon?"

"Little Stamen, the rat terrier, will be our path through Hester to her father. Hester has insight into what happened."

"Hester could be our path because she *is* the path, Stella. Face the inevitable. Hester poisoned Lucy and could have managed the deaths of all three people, although the jury's still out for me. Her parents' deaths likely resulted from natural causes." Aiden's tone is impatient. She believes he's preoccupied with concerns about Rosemary.

"I understand, Aiden. I need to find out for sure what happened—to Velma, to Leon, and to Lucy. If Hester is implicated, I'll accept the evidence."

"Good. Meet me at the farm tomorrow morning around nine. You may interview Hester if they let us into the house, and maybe we'll get to the bottom of this mess."

"The secret to Hester is discovering the right questions. I'll see you early tomorrow."

Chapter 24

Are You Here to Arrest My Sister?

Snow rushes past the porch door as they seek shelter between the weather and the warmth of the farmhouse.

"Do I need to contact our lawyer? What do you want?" Opal doesn't invite them in.

Penetrating Opal's defenses will be their most difficult challenge.

"We've come over this morning to speak with Hester, Opal." Aiden remains formal despite her abruptness. "Jacob is home. Please call him to support her during our interview. We'll wait until he's here."

"You can't talk to her without me."

"Your attendance is not required. I saw Jacob's truck in the back. Please find him. And where might Hester be right now?"

"Are you here to arrest my sister?"

"We intend to have a conversation with your sister. There are a number of outstanding questions answerable by her alone." Aiden places one booted foot on the threshold.

Opal pulls the oak door open and steps aside. Her voice is resigned. "Hester is up in her room. Stella knows the way. I'll locate Jacob."

Without words, Stella and Aiden remove their coats but remain at the bottom of the stairs until Jacob rounds the corner.

"I was in the barn. Your visit must be important to come out to the farm so early."

Aiden remains in control of the conversation. "Yes—follow-up issues resulting from our interview with Opal yesterday. Now we want to discuss those issues with Hester. Since the family has requested none of you be seen individually, we require you to sit in with her. Will this arrangement be suitable?"

He frowns but cooperates. "Of course. I'll help in any way I can, Detective North."

Stella considers his allegiances.

Hester sits cross-legged in the centre of her bed, hair combed and pinned. Her sweater and skirt both appear relatively clean. The expression on her face is serene. *She has prepared for this visit.*

"Good morning, Hester. Detective North and I came to ask you a few questions and find clarification after our interview with Opal yesterday. Jacob has agreed to be included. Will you meet with us?"

Her smirk is secretive; mischievous. "I wondered how long you would need, Stella. You are a smart woman. You can deduce and reason. You ask pertinent questions. Of course, I am smarter, but I am pleased, and I must add, grateful, to answer any questions. The correct questions may lead to surprising answers."

She knows the truth.

"Hester, please tell us what you recall of your mother's death."

"Be more specific, Stella."

"Let's start from the day or two before your mother died. You said you remembered an unusual scent."

Squinting at them, she smooths her skirt. "The mention of an odour was a hint, Stella. You never asked me what I saw."

"You were ten, Hester; a child. Do you remember more?"

"Oh, yes." She leans over toward them, seated on chairs beside the bed. Her elbows rest on her knees. "I will not tell you a story, Stella. I will be honest and truthful when I answer your questions. You are smart, as I said. You must use deductive reasoning. I refuse to implicate a member of my family in a crime."

Jacob remains in the doorway.

Stella hopes the sound of her swallow doesn't reverberate throughout the library-like bedroom. "Okay, Hester. I'll start."

She glances at Aiden for a second. He nods.

"What was the smell you detected in your mother's room and what was the source?"

"That's better, Stella." She giggles. "I smelled parsnips, and the odour came from the tea my mother drank after she gave birth to Jacob."

"Why did she drink the tea?"

"She told me Opal said that particular brew assists in restoring strength."
"Was it helpful?"
"No."
"Did she drink the tea often?"
"She drank many cups. Maybe four."
"Why didn't the tea help her?"
"I suspect it was made from water hemlock and therefore killed her." Her eyes focus first on Stella and then Aiden.

"Were there unusual happenings before Velma died?"
"Opal locked the bedroom door and told me she didn't want anyone inside but her."

"Tell us if there were other unusual events or circumstances in your mother's room after she died." Aiden's voice holds a quiet authority.

"Once Opal unlocked the door, I observed Mom. The sleeve of her nightie was ripped. If she bled in the bed, I cannot identify when or how. The teacup was chipped, and a piece fell on the floor."

"Did she hemorrhage when you weren't nearby?"

She indulges them both with a patient expression. "I was always around, Detective North. I watched over my mother, although from outside the room for a brief time. I stood guard. She did not bleed. There were no bloody linens."

Stella hears a scuffle and turns. Jacob is still at the entrance to Hester's room. She fears he'll faint.

"I need to go downstairs to find Opal. She was on the phone to Cavelle's office when we came upstairs."

Aiden intervenes. "Please stay here for now, Jacob. Sit, if you prefer." He acknowledges Hester. "There's additional information to gather from your sister."

"You gave me particular clues regarding your little dog's death, as well as your father's. Am I correct?"

Hester sighs, as if forced to make the obvious more obvious. "I gave samples to you, Stella. I loaned you my books. Monkshood is extremely poisonous." She peeks up from under her lashes. "You studied poisons because of me."

"Indeed. Did monkshood kill Stamen? And if so, how can you be sure?"

Without a sound, Hester unfolds her legs and pulls herself off the bed. She disappears behind a bookshelf. Stella jumps up to gain a better vantage point from which to observe her. Hidden by a row of small pamphlets, Hester reaches for a tiny tin. It has a decal depicting toffees on the top.

She turns, nods in Stella's direction, and takes her place back on the bed. She offers the tin to Aiden. "I cannot be certain monkshood killed poor Stamen or my father, either. My dog threw up before he died. I discovered little pieces of root in the vomit. I dried them and then saved them in a bag with his name and the date. I keep the bag in my tin."

"And in your father's case, Hester? Did he vomit?" Stella is anxious to find a way to encourage Hester to reveal what she knows. Her laborious questions create an anxiety where she fears she'll miss a critical point.

"Cavelle found Dad in the barn. The doctor said the problem was his heart. Nobody paid much attention to the vomit mixed in with the straw. We kept a cow back then."

Aiden wiggles the top of the small red tin with the picture of candy embossed on the lid. "Did you collect a sample of your father's vomit, Hester?"

"Of course, Detective North. It's in the tin, along with the piece of the teacup from my mother's tea." She directs an instructional finger toward the object. "Squeeze the sides and the top pops off. My tin is airtight because it once held candy."

Stella is grateful Hester will not be implicated in the three deaths at the Painter farm. She knows, now, what happened. Hester's evidence may not be enough to prove culpability. A confession is in order. "Were you suspicious Lucy was murdered with destroying angel mushrooms before we discussed the issue, Hester?"

"No. She fell into the basement of her new house and died. She threw up. I told you how she threw up in my room. I guess I might have assumed she hurled because she was expecting a baby if I had known. We both decided she had the flu."

"Did you keep a sample of her vomit as well?"

"No. I was not suspicious." Her voice takes on a more conspiratorial tone and she volunteers, "But once mushrooms became your focus, I needed to find evidence."

"Will you tell us in greater detail how you found this evidence you provided?"

"Of course, Detective," she repeats. "The farm's dried mushrooms, that we set aside for sale, are stored in a carton in the basement—in the dried goods pantry. Each is labeled. You took away examples I supplied. There's another box of dried goods for use here in the house. I examined those mushrooms and saw no unusual indications except for the box. I found dried mushrooms under the cardboard flap in the bottom. They were hidden. I was suspicious. I gave them to you."

"But you labeled them as destroying angel mushrooms."

"I made an assumption, Detective." She smirks. "The collections I've shared with you are my assumptions."

"Do you have an idea who killed your parents and Lucy, Hester?" Stella decides the direct question needs to be asked.

"Certainly, but I will not accuse a member of my family. Stella, I provided you with an abundance of clues, samples, information, and evidence. I waited a long time for a person outside the family to care enough to investigate the deaths of my parents. Detective North must be the accuser. I will not be the accuser."

The heavy front door crashes open and startles the four occupants of Hester's room. "Opal, where the hell are you?"

"We need to adjourn downstairs." Aiden rises from his chair and addresses his comment to Hester. "You may join us in a conversation with your sisters."

"My family will be cross with me. I want to wait up here, thank you."

****

When they arrive in the kitchen at the back of the farmhouse, they find Opal, stoic and statue-like. Stella is reminded of her conversations last Friday at Cocoa and Café, and then at the detachment on Sunday, when Opal sat at the table, rigid and expressionless. She detects a thin wet film across Opal's eyes. *She is resigned.*

Cavelle has removed her coat and boots, poured a cup of coffee, and wedged herself into the corner of the kitchen cabinets. It appears she's attempted to confine herself to stay calm. "Okay, you people. I've notified our lawyer. Are you arresting Hester?" Cavelle is all business.

Jacob slams his body onto a kitchen chair and drops his forehead into his palms.

Aiden directs his remark toward Cavelle. "We are not here to arrest Hester, Cavelle."

"No," Stella adds. "We had a conversation with her and now we need to talk with Opal once more. You may remain or go upstairs with Hester. She preferred not to join us."

"I'll stay."

Much to Stella's surprise, Jacob addresses his sister. "Opal, did you kill our mother because you wanted a baby of your own and I was to be your baby, or did you kill her because she decided to send Hester away to school?"

"What?" Cavelle shouts her shock.

Aiden raises his hand to encourage her to contain herself. "Cavelle, I need you to curb your responses and Jacob, you may listen but not intervene. You cannot take our investigation into your own hands."

Opal turns to Jacob with lifeless eyes as if he's a stranger. They burn black with no reflection of her brother. "I didn't expect Hester to be taken seriously. She is focused and intelligent but dramatic and unreliable. She fabricates. She harbours beliefs untethered to reality. She has a mental deficiency. Her challenges and social difficulties are pronounced. We protect and love her despite them." Her sentences have a recorded and rehearsed quality.

Stella pulls the kitchen chair closer to Opal. "May I talk with you, Opal?"

She nods. "I can't stop you. You torment my family unmercifully. You remind me of Hester's little dog—an aggravation."

Ignoring the remark, Stella asks, "Did you use water hemlock tea to kill your mother and did you lie to the doctor and suggest she hemorrhaged?"

Opal's tone is flat; her face expressionless. "You already know I did. I wanted to strangle her with my bare hands. She was blessed to be given Jacob. The family was blessed, but she was interested in herself and not much else except Dad now and then. I did the work and guess what she said?" Opal's blank eyes search for Stella. "She gave me permission to go back to school when she was up and around. She told me she intended to send Hester away; to give her more time to spend with Jacob." Opal surveys the kitchen for a moment. "Now, you understand I was not willing to let her send Hester away. Besides, she showed me she wasn't fit to care for a baby boy."

Jacob chokes on a sob. Cavelle's mouth hangs open as she stares at her sister.

"After your mother died, your father started to see Paulina McAdams, correct?"

Her attitude becomes snide as she mocks her father's perceived clandestine affair. "Oh yes. He assumed he covered his tracks, stupid man. He took Hester over to Paulina's house because of the library. She gave her piles of books. Hester loved Paulina."

"You were compelled to interfere in Hester's new friendship?"

"Of course. I wanted to poison Paulina, but whenever they came to the farm, too many people were around."

"And Aunt Del?"

"Del tried to convince Dad to send Hester away, like I said. She was the final straw."

"Did you practice on the dog?"

"Yes, of course," she repeats. Her eyebrows lift, as if her answers should be obvious.

Stella is struck by how Opal portrays her behaviour as the logical consequences and choices anybody might make under the circumstances.

"How did you discover monkshood?"

"Oh, research was easy, thanks to Hester. I experimented with the damned dog. My plan worked. I made Dad soup with shaved roots. No one else ate the soup. I was careful."

"Was Hester aware you borrowed her books? Did she understand you killed her parents?"

"I never asked her."

"Tell us why Lucy needed to be eliminated from your family, Opal." Stella understands the woman's twisted rationale but wants Opal's confession before they leave—and Jacob must hear his sister in her own words.

"Lucy gave Hester her own room in the new house. She said they designed space for a real library, like you see in magazine photos." She gazes around her, as if looking for confirmation. "They showed her pictures and allowed her to pick colours. Hester made sure I understood she was invited over any time she wanted to sit in her library with her books."

"You were afraid Lucy, who first took Jacob from you, was taking Hester as well?"

"The children were being taken from me. It was Mom, Paulina, Del, and Dad all over again. Jacob and Hester are my children. They are mine. I raised them. It's my right to be with them and I refuse to be abandoned for a usurper. Lucy was the problem. The possibility of her falling into the basement because she had a dizzy spell from being pregnant never crossed my mind. All that work to make sure she ate the bad mushrooms and no one else did…wasted."

Aiden stands. "Opal Painter, I am arresting you on suspicion of murder related to the deaths of Velma Painter in 1951, Leon Painter in 1959, and Lucy Painter in November of last year." He advises her of her rights and her need for an attorney. Cavelle sprints to the phone in the hall and speaks with their lawyer's office again.

Stella, since she drove her own vehicle to the interview, remains behind. Aiden assists Opal into his car. Cavelle will accompany her sister to the station.

****

Jacob resembles a lost child. Tears stream down his unshaven cheeks. His face has taken on a purplish cast. Stella fears for his health. "Jacob, I'll stay for a while. What can I do for you?"

"I don't understand, Stella. We loved Opal. How could she ever think we would abandon her for other people? Opal has been my sister much longer than Lucy was my fiancé or wife. Why was she threatened?"

The truth can be complicated. "Opal's fears didn't start with Lucy," Stella attempts to explain. "Opal, although the oldest child in the family which normally dictates security, felt threatened by your birth. You were the first, and most likely to be the only, son. To retain her importance, she needed to take on your mother's role. She imagined her strength and value related to her abilities to parent and guide both you and Hester. Paulina became another obstacle later."

She stops for a moment before she decides to share Paulina's story. "Paulina never seriously considered marrying your father. She was overwhelmed by you children. She wanted a quiet affair. She loves Hester. Opal may have avoided killing Leon if your Aunt Del hadn't wielded so much influence after your mother's death. She fought with him to institutionalize Hester."

Jacob is inconsolable. His body shudders while he sobs into his hands. It will take him a long time to fully comprehend Opal's view of their world. "There were no signs. Poor Lucy. She didn't stand a chance with Opal." He looks up toward Stella. Tears stream. His face is flushed with unimaginable pain. "Poor Lucy," he repeats. "She was such a kind, sweet person. Opal's goal was to keep me here. The build next door was her final insult." His chest heaves.

There are lines on his face not visible before today. She's distracted by a motion in her peripheral vision. Hester has crept part-way into the kitchen.

"Where did the others go? I waited for Cavelle, but she never came."

"Opal has been arrested, Hester. Cavelle went with her to the police station. Jacob is here with you. I can stay, too, if you want. You aren't alone."

The clouds of doubt wash from Hester's expression. She approaches her brother. "I'm sorry Lucy died, Jacob. She was good to me, but I couldn't help her. I'm afraid of Opal."

She looks over at Stella. "Opal won't come back home, will she?"

Stella shakes her head.

Hester turns back to Jacob and pats him gently on the back. "After you're finished being sad, may I please get a dog?"

Chapter 25

Debriefing the Parties Involved

Rosemary was discharged from hospital a month ago. Aiden is a man defeated by his circumstances when he speaks to Stella. He said Toni and Mary Jo did most of the heavy lifting until recently. Since the Painter case is resolved, they expect him to take well-deserved time off and stay home with her; take her to Florida for a week or two; pay more attention. Stella invites them to supper. She wants him to know the struggles with Rosemary do not and will not influence their future interactions—professional or otherwise.

They also discuss the process of debriefing the parties involved. Aiden met with Lucy's parents, her employer, and her friend Maeve. Of course, he was in regular contact with the Smithers family. He asks her to visit Del Trembly and Paulina McAdams to explain details regarding the case. Rumours abound in the community. Now, loose ends have been braided. Opal will go to jail for fifteen years. Her lawyer negotiated with the Crown to avoid a protracted trial and the resulting misery for her family. Stella finds Opal's concern for the welfare of her siblings to be contradictory at best.

After her conversation with Aiden, she calls Trixie. "Will you come with me to Harbour Manor on Tuesday? You can visit with Dad while I see Del Trembly." Trixie is reluctant but agrees, because she wants the facts from Stella as to exactly what happened in the Painter case. Information is now a matter of public record but very little has been reported in the papers.

Although still not the end of March, Stella feels as if spring is strutting with reliable expectation toward them. The asphalt is dry. The mounds of dirty snow are smaller each day. The sun warms her cheeks.

The windows of the Manor twinkle as they approach. Trixie climbs out of the Jeep. Her shiny yellow leather boots, purchased on her trip south with

Russ, reflect the morning light.

"You come in with me to see Dad and afterward I'll pop along to Del's with you. I want the whole story, okay?"

"Dad won't recognize me. Another visit is a waste of time."

Trixie pouts. Stella relents.

Much to the pleasure of them both, Norbert is in the middle of a good day. "Hi Trixie. Hi, Stella. You girls didn't tell me you were comin' to see your old man today."

Stella forces herself to take a stab at normalcy. "Nick says he'll be out next time. Work needed to be done at the park since the weather's clear."

Norbert nods as if he understands and turns to Trixie. "How're Brigitte and baby Mia? When are they comin' over to see their old granddad?"

Trixie glances at Stella and raises a brow. "I think I might send them as soon as they can come, Dad. I can't get over how well you are."

Their father smooths his heavy brown corduroy pants and rams his hands further into the pockets of his sweater jacket. "Love my sweater." He reminds Trixie it was a gift from Stella last Christmas.

Stella's throat turns raw. Her breath comes in short gasps. She and her sister have been graced with a rare lucid moment from their father. Her eyes well with tears. "The colour's good on you, Dad."

The visit lasts a healthy thirty minutes. At no time does Norbert indicate he isn't aware of who they are or why they're in his room. When they prepare to leave, Stella invites him to a family dinner in a few weeks. "I'll send Nick out to the Manor to pick you up," she adds. He tells her he will hold her to her promise, kisses them both, and walks with them toward his door. He doesn't sit in his recliner, stare at the television, and dismiss them with a wave. It's more than Stella can bear.

They arrive at Del Trembly's room near eleven o'clock. She's stretched out in her easy chair, legs spread, with a coffee cup clutched in both hands and supported by her ample belly. "Don't mind me, girls. Too much work to get up. They gave me the message you were on your way."

Stella begins. "Detective North asked me to tell you what happened with Opal's case, since a resolution has been reached. Have Cavelle or Jacob been to see you?"

"Neither one." Her tone is harsh, but then she has a sudden change of heart. "Well, I expect they thought they couldn't discuss Opal and they might be mad because I opened a can of worms. I have some bridges to build, I guess. What did Detective North want you to say to me?"

Stella sits on the corner at the foot of the bed. Trixie opted for the chair brought in for company. "Opal pleaded guilty to three counts of premeditated murder. Aiden told me she agreed to a deal in order to avoid a lengthy trial spelling out how her disabled sister collected evidence against her for years."

"What's going to happen to her? Life in jail and no parole?"

"No. She accepted fifteen years for the three murders. She might get out early, but Aiden suspects the full term will be served. She'll receive psychiatric support while in custody because the psychiatrist who examined her expressed concern she isn't remorseful."

"Opal's not sorry for what she did?" Del's chest puffs out and her recliner rocks in a reflection of her agitation.

"Aiden told me the report suggests she saw the deaths of her parents and Lucy as a means to an end. Her goal was to mother both Hester and Jacob forever despite the consequences. Therapy will assist her with self-awareness."

Trixie remains quiet throughout Stella's explanation, before she asks, "What do you think, Stella?"

Stella turns to her sister. "I think fifteen years of psychiatric care might not be enough."

Del snorts her agreement. "Fifteen years in jail isn't enough, period. On the other hand, I'm glad, for Hester's sake, a trial has been avoided. I hope I can get to know my nieces and nephew better now that this is all over." Her tone has become wistful. "Thanks for explaining in person, Stella."

From Harbour Manor, Stella and Trixie drive to Paulina McAdam's house for lunch. As always, Paulina stuns in her red wool trousers and winter white cardigan peppered with crimson dots. She bustles around her cozy kitchen. They spoon squash bisque out of large soup plates. She adds crusty buns but admits they came from Cocoa and Café. Stella thinks the minty pudding Paulina serves for dessert tastes like spring.

Afterward, Stella reviews the case and the ultimate resolution.

Paulina's eyes become distant and sad. "Poor Leon." In a sudden realization, her expression changes from sadness to shock. "Opal's initial goal was to kill me, correct? I wish I had showed her more appreciation for all the help she gave her family. She was always busy with work in the house or in the barn." She examines her perfect manicure. "Cavelle studied continually. The bond I created was with Hester. If I had understood Opal's fears, I would have included her. I thought I was doing her a favour when I occupied Hester for a time. Poor Leon," she repeats.

When Paulina stands from the table and turns toward the counter, Stella can see her shoulders tremble inside her fitted sweater. "Are you okay?"

She returns to her guests. Her voice is a whisper. "I never intended to marry Leon. I wish I had been more forthright with Opal. It might have saved his life."

The remainder of the luncheon is spent in the discussion of more pleasant matters. Paulina tells them how Jacob has brought Hester to Yellow House a few times since Opal's arrest. She explains how they have begun to research local tree species which have disappeared from the area. She and Hester plan to help reintroduce certain varieties back to Shale Harbour.

Trixie shares her Russ Harrison romance stories and describes their trip south. Trixie's commitment is out of character. In the past, her affairs never lasted. This could be serious.

With her flair for intrigue, Trixie mentions Paulina's rumoured liaison. "The word is you're involved in a secret affair." She wiggles her eyebrows at Paulina and leers in typical Trixie fashion.

"I cannot discuss details, girls. I must be the soul of discretion."

"Because he's married?"

She puts a slim finger over her lips. "You understand," she murmurs.

****

The next day, Stella calls Cavelle and asks if she can visit with the three siblings out at the farm. Yes, she's aware Detective North and their lawyer explained the details of the case already. No, she possesses no additional information. She simply wants to meet with them to follow up. Cavelle is hesitant but agrees.

When she arrives, Jacob is waiting for her. He must have decided to stand in the unheated porch to watch her approach because he is bundled into a warm jacket over his denim shirt. He opens the door wide and welcomes her with a sad smile not influencing the troubled expression in his eyes.

"Thanks for your hospitality. I wanted to see how the three of you have fared over the last month."

"It's been a long *four and a half* months, Stella." His reminder of the time passed since his wife was murdered is blunt. He moves aside to let her slide past him and into the front foyer. "Cavelle's in the kitchen making tea. Here, I'll take your coat. The house is warmer in the back."

"Thanks for seeing me today."

Cavelle turns from the counter and acknowledges Stella with a nod.

Stella feels uncomfortable. Her visit might well have been a mistake. "I want to catch up, Cavelle; see if you need me to help in any way."

"We try our best to put one foot in front of the other, Stella. Please sit." Jacob's voice sounds awkward and stilted. He struggles to communicate.

"Where's Hester?"

"I'm right here, Stella." Hester, dressed in baggy cotton pants and a poorly knitted sweater, rounds the corner. She clutches a black cocker spaniel puppy. "Stella, let me introduce you to Angel. Jacob and I brought her home last week. Isn't she sweet?"

Stella extends her arms and Hester sets a drowsy Angel on her lap. "Where did you manage to find such a glorious pup, Jacob?"

"I needed to talk to Borden Fisher. He still has the contract to build my house. Their dog had a litter and, since I promised Hester she could have a puppy, we went to his place, so she could choose."

Destroying angel mushrooms were the poison used to kill Lucy. Why did they permit her to call the dog Angel? "Your name choice intrigues me, Hester."

"Yes. I called her Angel after Lucy, because Lucy's an angel now, isn't she, Jacob?" She strokes the dog, settled with Stella, as she explains. "Not after the mushroom, Stella. Not after the mushroom."

Stella checks Jacob's expression. He purses his lips and closes his eyes for the briefest of moments.

"What's the plan for the house, Jacob?"

"Borden will finish construction in the spring. Cavelle and I have decided to improve our lives. We've hired a hand for me and a housekeeper for her. Hester will have company when we're both busy and I can avoid working eighteen-hour days. We've found a couple and they can live in the bungalow. Their wages won't be high, but they'll have a roof and food on the table."

"A perfect solution. What do you think, Hester?"

"I think Opal will be mad when she finds out we need two people to take her place. Jewel Winslow is nice. She has a baby."

Confused, Stella turns from Cavelle to Jacob. "Oh, we're hiring a couple," Jacob is anxious to explain, "who worked at the fish plant last summer and had a baby in the fall. They were interested in living at the farm. I'm sure you've met them. They rented Lorraine Young's apartment and stayed on after she died."

"Trixie put me onto them. She said they were laid off and couldn't pay their bills." Cavelle's face brightens. "They'll move out here with us the end of the month, because we need the help immediately, even before the house is finished." Her sigh is a whimpered shudder. "I expect the days will be different with a baby." She avoids Jacob's eyes.

****

A whiff of summer savory roasted chicken distracts Stella from self-admonishments. Her goal was to review pre-season reservations and complete an inventory of the campsites requiring attention in the spring. Rosemary and Aiden are expected for supper any minute and she didn't manage to finish. She grunts her impatience.

"Are you ready? They should be here shortly." Nick calls from the other side of the pocket doors, closed to create the temporary bedroom they are soon to abandon for their sanctuary upstairs.

"On my way." She runs a brush through her short hair, straightens the silk blouse which habitually twists itself around the waistband of her trousers, and slides open the doors. "Dinner smells terrific."

"Here's a glass of wine. I'll stir the roasted vegetables. The chicken is carved, salad is chilling, the potato casserole is cooked, and your apple crisp is ready to reheat once the veggies are out. We're in good shape."

She leans an arm against his shoulder. "Let's hope Rosemary's in good shape, too. Aiden sounded decidedly not good when we spoke last."

Aiden's car crunches on the damp gravel. Nick rushes through the living room and opens the door. When Stella reaches his side, they watch Aiden assist his wife from the sedan. Stella could be convinced he brought his aged mother for dinner. The woman who emerges does not remotely resemble the 1950s sock-hop queen of the rock-and-roll set they have come to expect. They wait, open-mouthed, as he supports her on her trek up the veranda steps.

"Come on in out of the damp. Nick's built a fine fire. Come in. Come in."

Stella is the first to find her voice and then can't shut herself up.

The detective's eyes hold a desperate appeal; an expression Stella cannot recall ever having seen, despite their adolescent friendship and working relationship now. "Supper smells great, even from out here by the door."

They squeeze inside. Rosemary stands, statuesque, while Aiden unbuttons her coat. He bends to unfasten her boots. Her stilettos are in a bag and he lifts each foot as he slides them on. She stares into space—at images Stella assumes she alone can see. She has not said a word. Stella attempts contact. She touches Rosemary's arm. "I'm happy you and Aiden were able to come to the park tonight. Nick and I are delighted to have the chance to spend time with you both."

Silence. Nick jumps in. "How was the drive, Aiden? The roads aren't frosting up much later in the day. Spring must be on its final approach." His chatter echoes around the hollow shell that is Rosemary.

Aiden guides his wife to the leather couch where she drops onto the cushions. He places himself beside her, close enough for their bodies to touch. He accepts a glass of wine but asks if Rosemary can have juice or soda. Nick rushes to accommodate.

Dinner is as awkward as the North's initial entrance. Rosemary sits in her place, eats very little, and does not utter a word. Stella is troubled by how she constantly checks her sweater and her slacks as if she doesn't know who owns them.

"Your sweater is lovely. I haven't seen you wear that style before." Stella tries to engage her, despite the blank expression and flat, emotionless stare.

No one hides their surprise when she mutters, "It must be my sister's because I certainly don't own an outfit as hideous as this."

Flustered, Stella wants to smooth out the exchange. "Oh, the sweater's very chic." She leans across the table to give Rosemary's hand a small tap. "Maybe not your exact style, but gorgeous regardless."

"Your opinion."

After supper is cleared away, Nick and Stella offer to show their guests the upstairs renovation. "We're approaching the finish line." Nick's enthusiasm is rooted in pure pride and joy. The project has gone well. The floors are sanded, the tile installed, the painting completed, and the walk-in closet kitted out. The plumbers and electricians return on Monday to set the fixtures. If there are no leaks or sparks, they expect to be enjoying their new space by the end of next week. Order will be restored before spring park preparations begin in earnest.

Aiden admires the room. Nick shows him the sinks, taps, and lights which are piled in the middle of the floor. "Duke has been a big help. He and I did the non-professional work." He grins at Stella. "She insisted we hire plumbers and electricians, though."

"Upstairs will be the ideal retreat for the two of you, especially in the summer when the house is full of staff and, on occasion, even guests."

Memories of the Search and Rescue team, and the storm which forced many to her home in the middle of the hunt for Lorraine, flood across Stella's mind. "Yes, we want to have a place to hide away if and when we need to." She leans against Nick.

"You two are lovers. I can tell." Despite her poor balance, Rosemary turns toward the door. The unsteady click of her heels echoes on the stairs.

About the Author

L. P. Suzanne Atkinson was born in New Brunswick, Canada and lived in both Alberta and Quebec before settling in Nova Scotia in 1991. She has degrees from Mount Allison, Acadia, and McGill universities. Suzanne spent her professional career in the fields of mental health and home care. She also owned and operated, with her husband, both an antique business and a construction business for more than twenty-five years.

Suzanne writes about the unavoidable consequences of relationships. She uses her life and work experiences to weave stories that cross many boundaries.

She and her husband, David Weintraub, make Bedford, Nova Scotia their home.

Email – lpsa.books@eastlink.ca
Website – http://lpsabooks.wix.com/lpsabooks#
Facebook – L. P. Suzanne Atkinson – Author

Watch for:

Sand in My Suitcase: A Stella Kirk Mystery #3

The third in a series of cozy mysteries, set in Shale Cliffs RV Park
Coming in the spring / summer of 2021

CPSIA information can be obtained
at www.ICGtesting.com
Printed in the USA
LVHW040117150120
643647LV00002B/2